P9-CLO-476

Praise for Tom Robbins and VILLA INCOGNITO:

"Robbins, as lyrical a counterculture hero as has ever tuned in and turned on, is to words what Uri Geller is to spoons: He bends sentences into playful escapades. Robbins is as frisky as ever. . . . Bottom line: Another bedside attraction." —*People*

"Robbins is an artist at play in the fields of language, a Merlin of the metaphor, and linguistic crown prince . . . his eighth and best . . . is smart and very funny." —*The Tulsa World*

"Robbins introduces a wild cast of characters and fashions a story that crackles with wordplay, wit, and political and philosophical digressions—all of which end up being great fun."
—*Milwaukee Journal Sentinel*

"Bursts with energy . . . Those who cherish his gift for metaphor, simile, and verbal riffs will revel in their plentitude here."
—*Entertainment Weekly*

"Robbins's latest is another wild romp. . . . Robbins's fans will not be disappointed by this latest book; it contains all his trademarks — the friendly tone, the careering plot lines, the impressively strange characters sprung fresh and vivid from his brain." —*BookPage*

"A[n] outrageous concoction that is a joy to the imagination . . . In vintage Robbins style, the plot whirls every which way, as the author, writing with unrestrained glee, takes potshots at societal pillars: the military, big business, and religion of all ilks. The language is eccentric, electrifying, and true to the mark. . . . This is a delectable farce, full of tantalizing secrets and bizarre disguises."
—*Publishers Weekly* (starred review)

"Vintage Tom Robbins. It's all there: the oddball fantasy, social criticism, and bizarre circumstances, marinated in Western dropout culture and Eastern philosophy. . . . [His] playful style tickles and delights . . . the novel cavorts to its own primal rhythm."
—*USA Today*

"Robbins's writing is a romp! . . . It can make you laugh out loud. It has more original metaphors than any ten books of poetry together. The man does have, as they say, a way with words. . . . [Stubblefield's] pontifications on the soul are wildly figurative and alone worth the price of the book." —*St. Louis Post-Dispatch*

"Replete with literary allusions as diverse as haiku master Basho, James Michener, and Franz Kafka . . . all of which give Robbins's prose a poetic quality, unique in contemporary literature."
—*The Rocky Mountain News*

"An entertaining read." —*Playboy*

"A trip through Tom Robbins's mind affords the same sensation as a ride through the fun house. It's smooth and bumpy; it's grotesque, exotic, and wildly entertaining. Robbins casually introduces topics other people don't talk about, and he does so in such beautiful language and with such fine appreciation for the field, the reader easily becomes part of whatever movement he is leading this time. . . . It's a good ride. Be glad you can tag along." —*Oklahoman*

"Tom Robbins pens his eighth and best novel yet."
—*The Cambridge Times* (Cambridge, Ontario)

"Novelist Tom Robbins is America's eternal pragmatic optimist. He writes boldly, fearless of exaggeration or of mind-boggling descriptives guaranteed to make you struggle, torn between laughter and letting that jaw drop. *Villa Incognito* positively vibrates with Robbins's perennial playfulness. . . . His is a brash, playful, BS-free zone, a delightful kaleidoscope of canniness, gusto, and chutzpah. . . . Robbins's satiric barbs [are as] sharp as ever." —*The Globe and Mail*

"Robbins dances and delights with words and ideas."
—*The San Diego Union-Tribune*

"Will entertain, provoke, and stimulate. With Robbins, it's always the ride and never the destination that makes the trip worthwhile."
—*The Orlando Sentinel*

"Zany, raunchy, and melancholic all at once." —*Seattle Weekly*

"Like the best of Robbins's previous novels, *Villa Incognito* reads like an elaborate farce, with truths about life, love, and society wrapped up in deeply interwoven philosophical metaphors . . . balances his philosophical and creative storyteller sides."
—*The Charlotte Observer*

"This is perhaps the funniest of Robbins's eight novels. . . . Robbins has pulled off an impressive high-wire act—working, as usual, without a net. I can do nothing but look up in wonder and delight, and applaud." —*Edmonton Journal*

"Dependably wacky, staunchly irreverent, and faithfully off-beat . . . A wonderful ride." —*Saint Paul Pioneer Press*

"Tom Robbins occupies a singular place in modern fiction: No one else makes readers laugh as hard as he makes them think, while leaving them openmouthed at his audacity. . . . It's not a place for the easily offended: Robbins has no sacred cows, tearing apart organized religion, U.S. intelligence agencies, and the American psyche with relish and more than a kernel of truth. . . . The star of this show is the puppet master, Robbins. He has a playfulness that makes the novel pulse with life. His unique style of description is the source for most of his humor. . . . And he has raised philosophical riffs to an art form." —*The Free-Lance Star* (Virginia)

A Featured Alternate Selection of Quality Paperback Book Club

BOOKS BY TOM ROBBINS

Another Roadside Attraction

Even Cowgirls Get the Blues

Still Life With Woodpecker

Jitterbug Perfume

Skinny Legs and All

Half Asleep in Frog Pajamas

Fierce Invalids Home From Hot Climates

Villa Incognito

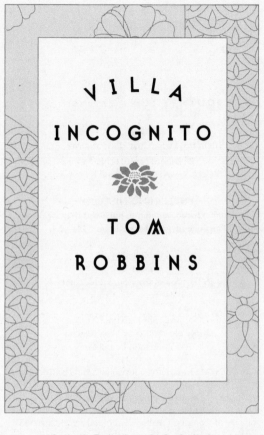

VILLA
INCOGNITO

TOM
ROBBINS

BANTAM BOOKS

VILLA INCOGNITO
A Bantam Book

PUBLISHING HISTORY
Bantam hardcover edition published May 2003
Bantam trade paperback edition / May 2004

Published by
Bantam Dell
A Division of Random House, Inc.
New York, New York

All rights reserved.
Copyright © 2003 by Tom Robbins
Cover illustration by Bill Slater

Lyrics to "Meet Me Incognito" copyright © 2003 by Tom Robbins

Book design by Laurie Jewell

Library of Congress Catalog Card Number: 2003040353
No part of this book may be reproduced or transmitted in any
form or by any means, electronic or mechanical, including
photocopying, recording, or by any information storage and
retrieval system, without the written permission of the
publisher, except where permitted by law.

Bantam Books and the rooster colophon are registered trademarks of
Random House, Inc.

ISBN 0-553-38219-5

Manufactured in the United States of America
Published simultaneously in Canada

10

FOR ALEXA, OF COURSE.

You never know to whom you're talking.

—BERTOLT BRECHT, *The Threepenny Opera*

PART I

I t has been reported that Tanuki fell from the sky using his scrotum as a parachute.

That is not so ridiculous when we take into account the unusual size of Tanuki's scrotum.

Well, okay, it's still pretty ridiculous—and no less so just because in relation to his overall body mass, Tanuki's scrotum is proportionately larger than the scrota of elephants, whales, and the Jolly Green Giant. In those days, his testicular balloon bag may actually have been even more voluminous than it is today, though that's difficult to imagine since his balls very nearly drag the ground as it is, and any increase in volume would surely have been an impediment to mobility if, indeed, not a source of some pain. There is also the possibility that Tanuki had (and perhaps still has) the power to increase or decrease scrotum size at will.

Yet, having said all that, we must concede that the role of anatomical size per se in Tanuki's descent is not easy to determine, and a more pertinent question might be not how the badger managed to use his significant seed sack to parachute to earth but, rather: Where did he parachute from? And why?

Knock! Knock!

"Who's there?"

"Tanuki."

"Tanuki who?"

"Don't be stupid. Tanuki. Himself."

"Oh, I see. Well, where did you come from, Tanuki himself?"

"From the Other World."

"What other world?"

"The one before this one, moron. The World of the Animal Ancestors." His voice could have been shoveled from a gravel pit.

"Ah so. Excuse me, then, honorable animal ancestor. How did you get here?"

"Parachuted in. It's strictly forbidden, of course. Against all the rules. But what the hell. . . ."

The farmer looked around for signs of equipment, for a silk canopy, specifically, and a harness.

"Never mind that," growled Tanuki.

"Well, what is it you want here?"

"To drink rice wine."

"Sake? Understandable, but I don't think so. From the look of the grin on your face, you've drunk too much sake already. Anything else?"

"Yes. Girls. Young, pretty girls."

The man snorted such a laugh that something shot out of his

nostril. "Forget about it. No girl would have anything to do with a funny-looking creature like you."

"Don't be too sure, old fool," snarled Tanuki, and with that he butted the farmer in the midsection with such force that the man fell to the ground, speechless, gasping for breath. Then, on his hind legs, round belly jiggling like a Santa Claus implant, the badger waddled over to the well where the man's daughter was filling water jars, and fixed her with his toothy, high-voltage grin, a smile so overheated and manic and wild it could crack a funhouse mirror or peel the lacquer off the chopsticks in a maiden's hair.

What immediately follows is a brief, and only partial, clarification concerning Tanuki's nature. To wit: while virtually everyone refers to him as a "badger," to the point where "Badger" is practically his second name, the scientific truth is, Tanuki is not a badger at all. Any zoologist will gladly point out that tanukis are a species of East Asian wild dog (*Nyctereutes procyonoides*), possessing the long snout, coloration, and markings of a raccoon, although lacking the raccoon's famous ringed tail.

The fact that tanukis are nearly tailless, coupled with their penchant for standing upright on their hind legs, undoubtedly plays a role in Tanuki's being so generally regarded in an anthropomorphic light. At the edge of a dark forest, it would be fairly easy for the impressionable to mistake a tanuki for a little man. But, thanks to his otherworldly powers, there happens to be an even more legitimate reason for Tanuki's anthropomorphic reputation, as we shall soon enough find out.

Before moving on, however, we must address the probability that the perceptive reader will have noticed in our narration an apparent and perhaps troubling inconsistency. Unless the author is simply too careless and sloppy to be trusted, why does he sometimes write "Tanuki" (singular, individual, a capitalized proper noun) and at other times, even in the same paragraph, write "tanukis" (plural, generic, an uncapitalized common noun)? The explanation is simple. This badgerish creature, like God, is both one and many.

Both. In the same instant. Like God.

As anybody who knows anything about the Unknowable well knows, "God" and "gods" are interchangeable. The exclusivistic patriarchal Jehovah/Allah freaks are not incorrect when they insist that there is but one Supreme Being and that "he" is immutable and absolute. However, neither are the wide-eyed inclusive pagans and primitives wrong when they recognize gods of fire alongside gods of rivers; honor a moon goddess, a crocodile spirit, and deities who reside in, among countless other places, tree trunks, rain clouds, peyote buttons, and neon lighting (especially the flashing whites and the greens).

Thus, if the reader is wise enough not to try to impose human limitations or narrow notions of uniformity on the Divine Principle, is nimble-minded enough to realize that he or she can be (perhaps *should* be!) simultaneously monotheistic and pantheistic, then he or she will have scant problem in accepting the paradoxical essence of our small friend, Tanuki of the tanukis.

At first, the daughter at the well seemed prepared to accept Tanuki's invitation to lie down with him. She was a farm girl, after all, and the mating activities of animals were as familiar to her as the sprouting of rice or the ripening of plums. Likewise, bestiality was not unknown to her, for she had brothers, cousins, and young male neighbors who, from time to time, were prone to so indulge. If we seldom if ever hear of girls participating in such sordid practices, it's certainly not because rural girls are any less lustful than their masculine counterparts. Perhaps it's due, rather, to the universal girlish character, which is cleaner, more restrained, sensitive, and finer-grained than that of the hopelessly coarse adolescent male. Or, it may only be a matter of logistics: it's one thing for a hormone-racked boy to mount a ewe, but a maid presenting herself to a ram is so awkward an enterprise as to be nearly unthinkable. It would test the girl's ingenuity and probably confuse the ram.

Still, Tanuki was no ordinary beast. He walked upright, had a charming accent, a confident and exotic manner, and a riveting, if somewhat unnerving, grin. So cute was he, and so persuasive, that she soon found herself loosening her kimono. Alas, when he commenced to boast about how he had recently parachuted to earth from the Other World, she grew frightened, ran away, and bolted the farmhouse door behind her. "I thought I saw a demon," she told her mother, to explain her blush and why she'd returned home without water.

Dejected, Tanuki stole a small jar of sake from its cooling place in the well and lumbered off into the forest to brood. At some point during the night, when he was quite tipsy, he began to drum on his protruding belly, as tanukis are wont to do, and the *pla-bonga pla-bonga* sound of his drumming eventually attracted a kitsune. A fox.

"You idiot," Kitsune scolded him, after Tanuki had bemoaned his woeful failure. "How could you be so naive as to tell a human being the truth? Men live by embedding themselves in ongoing systems of illusion. Religion. Patriotism. Economics. Fashion. That sort of thing. If you wish to gain the favor of the two-legged ilk, you must learn to fabricate as wholeheartedly as they do. Actually, by sabotaging their static illusions, we can sometimes help turn their stale deceptions into fresh possibilities for their race, but that's probably a mission you're neither interested in nor suited for. So, just lie to people any way you see fit and reap what benefits you can—but do bear in mind that you should never, ever lie to yourself."

Much of the fox's wisdom was lost on the drunken badger, but he'd grasped one important fact, and the following dusk when he approached the farmer's daughter at the well, he took a different tack. "My pretty cherry flower," he rasped, "I am, in fact, merely a simple beast of the woods who has become enchanted by your beauty and yesterday was driven to misspeak due to the intensity of my desire to hold your sweet hand and nuzzle your exquisite neck."

"Oh my," gasped the girl. And she watched him with a mixture of pity, vanity, and awe as his tiny fingers undid her sash.

Afterward, leaving the girl exhausted on the moss, Tanuki rapped at the farmer's door. "Ten thousand pardons, honorable sir," he said, bowing deeply. "In addition to the impolite interjection of my head bone into yesterday's conversation, I'm afraid I also told a little fib. Look at me, sir. Look me over. Obviously, I'm no Animal Ancestor. Damned ridiculous! No, I'm merely a poor orphan of the woodlands, temporarily down on his luck and maddeningly hungry. Both frogs and wild onions are scarce this season, and my ravenous self would be forever in your debt if you might spare . . ."

Somewhat apprehensively, the farmer set a bowl of boiled rice by the kitchen door. Tanuki proceeded to eat, taking deliberately dainty bites, chewing very, very slowly; and when his host grew bored and turned his attention to some household chore, the badger suddenly seized a cask of sake quite as large as himself and, short legs pumping, heavy scrotum swinging, escaped with it into the brush, one step ahead of the farmer's ax.

That night Tanuki got snockered so enthusiastically that the sake got snockered along with him. He thumped his full belly—*pla-bonga pla-bonga*—and his grin fought a duel with the moon.

Tanuki relished homemade sake. He liked dancing his drum-belly dance in the moonlight, he liked gorging himself on fat frogs and yams, and as much or more than anything else, he liked seducing young women. After his initial success with the farmer's daughter, he embarked on a long spree of seduction. Over the years, he enjoyed a great many such successes, and the encounters brought him immense delight, despite the fact that some of the girls would later give birth to strange-looking babies, which, believing them to be demon children, the girls' families would drop over a cliff or drown in the nearest creek.

Eventually, however, Tanuki grew weary of country girls, with their frank and easy ways; and he commenced to wander into cities, where the women were glamorous and sophisticated, were wrapped in rich silks, recited poetry, served sake of a noticeably finer quality, and smelled of powders and perfumes instead of farm sweat.

After stealing into a garden or a courtyard or a courtyard garden, he would saunter up to a woman there, his scrotum swaying, his smile on fire. "Pardon me," he'd say, "I'm a lonely denizen of the purple hills, who has been pulled into town by nothing but the beacon of your own beauty, which in my innocent way I long to . . ."

Reaction depended upon the female's age. A really young girl—fifteen, sixteen, seventeen—would scream as if a godzilla egg had hatched in her bathwater, and run right out of her getas in her haste to reach the safety of the house. Girls in their twenties, on the other hand, would hurl their getas at him, would hurl books, flutes, teapots, iron lanterns, inkwells, and stones; hurl them with such bone-bruising force that it became his turn to scramble to safety. If the object of his intentions was thirty or older, she'd usually regard him with calm contempt, wag a sharp, painted nail at him, and admonish him coldly, "You're stinking up my chrysanthemum beds, you obscene monkey. Crawl back to your filthy lair before my retainer treats you to a taste of his blade."

Each successive rejection took a larger bite out of Tanuki's confidence, until finally it was gnawed down to the core. With what passed for his tail between his legs, he did, indeed, slink back into the hills, so far back that the lights of no city, town, or village could muffle the silent beeping of the stars. After a half-hearted meal of shelf fungus, he slurped a jar of purloined sake (down-home variety) and began a halfhearted shuffle upon the fallen leaves. Around midnight, a fox appeared.

"What a pathetic excuse for tummy-thumping!" Kitsune chided him. "I could produce better *pla-bongas* by beating a steamed dumpling with a toothpick. Have you completely dissipated your sense of rhythm?"

Resisting an impulse to bludgeon the kitsune with the empty sake jar, Tanuki instead embarked upon a mournful litany of urban failures, not caring that he was losing face by the bucketful.

Kitsune shook his orangish head. "It's beyond me," he said, "how you ever acquired a reputation for cunning. Listen, lover-boy! All human beings can be deceived, but they can't all be deceived in the same way. The very hook that will snag a bumpkin, an educated cosmopolite will spit out or brush aside. Unless, of course, it's baited with money, that fatal lure that regularly makes a fish out of men of every station."

"I hear you can exchange it for sake," Tanuki objected. "The good stuff."

"True enough. But you'd have to steal the money in order to purchase the sake, so why not just steal the wine and cut out the middleman? Money! Before it was invented, men were nearly as savvy as us. Not that *you* are overwhelmingly savvy. All that hug-

me-because-I'm-a-furry-little-lost-animal crap. That's for ama-
teurs. That's for house pets and teddy bears. You still haven't
sorted out the knots and tangles of the human mind. Well, I'll
tell you this much: if you're going to recline on a lady's futon,
you're going to have to recline there in a gentleman's body."

"But how . . . ?"

"How? *How?* Are you an Animal Ancestor or aren't you?"
Properly exasperated, and convinced that food, beverage, and
worthy entertainment were irreversibly absent from the badger's
clearing that evening, Kitsune loped off into the shadows.

Tanuki lay down in the dead leaves to try to attain the degree of sobriety necessary for a full grasping of the fox's meaning.
A few snowflakes began to fall, falling slowly, very slowly, taking
their time, as if waiting for Tanuki—or *anybody*—to notice them;
as if stalling until some wonderstruck bystander might remark on
their beauty and how no two snowflakes are ever exactly alike.
At what point, it's fair to ask, did snowflakes start believing their
own publicity?

That had been the first snowfall of the season. When the last
snow fell at winter's end, toward the middle of March, the figure
that stood in the badger's clearing was casting a humanlike shadow.
Falling only marginally faster than November's intrepid trailblazer;
preening on the breeze; boasting in a fluttery stage whisper,
"*Regardez-moi.* The likes of me has never been seen before and
will never be seen again," the very last flake in line (self-delusional
to the finish) landed on an eyelid that could have belonged to
Toshiro Mifune, complete with epicanthic fold. There, it was
summarily flicked off by a thumb. Not a claw, but a thumb.

It had taken Tanuki most of the winter to perfect this
change—if perfect it he had. Shape-shifting was surely within the

scope of his otherwordly talents, but it was hard work, and for a tanuki, hard work holds a minimum of charm. Metamorphosis, however temporary, requires intense concentration (it doesn't just occur with a wand and a *poof!* as in fairy tales); while sake, consumed injudiciously, has the effect of loosening the screws of one's focus. Consequently, due to indolence and periodic inebriation, certain flaws could be detected, upon closer examination, in the figure that stretched its limbs at the mouth of the den.

Tanuki wasn't worried. He preferred his badgerish form anyhow, regarding it (not entirely without justification) as a softer yet stronger, more agile and energetic vessel than the one occupied by the most celebrated actor, athlete, or warrior. He might not yet comprehend the human mind, but he knew, now more than ever, the biomorphic restraints of the human body. His new lady friends would just have to accept a patch of fur here, a sharp tooth there, along with his elegant animal grace and splendidly gamy odor.

April. Spring was on the land like an itch. The whole countryside seemed to be scratching itself awake—lazily, luxuriously, though occasionally scratching so hard its nails hit bone, that old cold calcium that lies beneath our tingles. Tiny frogs, raked into alertness, were being scratched from muck and mud. Tiny buds, as bright as blisters, were being scratched from hardwood. The trees themselves, as juiced on sap as Tanuki ever was on booze (though the trees had a great deal more dignity), were scratching long blue notes from the sky.

A thousand insects tested their motors, anxious for this year's grand prix of nectar and blood. Crows that had looked so black against December's drifts now found their stark menace diluted, the tints of spring doing to them what Technicolor was to do to

Boris Karloff. No mild yellow ray had sweetened their spooky cries, however, and the crows went right on auditioning for the demon role in some imaginary Kabuki, their squawk periodically obliterating both peep and buzz. Those caw calls must have had a bugling effect, because nature was definitely out of bed and getting ready to put its shoulder to the wheel.

Tanuki was up as well, squinting at the morning sun, washing his face, taking inventory of his larder, wrapping a few things in a blue and white bento cloth. Spring has a way of erasing doubt. Violets, come April, no longer worry that their careers may be over. The miller's son starts to believe once more that he can win the princess. The grass and the spinster alike toss aside their armor of frost. Tanuki, apparently, was similarly optimistic.

In his animal body, he clambered up a flowery slope, climbed a crag upon which lichen gleamed like a rash, and stopped near the base of a waterfall. There, he commenced to cut bamboo and gather vines, obviously intent upon constructing some kind of raft. Alas, trimming poles and tying them together proved more labor intensive than the badger had bargained for, and after a sweaty hour, he gave it up.

What he did then was to wade into the river and position his bulky scrotum upon its surface so that his testicles were like a couple of pontoons. Next, he leaned forward and gingerly balanced his weight atop this most improbable of boats. *Banzai!* He gave himself to the current. And the river, high and swift with snowmelt, carried Tanuki downstream. For fifty miles. All the way to Kyoto.

Meet me in Cognito, baby,
In Cognito we'll have nothing to hide.
Let's go incognito, honey,
And let the world believe that we've died.

Incognito, disguised (to the bone) as a man, Tanuki spent his first day in Kyoto dodging trolley cars and rickshaws and ducking to keep his head from banging (he was unaccustomed to his newly acquired manly height) against both candle-hearted paper lanterns and raw electric lightbulbs. Kyoto was in a transitional state, mince-stepping from the feudal world into the modern, a contrastive state well-suited, in a sense, to this strange visitor, for Tanuki, an Animal Ancestor, lived outside of time. But while he might eat anachronisms for breakfast, urban life proved not his milieu. Unfortunately for every one of us, civilization and wild nature have never mixed, and in this case, you could take the quasi-badger out of the woods, but you couldn't take the woods out of the quasi-badger.

In the furtive way that he would slink about town, sniffing at the noodle carts and ogling the geishas; in the ferocity with which he lapped his sake and gnawed his meat; in the casual brashness with which he'd thump his belly or pick his teeth on those social occasions when he ought to have been praising the emperor or reciting a favorite haiku; in the sheer intensity of his gaze when he caught sight of the moon or a wedge of migratory geese passing overhead, Tanuki showed himself in Kyoto to be rather a rube.

Sure, as cataloged earlier, he had his charms and wiles, attractions that survived the metamorphosis from beast to man, and there were high-bred city women for whom his backwoods manners were actually a kind of turn-on, a thrilling intrusion of the rustic into the overly refined. Rustic airs are one thing, patches of rank gray fur behind your lover's knees, quite another; and many ladies and courtesans, once he'd disrobed for them, found themselves streaking back to refinement as fast as their trembling legs would carry them.

But all was not lost. As the sages have warned us, there's no accounting for taste, and evidently some women favor hairy men, favor them to the point where they might be fairly unfazed by the discovery of shaggy clumps, like misplaced doll wigs, blooming here and there on their bed partner's flesh. There had never been any doubt—had there?—that Tanuki was a wild one. The furry outcroppings went with the territory. More or less.

There was yet another problem, however, a veritable coup de grâce. Let's say that a woman has succumbed to his crude charisma and that his errant tufts have inflamed rather than dampened her ardor. The woman has positioned herself on her silken pillows, ready to receive his opening thrust, when all at once his tail flies up: the stubby little appendage that in his carelessness he has neglected to transform and that in her heat she has heretofore failed to notice. But now, as excitement overtakes him, the tail pops out of its hiding place—and begins vigorously to *wag*! (A tanuki's plasma, remember, fairly yaps with canine genealogy.) Well, that was usually the end—the tail end—of that. If coitus interruptus was a country, then Tanuki's tail would have been its flag.

Only one of Kyoto's beauties, Lady Ogumata, ever allowed the play to proceed once Tanuki's tail had burst onstage. Needless to say, that triumph elated him, and a few nights later he optimistically returned to her door, only to be informed by a servant that "Lady Ogumata has repaired to the seashore for a long, recuperative rest."

Tanuki grew sick of Kyoto. Its women were too finicky, its air too smoky, its streets too crowded, its crowds too noisy, and it had far too many rules. You couldn't hear the crickets, you couldn't see half the stars, and the trees were being chopped down to make way for more houses and shops. "Why," Tanuki grumbled, "would they fell trees but leave men standing? Trees are a damn sight more useful than people, and everything in the world knows that except people."

Maybe he had a point. Trees do generate oxygen; men just

breathe it up, stink it up, and generally misuse it. Trees hold the soil in place, men are constantly displacing it. Trees provide shelter and protection to countless species, men threaten the existence of those species. When in sufficient number, trees regulate atmospheric temperatures, men endanger the planet by knocking those regulations askew. You can't rest in the shade of a human, not even a roly-poly one; and isn't it refreshing that trees can undergo periodic change without having a nervous breakdown over it? And which has more dignity—the calmer spiritual presence—a tree or a typical Homo sapiens? Best of all, perhaps, what maple or cypress ever tried to sell you something you didn't want?

Trite? Probably, but so what? The point here is that our pal was getting a bit fed up. The evening that he learned of Lady Ogumata's flight, he repaired to the outskirts of town, where, between a solitary pine grove and an old stone wall, he went through the now ten-minute process of turning back into a *Nyctereutes procyonoides*. It wasn't the first time he'd reassumed his animal form since coming to Kyoto, but it had never felt more right. The instant that the transformation was complete, however, just as he was starting to glory again in the nimble toughness of animal sinew and the reassuring heft of ponderous balls, he heard a low whistle from the direction of the wall and a soft, feminine voice exclaim, "Well, well. Ah so. You really were some kind of otherworldly magician all along!"

Tanuki bristled. Somebody, some shameless human, had spied on him and watched him change! That would never do. Spinning to face the voyeur, he reared up on his hind legs, bared his fangs, and hissed.

"You weren't so unfriendly the last time we met, Tanuki-san." The voice was gentle but had a mocking tone.

The badger could make out a figure standing in a narrow gateway that was recessed unobtrusively in the wall. "Do—do—do I know you?" he stammered.

"Oh, indeed." The woman stepped out of the doorway.

"But it's been twelve years, and I'm sure you've since done to many a poor girl what you did to me."

What the young woman didn't realize was that for a being such as Tanuki, twelve of her years might be a full century. Or, about four minutes. She only knew that, at twenty-nine, she was a dozen years older than she'd been when he had laid her on the moss that dusk beside her family's well.

For, yes, this was Miho, the farmer's daughter who'd been his very first conquest upon parachuting to earth from the Cloud Fortress, where the badger had been summoned for a reprimand by an irate council of divinities, presided over by a disapproving God of Moderation and a pretty pissed-off Goddess of Wet Noodles. (Incidentally, if his patrons—the Goddess of Petty Thievery, the God of Burps and Belches, and the Monkey Business God—had not helped him escape, Tanuki might have been banned from our world forever. Or, so the story goes.)

Miho reintroduced herself and then as he came closer, helped her erstwhile seducer remember their wellside liaison. She told him how that encounter had left her pregnant, how she'd given birth to a wonderful baby, a lovely infant normal in every respect—except that it had been born with a full set of teeth. And its ears had been a teeny bit pointed. And it possessed what an overly critical person might infer was the faintest suggestion of a snout. And, yes, its scrotum was half the size of its head. But it was beautiful. Beautiful and sweet. And *hers*. Alas, her mother had cursed it, her brothers had laughed at it, and her father had hurled it down a ravine. The ravine where the wild boars fed.

"The ignorant yamhead," growled Tanuki. "I should have hit him harder." He paused. "But he does cook up an acceptable jar of sake."

In disgrace, Miho had fled the farm and made her way to Kyoto. "I'd hoped to find a career as an entertainer," she said, "but each time the mama-san at a geisha house inspected me, she'd see the stretch marks that that big baby of yours left on my tummy, and she'd send me away. I was starving, I had no place to sleep, and I was on the verge of having to become a common prostitute when the monks at the temple here found me huddled in this very doorway and took me in."

"Monks?" For the first time, Tanuki noticed the familiar angular silhouette of a temple roof rising in the gloom behind the stone wall. "I didn't think monks allowed women about."

"Oh, but these are *Zen* monks. Unlike those regular Buddhists, they aren't afraid of temptation. And unlike those blue-eyed European devils who are ranting all over Kyoto these days, they aren't scared to death of any idea that might be at odds with their own. Zen priests aren't afraid of *anything*." There was a measure of pride in Miho's voice. Then she added, "But they work me very hard, scrubbing and cooking. I'm up at four every morning and seldom get to bed before midnight."

Although the light was dim, Tanuki could see the fatigue in her face. Her nose was a bit too lopsided, her mouth one pucker gene too akin to a persimmon for her to be considered a classic beauty, but she possessed the long, graceful neck so admired by her countrymen, and overall was most pleasing to behold. *She'd be even prettier*, Tanuki thought, *if those monks weren't so damned fearless when it comes to someone else's manual labor.* "I suppose you hate my guts," he said. He was shuffling his feet, as if preparing to be on his way.

"Oh, no," she answered quickly. "Not in the least. If not for you, I never would have seen Kyoto, with its bright lights and street musicians and shrines and samurai and festivals and fine kimonos. I'd still be on the farm, feeding the chickens and serving some dull lummox of a husband night and day instead of a flock of lively Zen sensai. You disrupted the predictable pattern of my life, and although uncertainties and changes can be quite uncomfortable, a life is only a paper puppet show without them."

"Sounds like your monks talking," Tanuki grumbled.

Miho blushed. "Yes, I suppose they have shaped my views."

She hesitated. "Listen, Tanuki-san, I don't wish to overstep my bounds . . . but I happen to have met a couple of other girls in Kyoto who also bore your illegitimate spawn, and they say the same thing. Each of us is heartbroken, naturally, that our babies were exterminated, it's our everlasting sorrow, yet we're also grateful that by taking advantage of our uncomprehending yearnings, you turned our lives upside down and rerouted us into new lives that we could not otherwise have imagined. I'm sure I speak for every one of us when I say that we're thankful to you for having ruined us." Smiling discreetly, Miho lowered her eyes.

Tanuki, who a few minutes earlier had been as spitty with unwarranted arrogance as a spoiled child or a college basketball coach, now became uncharacteristically thoughtful. His face, which, with its long, rounded snout, must have reminded Miho of a bicycle seat, took on such a pensive, faraway demeanor that the "seat" might have been straining under the weight of the bountiful buttocks of Buddha.

He was thinking about Kitsune and how the fox continually played mean tricks on human beings, yet claimed that his mischief was actually a benefit to men because, in the end, it forced them into the flexibility and resourcefulness essential to their advancement. Tanuki had always believed that the fox was merely rationalizing his behavior, and needlessly so, since, as far as he, the badger, was concerned, pleasure was its own excuse and the advancement of human culture was never a priority. Now, however, if Miho spoke the truth, his own careless indulgences had unwittingly precipitated positive change in several women's lives.

How should he feel about that? Tanuki was unsure. He was feeling *something*, however, an emotion so unexpected, so foreign that it was unprecedented in the annals of tanukidom. Before he could quite get a handle on it, Miho interrupted his reflection.

"I have to go clear away the dinner dishes," she said. "I'm happy to have had the opportunity at last to speak my mind to you. Now, Tanuki-san, I'd enjoy hearing sometime why an arboreal character such as yourself has ventured into the big city. Stop by again and I'll serve you tea."

"Sake," snapped Tanuki, although whether he meant that he was in the city for reasons of sake or wanted sake served to him instead of tea was left forever unclear.

Tanuki had intended to return to his old stomping grounds ("belly-thumping grounds" might be more precise), those being chiefly in the mountain range that buckled along the length of Honshu's spine, though he also was known to have frequented rural Hokkaido. He got no farther than the foothills west of Kyoto, however, before he chanced upon a shallow abandoned cave and crawled inside. To grieve.

That's correct. The strange, novel sensation that had blindsided Tanuki was nothing other than grief. Specifically, grief for his dead offspring. The emotion was as irritating to him as it was unfamiliar. He didn't like it one bit, cursing the lack of drink with which he might have chased it away. Yet, rather than raiding one of the farms in the vicinity for a jar or two of sake, he remained at the cave and dealt with it.

In the stiff black book that the "European devils" carried with them wherever they went, it was written, "God can forgive everything except despair." The missionaries steadfastly avoided discussing such statements with the Zen priests who politely debated them ("The blue-eyed ones can attain neither wisdom nor tranquillity," said one of Miho's sensai, "because they're too busy clapping their hands in glee over the suffering of the damned."), and certainly the illiterate, disinterested Tanuki could not have come across it. Nevertheless, he possessed the instinctive knowledge (an intuition that, admittedly, had to be awakened from time to time by Kitsune) that despair is ultimately destructive to oneself and a burden to others; and that if one persists in it, the gods will sooner or later lose patience and give one something to really despair about.

What portion of Tanuki's grief was a sense of personal loss? What portion was a painful reaction to the general tragedy of infanticide (historically a common practice in parts of Asia)? And what portion was simply curiosity about the kind of children that might have sprouted from his cross-species union with women? We'll never know. Even were it largely curiosity, however, it would not be uncommendable, for curiosity, especially intellectual inquisitiveness, is what separates the truly alive from those who are merely going through the motions. Among human beings, at any rate.

Whatever the composition of the badger's sorrow, he indulged it for only a week. Then, one sparkling October morning, he acted. With a great popping of tendon, crackling of tissue, snapping of muscle, and grinding of bone—a corporeal cacophony that sent every mouse, rabbit, and bird in the vicinity dashing for cover—he resumed human identity and took the main road back to Kyoto.

Meet me in Cognito, baby,
Of course we'll have to color our hair.
The best thing about life in Cognito
Is that everybody's nobody there.

Knock! Knock!

"Who's there?"

Before Tanuki could respond, the gate opened slightly, and Miho's face appeared in the crack. She seemed puzzled. "Excuse

me, sir, this is the tradesmen's entrance." Apparently, the likes of
the rich Tokugawa kimono that Tanuki wore (he'd liberated it
from a clothesline in an exclusive neighborhood) had never been
seen at the back gate of the temple. "What do you . . . ?"

"It's me. Himself."

Tanuki's voice could have been raked from a dry creek bed
with a pair of rusty pot lids. It was a distinctive voice, to be sure,
but she couldn't quite place it, couldn't connect it to the jaunty if
somewhat disheveled gentleman who stood before her.

"Me, damn it! Your ruination."

A lightbulb went on in Miho's head. Or maybe it was a good
old paper lantern. "Oh! Ah so! Tanuki-san! You've done your
change-o change-o trick again." For some reason, she was feeling the same discomfort talking to Tanuki in his human guise as
she experienced when the abbot recited sutras to her from his
seat in the privy. In spite of that, she invited him in.

It seems abbot and monks had departed en masse that dawn
for the mountains: their annual retreat to view the autumn
leaves. Tanuki had doubtlessly passed them on the road. Miho
and three teenage apprentices had been left in charge of the temple, and not long after finishing morning zazen, the boys had
taken advantage of their new freedom, hopping a trolley into the
pleasure district to attend some Kabuki performances. Tanuki
and Miho had the temple to themselves.

Knowing Tanuki's proclivities and suspecting Miho's suscep-
tibilities, the reader can, within limits, imagine what transpired
that late afternoon and evening. The one thing that may be surprising is that Miho refused to have anything the least bit inti-
mate to do with Tanuki—would neither dine nor drink, dance
nor diddle with him—until he snapped, crackled, and popped
himself back into badger mode.

Certainly Tanuki was surprised by her demand and, to the
extent that he was capable of sentiment, touched by it as well.

"A real villain is always preferable to a fake hero," she said serenely, by way of explanation. Without question, her odd preference was a good deal more psychologically complicated than that, though she wasn't about to elucidate.

As for Tanuki, he believed she was just spouting more obtuse Zen philosophy but nevertheless took her statement as a compliment and was more convinced than ever that he'd been wise to select her above any other woman for . . . what he had in mind.

Pla-bonga pla-bonga. The sound, large and round yet somehow hollow, resounded throughout the temple and its environs. *Pla-bonga pla-bonga.* For miles around. Sometimes it was his paws drumming his paunch, providing the rhythm as the couple danced in the courtyard; sometimes it was his big hard belly bouncing against her flat soft one as they. . . . *Pla-bonga pla-bonga.* She, five-three; he, almost two feet shorter; yet somehow managing to. . . . *Pla-bonga pla-bonga.* Nearby residents, those from rural backgrounds, glanced at one another gravely. "Looks like it's going to be a long harsh winter," they said. "The tanukis are moving into town."

The neighbors didn't connect it to the drumming, but from a distance the temple seemed to glimmer and shine. Fluids, not all of them spilled sake by any means, glistened on Miho's futon cover, on the tiles beside the bath, on the tatami mats in front of the shrine, on a couple of low tabletops and one cedar chest.

He filled her tank. Then he topped it off. Enough was left over to glaze several rooms and their furnishings. When enriched by her own contributions, not to mention rays of silvery moonlight and splashes of the abbot's best wine, the whole temple became lustrous and, though outsiders couldn't detect it, slippery as well. Venturesome mice, drawn from their nests by the aromatic

promise of unusual dining opportunities, skidded into one another like midget cars on an ice track. Twitching to free themselves, moths and mosquitoes stuck to the walls. On the floor a
cricket rubbed its legs together—and couldn't pull them apart.

Miho spent the next two days sponging and mopping the
place. By the time the monks returned, there were no visible
signs of Tanuki's outpouring, though she still sloshed a bit when
she walked. As for the missing sake and broken cups, the young
novices had to shoulder the blame.

Nearly three months passed before Tanuki returned to the
Kyoto temple.

Knock! Knock!

"Who's there?"

"Me. Himself."

"The Me Himself who made me crazy and then abandoned
me?" There was no recrimination in Miho's voice—she had expected nothing less—but there was a pith of sadness. There was
sorrow in her face as well, and after she opened the narrow gate,
he asked about it.

"I must quit the temple," she said. "I shall have to leave my
wise monks."

"Because of the sake?"

"Because of the child." She patted her belly, which had not
quite yet begun to distend.

Tanuki grinned. One could hardly say he was taken unaware. After all, hadn't he provided enough seed to repopulate
Atlantis and half of Pompeii? (Repopulate with what sort of citizens, exactly, was another matter.) "Good," he said matter-of-
factly. "Mission accomplished. I've come to take you away to be
my wife."

Miho seemed stunned. "But—but I can't marry a—a badger."

"I'm not a badger. And who says you can't?"

She thought for a moment. "Well . . . nobody." She thought some more. "But I can't go live in the woods like a wild animal."

"Of course you can."

"Oh." She paused. "I never considered it from that angle."

Within the hour, as soon as darkness fell, the strange couple set off for the hills.

The road was lightly talcumed with snow. Occasionally, a gust raised a small billow of powder that was sometimes difficult to distinguish from the pale, papery rice-husk of moon overhead or from the couple's own condensed exhalations. They held hands for the warmth that was in it, and the way uncoiled before them, narrow and stiff.

They'd covered no more than three or four miles when they found their path blocked by a trio of *ronin*, or unemployed, freelance samurai; aging relics from a more feudal time. Initially, the seedy ronin thought that Miho had a child in tow, and though there was no mistaking the meaning of their leers, they were inclined, by what little remained of their honor, to allow the young mother to pass. Unfortunately, a cloud slipped away from the moon just then.

"Ah so!" one of the ronin exclaimed. "Do you see what I see? This tasty strumpet is out walking her pet." He didn't say pet *what*. While he'd occasionally heard them drumming in the forest next to one battlefield or another, he'd never before seen a tanuki.

"He's not my pet," Miho snippily corrected him. "He's my—" She broke off. She couldn't say the word, and it's probably just as well that she couldn't.

The men closed in around her, which set Tanuki to growling. One of the men drew from its scabbard a sword, nicked, corroded, and more in need of an oil bath than gore. He swiped at the quasi-badger's head, but he was half-drunk and long out of practice. Ducking easily, Tanuki then sank his fangs to the gum in the derelict samurai's kneecap. His anterior cruciate shredded, his medial meniscus unfastened, his lateral collateral bitten completely in half, the attacker howled and grabbed his knee, dropping the sword in the process. As the savaged leg would no longer support his weight, he collapsed.

Tanuki bared his teeth at a second ronin, but the third one came up behind him and kicked the animal so powerfully in the small of his little back that he flew completely off the road, landing facedown in the freezing muck of a rice paddy. Laughing and drooling, the two men grabbed at Miho. One of them was undoing his underdrawers, the other brandished his sword.

Now, back on the farm, during playtime, the young Miho had fought many a wooden-sword duel with her brothers. Moreover, her muscles were working-girl hard. So it shouldn't be totally surprising that she snatched up the fallen blade from the roadbed and with one dynamic, well-placed swing, separated the brandisher's sword hand from his wrist. Actually, it wasn't a clean separation: the severed hand dangled by a single bloody tendon, as if the hand were slurping an *udon* noodle and enjoying it too much to let go.

In the nearby thicket from where he had been silently watching this confrontation, a fox said to himself, "It appears that that reckless Tanuki has paired up with a human female, which is not very smart—but at least he's chosen a spunky one."

At that moment, Tanuki rose from the paddy, dripping mud, water, ice crystals, and manure. He commenced a ferocious snarling. He beat his belly. He jangled his great balls. Lines of blue electricity zigzagged from his eyes. Kitsune, for the fun of it, chimed in from the thicket with a barrage of wild fox barking. The three thoroughly spooked ronin, already maimed and dazed, staggered or crawled to the side of the road, clearing the way for woman and beast to proceed toward their future home in the hills.

As they walked out of sight together, she wiping the silt and excrement off Tanuki with an obi sash from her sack of spare clothing, he uncharacteristically praising Miho for her skill and courage, the still-hidden kitsune clucked and shook his foxy orange head. *"Ah so desu' ka?"* he muttered. "What do you suppose is going to come of this?" Then, he returned his attention to the plump pheasant that the gods had provided for his winter's eve meal.

Fit though Miho was, by the day they arrived at the wilderness north of Lake Biwa, the location of Tanuki's favorite den, she felt quite exhausted. It was a spacious cave—Miho found she could stand upright in it—but being dirty, sore, cold, and weak, she didn't remain standing for long. With a sigh, she dropped down onto the soft, sweet-smelling bed of pine boughs, dead leaves, and dried moss. Tanuki blanketed her with the futon cover she had carried all the way from the temple. Then he crawled in beside her and loved her so aerobically she was soon perspiring like a sumo wrestler on a treadmill. Afterward, she slept for twelve hours.

When we sleep on someone else's pillow, we sometimes find ourselves having that person's dreams. If a married couple switches sides of the bed, for example, he will have her dreams for a while and she will have his. Nothing of the sort occurs in a hotel bed, naturally, for the simple reason that no one person has slept there long enough to leave a psychic imprint. Is the connection to the bedding place or to the space below it? Perhaps we draw up transneurological info-bits from the underworld to form dreams the way that exposed metal draws down oxygen molecules from the air to form rust. Dreams, then, may be a form of psychic oxidation. Each morning, the greasy rag of wakefulness wipes us clean. Sooner or later, however, we rust completely through, at which point we lose tensility, conductivity, and clear definition; turn senile or go bonkers; fade away. If we applied the rag more rigorously, this might not happen. Which is why the message of Miho's Zen monks—the message of mystic masters everywhere—was and is, "Wake up! Wake up!"

At any rate, during her first long snooze in the Biwa cavern, Miho dreamed dreams unlike any she'd ever dreamed before. Unbeknownst to her, they were Animal Ancestor dreams. Dreams from an age when the stars were like resin drops and could sometimes be licked by deer. When certain storm clouds were the product of lobster farts. When the gnawing and crunching of bones rivaled the music of the spheres. When an individual snowflake really *was* unique: its picture could have been posted on a police station wall. Miho dreamed dreams that made her blush. And tremble. And occasionally howl. In her sleep.

Nevertheless, she woke refreshed. "Is it true, do you think," she asked, stretching, wiping away a last smear of dream, "that honeybees invented arithmetic, which pissed off the gods?"

"I don't know what you're talking about," Tanuki said, scowling. Precariously balancing a bark platter of dried berries and fresh trout sashimi, he served her breakfast in bed. Then he trotted off on a forty-eight-hour foray to steal a sack of rice for her (and perhaps a drop or two of sake for himself) from the nearest farm, leaving Miho to set up housekeeping in the cave. Their new life had begun.

For Miho, the cave was as different from the Zen temple in Kyoto as the temple was unlike the farmhouse in which she'd been reared. She adapted to it with relative ease, however, experiencing a sense of coziness, comfort, and even familiarity there. That's entirely understandable, for quite aside from obvious uterine associations, there remains a fair amount of actual cave memory in every human's DNA. Cave heritage, as well.

After the monkeys came down from the trees and learned to hurl sharp objects, they had had to move into caves for protection—not only from the big predatory cats but, as they began to lose their monkey fur, from the elements. Eventually, they started transposing their hunting fantasies onto cave walls in the form of pictures, first as an attempt at practical magic and later for the strange, unexpected pleasure they discovered in artistic creation.

Time passed. Art came off the walls and turned into ritual. Ritual became religion. Religion spawned science. Science led to big business. And big business, if it continues on its present mindless, voracious trajectory, could land those of us lucky enough to survive its ultimate legacy back into caves again.

Whether or not that synopsis of human history was encoded in Miho's genes is a matter of conjecture, a topic perhaps best left to minds such as those at Villa Incognito. One thing was certain, though: Miho adjusted to habitation in a cave much more smoothly than she adjusted to cohabitation with Tanuki.

Oh, she couldn't fault him, really. No creature of his ilk ever made a more sincere effort, but domesticity was just not in his marrow. And as difficult as this is to believe, Tanuki, when it came to fathoming the needs and dispositions of women, was even more clueless than the average human male. For example, he had her hauling water from the spring and gathering firewood (he didn't require fire for warmth, but he loved her fried food) long after she should have given up heavy lifting. He couldn't comprehend why, as her pregnancy advanced, that she or he or both of them couldn't take advantage of her swelling belly and employ it as a drum. It took her months to convince him not to urinate in their sleeping and dining areas. And on those full-moon nights when tanukis from miles around would gather outside the cave to dance and jam, well, she was never completely sure, once she tired and went to bed, whether it was her Tanuki or some visiting tanuki (or a whole succession of them) who was fucking her. Physically, it didn't matter, her orgasms cascaded with the same frequency and intensity, but emotionally. . . .

Emotions of that complexion were responsible for her pestering Tanuki to arrange some kind of marriage ceremony. After all, he referred to her as his *wife*. He didn't particularly object to a wedding, he simply didn't know how to go about it. Finally, he consulted the fox. Kitsune thought the idea of a tanuki marrying a human grotesque and preposterous, but for that very reason it appealed to him. If nothing else, it would outrage both men and gods, and Kitsune, who had been known to promote human improvement and who served as the gods' principal messenger on earth, was well-acquainted with the far-reaching benefits and private joys to be derived from fracturing taboos.

As it turned out, the nuptial rite that the fox suggested was the very Shinto ceremony that Miho remembered from her girlhood. Called *san san ku do*—"three three nine times"—it involved the wedding party sitting in a circle while the Shinto priest poured warm sake. A sake cup was then passed thrice around the circle, with each participant taking three sips on each revolution. After the last person had taken his or her ninth sip—*banzai!*—the priest would declare the couple to be husband and wife. Kitsune volunteered to serve as priest.

Under those conditions, needless to say, Tanuki made an enthusiastic bridegroom. It may be equally superfluous to report that neither groom nor priest was satisfied with nine sips of sake. The cup kept going around and around. Around and around. In the end, Miho was positive she was married at least twelve times over, and as for the badger and the fox, they had probably married each other so profusely that every divorce court in the land would have had to work night and day for a year to put them asunder.

The baby rode in on a sweet summer wind. Miho squatted, animal style, on a bamboo mat and gave birth with scarcely a pang. Describing it later, she made it sound as if, following an hour or two of pressure in her lower abdomen, a big quivering gob of plum jelly had suddenly shot out of her to slide down her thighs. Slick, wet, and tickling. Like a tadpole winnowing out of a cocktail straw.

The baby girl was perfect. Well, she was virtually perfect. Like her mother's, her nose was slightly lopsided. Ah, but the nose possessed not the remotest suggestion of snoutness. Nor did her ears point toward Polaris. She was beautifully bald from head to tiny toe, her gums were as devoid of teeth as a vegetarian's bear trap, and scrotum size was hardly an issue. In fact, the single physical trait she had inherited from her father was a goofy yet galvanizing grin, that tantalizing tanuki smile that seemed to advertise both fun and ferocity, merriment and menace.

Tanuki was sorely disappointed. His nearly yearlong mission, his experiment, his atonement, his sacrifices had resulted in *this*? Just another ordinary two-legged brat! Weren't there more than enough of them already?

True, very true. Yet, this one wasn't *quite* ordinary. She did have his smile. And, when the light was right, a hint of something ancient and forgotten in her eyes. He was captivated by the bubbles that were always percolating at her lips. By the way she'd pee anywhere, anytime she chose, just as he did. And by the fearless innocence with which her miniature hand would close around one of his claws. "We'll name her Kazu," he abruptly informed Miho after nearly a fortnight of skeptical observation. Since *kazu* was the word for the sticky, sweetish residue that collected at the bottom of sake casks, Miho happily considered the naming a sign of paternal approval.

Indeed, as the months passed, Tanuki seemed increasingly fond of his daughter. That fondness was strongly reciprocated. Kazu took endless delight in Tanuki—and why not? She was the only little girl in the world with a stuffed animal for a father. They played with each other like a pair of sentient toys.

It would be nice to report that this true story is now poised to come to an imminent and happy conclusion. Alas, that is not the case.

Once the naked monkeys got out of hand, the gods became fed up with life on earth. Disgusted, they moved their abode to loftier dimensions, and while they continued to exert considerable influence here, that influence, over the millennia, has become gradually more and more subtle and indirect. At the time of our story, and in the particular land where this story transpired, they remained moderately active in the affairs of mortals, especially active when those affairs concerned an interface between men and the natural world. Which is why, as Kitsune had predicted, the gods were incensed by the marriage of Tanuki and Miho. Only Kitsune's persistent pleadings (the sly, shifty fox was invaluable to the Cloud Fortress as a go-between) had prevented divine retribution.

For approximately two years, Kitsune succeeded in concealing from the gods the news that the forbidden union between an Animal Ancestor and a mortal female had produced an offspring. One morning, however, as the fox lapped water from a stream, he was singled out by a shaft of sunlight so solid it whacked him like a club, and an unseen hand grabbed him by the tail, yanking him,

yelping, hundreds of feet in the air. Instantly, he knew that somebody had tipped off the gods. Most likely, it was a cuckoo. While
all birds are tattletales, the cuckoo is a special case. Its name in
Japanese is *hototogisu*, which means, depending upon the calligra-
phy, "bird of the other world," or "bird of time." As in the haiku
Basho composed upon returning to Kyoto after a long absence:

> *Here I am in Kyo again*
> *yet I am lonely for Kyo—*
> *O bird of time!*

Which is a more exquisite, penetrating, and poignant way of
saying, "You can't go home again." But we digress.

The point is, the cuckoo, with its eerie song, crosses zones
where other birds don't fly. But that doesn't matter, either.
What's important is that *someone* had let the secret out of the jug,
and the consequences weren't likely to be salubrious.

The gods, who, like our governmental and military leaders, have
never much minded sacrificing innocent lives for "the greater
good," whipped up a mighty typhoon off Honshu's west coast. By
the time it reached the inland mountains, however, it had lost
enough of its edge that it was a minimal threat to beings hunkered
in a cave. Pounding rains kept little Kazu indoors, but, along with
a modicum of seepage, that was the extent of its effect on Chez
Tanuki. Barely had the clouds blown over than the gods, unaccustomed to being thwarted, sent a mighty earthquake. It rattled the
occupants of the cave like aspirin in a bottle, yet the mountain
stood its ground, and although mudslides destroyed a village and
several farms near its foot, no creature who burrowed inside it was
harmed.

Barely had the last tectonic plate sighed with exhaustion and settled down into its new alignment than Kitsune lit out for the cave. He knew what was coming next. The deities would dispatch demons, armed with an assortment of demon stuff: fevers, retchings, deliriums, tumors, accidents, comas, ruptures, poisonous bites, etc. And all of this sorcery aimed specifically at Kazu. Kitsune gathered speed.

He was still a kilometer or so away when he spied the head of Tanuki protruding from a hollow log. Initially, the fox thought his colleague had been felled by the quake, but he quickly realized that the badger was, instead, sleeping off a bender. Tanuki reeked, not merely of sake but of a medley of vaginal perfumery, not every note of which, according to the fox's keen nostrils, was human. (There *were* female tanukis in the hills.) Moreover, he was bleeding from various wounds, administered, doubtlessly, not by the earthquake but by men whose wives or daughters he had been caught romancing. His short legs were swollen from excessive dancing, his round belly had been drummed to the point of baldness.

"Forgive me if I don't pay immediate homage to your suave grooming and elegant mien," said Kitsune. "Compliments, however well deserved, must of necessity be postponed. You've got to run to your den at once and send your family away." When Tanuki groaned in protest and made to turn away, the fox seized him by the ears. "Listen up, you worthless rascal!" Then he briefed an increasingly sober Tanuki on how the Cloud Fortress was intent upon eradicating tiny Kazu.

Tanuki's immediate impulse was to fight back—but though he had a lot of tricks in his bag, they would have been no match for the combined forces of the Cloud Fortress, and he was somehow astute enough to realize it. As for Kitsune, he had outwitted the gods on any number of occasions, but this was not a cause for which he was prepared to risk anything more than he had already. "You have no choice," he said. "You've got to send them out of the country immediately."

The badger grew solemn. "That Miho," he mused, and his voice was less gravelly than usual. "That Miho made a fine wife woman. As wife women go. Of course, she hasn't been overly friendly to me lately. . . ."

"I can't imagine why not," said the fox, his flame of a tongue curling with sarcasm.

"And Kazu. How could such a thing as this be happening to my precious little Kazu? What will become of her?"

"You should have thought of that before," chided Kitsune. "To bring a child into the world without preparing in advance for its security and happiness is a criminal act, and the parents responsible should have their genitals removed." He might have said more in this vein had he not noticed that there were tears— actual teardrops—in the badger's beady orbs. Kitsune rested a paw on Tanuki's shoulder. He'd never seen him look so despondent. "Everything will turn out all right. Let's take you over to the creek and get you washed up. Afterward, I'll accompany you home if you'd like."

"Okay," muttered Tanuki. "Thanks." Then he hesitated. After a thoughtful moment, he said, "I need to find something first."

The fox's green eyes grew slitty with suspicion. "Oh? You need to find *what*?" He was imagining a jar of sake stashed in the bushes somewhere.

"A chrysanthemum seed," Tanuki said quietly.

"Ah so," said Kitsune. He nodded understandingly. "I see. Yes. A chrysanthemum seed. I'll help you look for one. Let's go."

Pausing about thirty yards from the den, the two animals, who'd been scampering through the woods on all fours, caught their breath and surveyed the situation. It was nearly dusk and very still. Under a pine tree not far from the cave's entrance, Kazu was playing with a crudely fashioned stick doll. At the entrance, yams were roasting over supper coals. Their aroma set Tanuki's mouth to visibly watering, and Kitsune practically had to hold him back. "Miho's inside," said the fox. "Good. I'll go in alone and talk to her, save you getting brained with a rice pot."

"Thanks. My head's sore enough already."

As Kitsune disappeared into the cave, Tanuki approached Kazu. She squealed with pleasure when she saw him. "Papa!" He reared and they embraced. "Papa go for eat?" she asked, always amused by the gymnastic vigor with which her father addressed his food.

At the mention of eating, Tanuki's head swung involuntarily in the direction of the roasting yams, and his oral cavity again flooded with anxious saliva. However, exhibiting more restraint than experienced tanuki observers would have thought possible, he turned back to his daughter. "No eat," he said through the drool. "But I want you to open *your* mouth. Open it wide for Himself."

The little girl did as she was asked, expecting to be fed a tidbit of honeycomb or some sweet berry. "No, this is not for chewing," said her father. "Now open wide. This is going to pinch a little, but it won't hurt for long. Be brave. Like a tanuki."

With that, he pressed the chrysanthemum seed against the roof of Kazu's mouth. She flinched, and tears formed, but she did not pull away, and he pressed harder and harder until the seed was embedded fairly deeply in the soft tissue of her palate. When it was as fixed as he could make it, he sealed it with a smear of beeswax to help hold it in place until the impacted tissue would grow over it.

"You must make Himself a promise. Okay? This is very, very important. Are you listening?"

"Yes," she assured him with a bit of a choke. And she was.

"You must never ever, even when you're a big girl, even when you're a grown lady like your mother, you must never ever take out of your mouth what I just put in it. Understand? You promise?"

Kazu was no more than two and a half, but she was quick. She got the picture. She made the promise. And she was rewarded and consoled with a morsel of sugary rice cake that Tanuki had fetched for her from the stash of stolen goods he kept midway down the mountain. He hugged her again.

"Now, why don't you run inside and see what your mother and that old fox are up to?"

For several moments after his daughter disappeared into the cave, Tanuki stood watching after her. Then, with a swish and a clunk of his giant scrotum, he turned and vanished into the forest.

Not many hours later, after the moon had set, when the night was so black not even Michael Jackson's cosmetic surgeon could have lightened its hue, Miho and Kazu began to steal their way down the mountain.

Acting on Kitsune's advice, Miho's plan was to trek directly to the sea. "Maybe you can convince a boatman to sail you down the coast," the fox had said. "Barter him your body if necessary. From Kyushu, you'll need to find another sailor to take you across the strait. Maybe in one of those noisy, newfangled boats, the fast ones they call 'motorized.' You may have to fuck him, too, but try first to rely on your disguise."

Miho was dressed in a masculine kimono left over from Tanuki's clandestine days in Kyoto. From dried moss, Kitsune had helped her fashion a wig and false beard. Secured in a covered basket with twigs protruding from it, Kazu was strapped to her back. The appearance, if one didn't look too closely, was that of an old man packing a load of firewood.

Meet me in Cognito, darling,
Sure, some may think that it's rash,
But you'll look chic incognito
With your fake nose and Groucho mustache.

Admittedly, the prospect of this new adventure excited Miho. For most of her existence, she had been tweaked by curiosity. It was her abiding curiosity, in fact, that had prompted her to do the unthinkable, to make the romantic decisions that had resulted in her current predicament.

The pain of her departure was tempered somewhat by its inevitability. Even before learning that she had angered the gods—what a bunch of hypocrites!—she had been preparing herself for an exit. Tanuki was staying away for increasingly long periods of time, and when he did come home, he was drunk or hung over, dirty, bedraggled, stinking of fornication. It wasn't really a surprising development. Neither was he totally to blame. After all, she had willingly married a tanuki. And a tanuki was . . . a tanuki. Still, it was not a healthy environment in which to raise an impressionable child. Especially, perhaps, when that child, herself, had tanuki blood in her veins.

Upon Miho's previous exodus, as she'd been packing to leave the temple, the abbot had come to her room to bid her farewell. His gaze was pellucid, his nod curt. "Remember this," he said. "It is what it is, you are what you it, and there are no mistakes."

She wasn't sure what his words meant. She wasn't sure they meant anything at all. Maybe they were just another of those cryptic Zen ploys designed to slip a silver bridle onto the wild horse of the mind. In any case, the words gave her a sort of solace, a strange sense of elasticity and liveliness as she picked her way around rock piles and descended slippery slopes, and she whispered them to herself for the sheer tingle of hearing them spoken.

"It is what it is."

"You are what you it."

"There are no mistakes."

A kind of boil was forming around the seed in the roof of Kazu's mouth. Honoring her promise, she didn't touch it, not even with tongue tip. But from time to time, the soreness caused her to whimper. Believing the child's discomfort the result of sleepiness and confinement in the basket, Miho cooed soothing words to her. She jostled her as little as possible. She sang her a low lullaby.

Thus, mother and daughter went on through the night. No rest. No regrets. They just pushed onward, onward toward whatever lay in store. At one point, however, Miho came to a complete and sudden stop. From somewhere above them, far up the mountainside, she and Kazu—who had just as abruptly ceased fretting—heard a familiar sound, a faint rhythmic echo of some terrible unnamed and untamed joy.

Pla-bonga. Pla-bonga. Pla-bonga.

PART II

She was the kind of woman who thought that the changing of the seasons was cute.

Her sister, if anything, was even worse. *She* thought that clowns were sexy.

"Isn't it cunning, isn't it adorable," marveled Bootsey, "how gradually, on their own, the days are getting a teeny bit shorter? And how there's an itty-bitty kiss of fall in the air?"

Pru sniffed. Pru shrugged. To ascribe osculatory attributes to a season characterized by rot and decay struck her as a textbook example of metaphoric excess. Now that she no longer looked good in a swimsuit, Pru frankly didn't give a damn about the length of summers. The single thing about the end of a typically anemic Seattle summer—and, hey, kiss of autumn or no kiss of autumn, it was still only August—that meant anything to Pru was the high probability that a circus or two would soon be rolling into town.

Sure enough, scarcely a fortnight passed before just such an event was announced. The sisters were watching the six o'clock news together, as was their custom, when on came a commercial for the so-called Mother of All Shows, scheduled, an offscreen voice intoned, to open at Seattle's Key Arena in about ten days.

A staccato montage of animals, props, and spangled performers assaulted them, accompanied by exuberant brass band music. Then the camera stilled, focusing on an alluring Asian woman in riding breeches and high, black patent-leather boots. The woman, glaring theatrically, was cracking a whip in a playfully menacing manner, while behind her a semicircle of funny, almost cartoonish animals, seven in all, were perched on their hind legs atop seven separate red and yellow stools. The animals—snouted and barely more than three feet tall—seemed poised to perform some feat or other, their beady eyes and pointed ears alert for their mistress's command. A couple of them were dancing in place.

"For the first time ever on the North American continent," proclaimed the disembodied ringmaster, "a titillating troupe, a curious congregation, an exotic ensemble of one of the rarest animals on earth—the tremendous tumbling tanukis from the jungles of Southeast Asia, genuine mystery beasts: captured, tamed, and trained to execute amazing and amusing antics by the glamorous adventuress, Madame Ko."

"Oh, my goodness," said Bootsey. "Aren't they just precious?!"

"Kind of goofy-looking, if you ask me," said Pru. In truth, Pru did find the tanukos (she hadn't caught the name) oddly appealing, but so disappointed was she by the lone fleeting image of red nose, greasepaint, ruffled collar, and pantaloon during the entire thirty-second circus commercial that she wasn't about to speak favorably of it. The instant the ad ended, in fact, she arose in a mild distemper and went to the kitchen for a glass of tomato juice. There'd be no shortage of clowns at the actual circus, naturally, but still. . . .

"But what was that hanging between their legs?" Bootsey asked as Pru left the room. "Was it their . . . ?"

"No way. Couldn't have been."

Pru decided the canned juice might be improved by a squeeze of lemon. She was rummaging in the refrigerator's fruit-and-vegetable drawer when Bootsey called from the den. "Pru! Come here! Quick!"

There was just enough urgency in Bootsey's voice to prompt her younger sister to slam the refrigerator door and walk rather briskly back into the TV room. *What now?* Pru thought. She'd neglected to bring the tomato juice.

"Look at that man, that priest," said Bootsey, pointing at the screen, where an ostensible man of the cloth, his hands cuffed behind his back, was being led through what appeared to be one of those palmy, breezewayed, stucco terminals that one finds at tropical Third World airports.

Before Pru could focus clearly, the scene shifted to a close-up of a cardboard box into which were being placed a number of plastic baggies filled with beige powder. Then, just as abruptly, the camera returned to a view of the handcuffed man, now being ushered into a Jeep operated by what appeared to be U.S. military police.

Piecing it together, Pru gathered that a French Catholic priest on a flight from Bangkok to Los Angeles with a stopover in Manila had been apprehended at the airport in Agaña, Guam, with bags of narcotics taped to his torso and legs beneath his ecclesiastical garb.

"Doesn't he look like Dern?" Bootsey said. "Look! I mean, doesn't he?"

"Hmm. Well, yeah, I guess so. I can see that. There's a resemblance. Although he's quite a bit older."

Bootsey regarded Pru with the compassionate dismay she usually reserved for the more spectacularly incompetent clerks at the post office where she worked. (By this time, the newscast had moved on to coverage of student protests against the proposed U.S. missile defense system.) "Older? Older than Dern? Not any more. Honey, Dern's been missing for—"

"I know. I know." Pru sighed. "Dern's been gone for twenty-seven years."

"Twenty-eight."

In front of the shill and flicker, the sisters slowly sank into a state somewhere between reverie and paralysis.

At about that same time, give or take a few hours, a pretty, twenty-year-old woman was waking up in a strange bed in Bangkok. The woman's street name, her professional name—her nom de guerre, as she would prefer it—was Miss Ginger Sweetie. Her real name is not important.

In Miss Ginger Sweetie's cerebral railyard, germ-sized boxcars were starting to couple. With an electrochemical creak, the train lurched forward. First, Miss Ginger Sweetie remembered that she was at the Green Spider, a cozy backstreet boutique hotel that catered to a clientele, mainly foreigners, who possessed a certain aversion to paying by credit card, showing identification papers, or entertaining unannounced guests: not a low-life element, exactly, just careful.

Next, as the brain train picked up speed, Miss Ginger Sweetie recalled the man who lay beside her and to whom her smooth, bronze back was turned. My, wasn't *he* the odd one? Nice. Likable, actually. But decidedly unusual.

He claimed that he was French, but he spoke Americanized English. He spoke, in fact, the way she imagined William Faulkner would have spoken. And his name was Dickie. *Dickie?* Now, Miss Ginger Sweetie was no world traveler (until a few years ago, she'd never been out of the slums of Chiangmai), but neither was she some ignorant paddy girl. She was, she'd have you know, a full-time student of comparative literature at an accredited university—and, yes, it's true, she whored in Patpong, but only to pay for her education. Miss Ginger Sweetie knew that *Dickie* was a name no French mother would have christened her son.

And this Dickie hadn't touched her. (She felt between her legs now to make sure.) He was a handsome man, tall, slender, too old for his face; which was to say, while his hair was rather liberally salted, he looked as boyish as she thought Tom Sawyer might have looked. And while Miss Ginger Sweetie appreciated the holiday, the respite, she wouldn't have minded terribly much if he had taken what he paid for.

But he hadn't touched her. At least, not in any regular sense. What he had done was to smell her—although, she was quick to remind herself, not in the crude manner of a pervert or a dog. He'd looked her over thoroughly in an admittedly flattering way, and then he'd carefully sniffed her as if he were a wine connoisseur or something; sniffing her perfumed neck, her nipples, her armpits, finally lowering the tip of his nose gently into her belly button. But that's as far south as he would go.

Now, the man had not been unaffected by this scrutiny, this olfactory examination, Miss Ginger Sweetie had noted with some professional pride. In fact, when he had lain upon his back, the protuberance that jutted from the depths to lift a section of the white cotton bedsheet was of such substance that, rising like it did, Miss Ginger Sweetie couldn't help thinking for one weird second of . . . Moby Dick. Two-plus years of Patpong service had left her jaded about, even bored by, masculine display, yet for some reason the indication of this lurking phantom, all shrouded in savage shyness and allegorical white, had aroused the exploratory instinct in *her*. When she attempted to lay claim to the object of interest, however, he'd pushed her hand aside.

Dickie was in love, he explained. He had a fiancée, traveling now thousands of miles from Bangkok. "Okay." She'd smiled as if he were noble and she understanding, but to her Thai mind it made no sense whatsoever. His girlfriend had gone far away, Miss Ginger Sweetie was right here. There was an opportunity for pleasure. Where was the problem?

Then she reminded herself that Dickie hadn't gone to Patpong seeking pleasure. Men went to Bangkok's entertainment district (a little Las Vegas without gambling or glitz) for the sex shows, the girlie bars, the disco, the go-go, the booze, the speed pills, the smack, the full-body massage, the freelance larks of the night. But Dickie, her Dickie, had gone there to buy a guitar.

Not that the purchase of the guitar hadn't made him happy. So delighted was he with the new instrument—a cheap Thai knock-off of a Martin D-28—that she suspected he'd picked her up primarily to have someone with whom to share the delight. There would have been secondary reasons, too, she thought: undercurrents of loneliness and yes, even desire, never mind how successfully he'd suppressed it. Consider. When he took her to his room at the Green Spider, a room aromatic with oiled teak and moldering silk, he'd tuned the guitar and performed for her that song she liked about a river and oranges and a girl with a perfect body, and while he sounded nothing like Leonard Cohen, he wasn't half bad. She'd applauded, and he might have gone on strumming and singing through his whole repertoire except that she'd slithered out of her underwear and the distraction was more than his musicianship could bear.

Miss Ginger Sweetie turned over. Dickie had appeared a bit sad when she kissed him good night, torn as he was, she supposed, between wanting her and wanting not to want her, but now he was propped up in bed with a jowl-splitting grin on his face. Dickie was beaming like an overlit showcase in a jewelry store. Maybe he'd made up his mind about something. "Why so smile?" she inquired. "I worry you explode for happy."

She was both mildly stung and mildly relieved when his joy proved to have nothing to do with her. "Ah, Miss Ginger Cookie," he said, getting her name wrong but smiling on, "let you be the first to know." He cleared his throat. "You see," he announced, "as of last night—this morning, actually—I have dropped out of dream school."

It was a reflection neither upon Miss Ginger Sweetie's English nor her intellect that she was totally mystified. She asked him to repeat it in French, which he did, but it was bad French, worse than her own, and she regarded him curiously as, with a long crimson nail, she scratched a grain of sleep from her eye.

"Well, you see," said her handsome but perplexing faux French Faulknerian bedmate, "for years, for my entire adult life, I've been plagued by a recurring dream, a *nightmare*, I think you could safely call it. In this dream, I'm always back in school. Sometimes college, but mostly high school. There's a test that day, an important final exam, and when I get to the classroom I realize that I haven't studied for it, not at all. I'm not going to know a single answer, and I can't find my textbooks for a last-minute cram. Sometimes, I can't even find the right classroom." He slapped his forehead to illustrate what a predicament it was.

"Or else," he continued, "I'm supposed to give a presentation in front of the class, and when I stand up, it's suddenly clear to me that I'm totally unprepared, I've got nothing to say. Or, I've lost my homework, or neglected to do it, and everyone is turning it in but me. You get the picture? There're variations, but the theme is always the same: frustration, embarrassment, anxiety, failure."

Miss Ginger Sweetie nodded. She enjoyed a discussion of "themes."

"You couldn't count the hundreds of nights that that dream has ruined for me. The times I've woken up in a sweat, in a panic, and even felt bad the next day. And the thing is, you can never graduate from dream school! Not ever! You're doomed to repeat those embarrassing failures until death, and maybe they continue in Hell.

"However—*however*—last night (or this morning), I dropped out. I threw down my bookbag and just walked out the door. And I wasn't coming back. I was gone for good. And now, I'm through with dream school. I know—I feel it and I know it—I'll never have that horrible dream again. It's over for me. I've dropped out." His smile widened. "You have no idea, sweetie cookie, how incredibly liberating it is, what a burden I've shed. I haven't felt this free since that day twenty-five years ago when I made the decision to stay in. . . ." He fell silent. His smile lost a modicum of wattage, but it was still bright enough.

"Good. Very good, Dickie." She clasped her palms together, fingers pointing ceilingward, and saluted him in the Buddhist fashion. "I like story for have happy ending." She glanced at her dainty wristwatch. There was time for a quickie, if he was inclined. Alas, the dropout was busy reveling in his newfound freedom. So be it. He was an odd one. She slipped out of bed, retrieved her panties (her steam-dumpling breasts did not require the services of a bra), grabbed her handbag, and padded into the bathroom to perform her toilette.

Mahidol University was in Nakhon Pathom, an hour's bus ride from Bangkok. There was a seminar class at noon, during which she planned to present her original theory that Rimbaud, the precedent-shattering revolutionary French poet, was greatly influenced by Shakespeare; specifically, that he'd based his whole approach to poetry on Mad Tom's speech from *King Lear*, and she wanted sufficient time before class to make sure her delivery was properly polished and prepared. She didn't wish to be a character out of Dickie's nightmare. She wished never herself to be troubled by similar dreams. For Miss Ginger Sweetie, failure in school couldn't be an option. Learning not only satisfied some inner need, it was also her ticket out of Patpong.

Periodically, she would force herself to dwell on her cousin, Sup (nom de guerre: Miss Pepsi Please). Miss Pepsi Please had been lovely—truly movie-star gorgeous—but after seven years in Patpong . . . well, the last time Miss Ginger Sweetie saw her, Miss Pepsi Please's face looked like a sink of dirty dishes: greasy, hard, worn, forlorn, and neglected. There were many others like her, and then there were the less fortunate girls withering away

with AIDS. As she glossed her lips, Miss Ginger Sweetie reminded herself of her insistence that her own story have a happier ending.

Bladder drained, eyes shadowed, long black hair laboriously
brushed, she returned at last to the bedroom. Dickie was sitting
on the side of the bed watching TV, watching with great intensity, his dazzling dropout smile replaced now by an expression of
shock, concern, and disbelief. "Jesus," Dickie swore. "Jesus.
Holy shit."

From the announcer's English, she could tell that Dickie was
tuned to CNN. Perhaps there had been a huge natural disaster
somewhere, or a terrorist attack. She'd sensed that Dickie was
the empathetic type.

When she was in a position to see the screen, however, the
image thereon was of a Western Catholic priest, handcuffed, surrounded by police. Miss Ginger Sweetie shrugged and raised her
freshly penciled eyebrows.

But Dickie . . . Dickie sat there looking stunned. "Jesus," he
repeated. "They've got Foley. They've got him. They've got
Dern."

At about the same time, give or take a few hours, that Miss
Ginger Sweetie was attempting to persuade an astonished instruc-
tor and a few disinterested classmates that some Shakespearean
babble about whirlpools and ditch-dogs had directly inspired
Rimbaud's incandescent imagery in such startling poems as *Une
Saison en Enfer*, another attractive Asian woman was also making
a case. This woman was approximately a decade Miss Ginger
Sweetie's senior; was grander, keener, looked more Japanese than
Thai, and was pacing the pavement in front of San Francisco's
Cow Palace while waiting for a taxi to take her to the airport.

"The show here in San Francisco three more day, right? Then it go Porkland."

"Portland."

"Okay, Portland. By time set up in Seattle, I probably be back. Back in show, same-o same-o."

"No, you won't, Lisa," protested her companion. "You know you'll be gone longer than that. And anyway, you signed a contract. You have legal obligations to the show. You're featured in all the damn commercials. They've invested tens of thousands of dollars in those ads. You can't just skip out whenever you get an ant in your pants." The person confronting Lisa Ko was Bardo Boppie-Bip, the clown (not to be confused with any secretary-general of the United Nations, past or present). An onlooker wouldn't have recognized Bardo Boppie-Bip, as she was out of costume, dressed, in fact, in jeans, a Harley-Davidson Motorcycles sweatshirt, steel-toed workman shoes, and a baseball cap set low on the apricot-colored hair that she wore mowed almost to the follicles in a commando crop.

"No ant in no pant," countered Lisa Ko, staring in the direction from which she expected the cab to arrive. "I tell you it is *emergency*."

"Yeah, you told me, all right. But you still haven't explained the nature of that emergency. I mean, you see something on the news—and there was nothing on about Laos because I checked—and you freak out, clam up, fret all night, practically ruin your act, and now you're hopping a plane to Asia somewhere without even notifying management."

"I leave note." Nervously, she glanced at the Cow Palace, hoping that no one on the circus staff would emerge before her taxi came. The fog that wafted in from the bay wasn't quite thick enough to conceal her.

"How gracious of you. How thoughtful. *That'll* hold up in court. In this country, we say the show must go on. Personally, I think your 'emergency' has something to do with that guy you're supposed to marry over there. If you're so hot to see him, why don't you just send him a ticket so's he can come here? It'd be better for everybody concerned."

Lisa shook her head, jostling every ebony layer of her piled-on hairdo, crinkling the high silk collar of her jade green dress. "Can't happen. No way." She paused. "And I not very sure I marry him."

Bardo Boppie-Bip became pensive. Eventually, she said, speaking softly, with a smile about a centimeter on the vulnerability side of sarcasm, "Does that mean there's a chance for me?"

Under her breath Lisa muttered something in Lao. (The primary language spoken in Laos is called Lao. Likewise, the properly informed refer to "the Lao economy," "the Lao climate," "the Lao civil war," etc. Around 1960, when events in that small Southeast Asian nation forced Western media to start paying attention to Laos, the Associated Press, networks, and news magazines decided that it would tax the American intellect—rigid yet porous—to comprehend that *Lao* was the adjective form of Laos, and, always preferring the dumbing-down of an audience to challenging it, they invented the term *Laotian*. a rather ugly Ohioan-sounding word that naturally, not being bumpkins, we shall not use here.)

A yellow cab, like a smoker's tooth in the cottony mouth of morning, flashed into view. Lisa, who'd been staring at the pavement, suddenly turned to Bardo Boppie-Bip with a pleading look. Her eyes were wet. "You take good care my kids? You will?"

"Yeah, you know I will."

"Please."

"Relax. Those little hams are so hot to perform I could put 'em through their paces myself. Hell, maybe I'll take over your act. Next winter I'll have tanukis on my cable TV show."

"No, no, please. You only take care. You remember how do?"

"You wrote it all down for me. Relax. Just get your ass back here as soon as possible. I'll watch after your critters and try to save your job."

"Thank you." It was a heartfelt thanks, but when Bardo

Boppie-Bip went to embrace her, Lisa opened the door and followed her carry-on luggage into the taxi. She did, however, call "Good-bye!" Then the car pulled away, carrying "the glamorous adventuress, Madame Ko," looking a bit less sure of herself than in the commercial, to the international terminal at the San Francisco Airport.

"See you this evening, Sis." Tin Winnie the Pooh lunchbox in hand, Bootsey was leaving for the bus stop, ultimate destination: Seattle's Queen Anne branch of the United States Postal Service. She paused at the front door of their bungalow. "I have to say, my heart's still in a tizzy over how much that French priest last night reminded me of Dern."

"Forget about it." Pru took a swallow of tomato juice. "A French priest is a French priest."

Bootsey grasped the doorknob. "Are you going to look for work today?"

Pru, who'd been laid off from her drafting job during a downsizing at Boeing, smiled hesitantly. "Well . . . yes . . . and no."

"What does that mean? Yes and no?"

"What it means," Pru answered, a bit sheepishly, "is that I heard that the circus advance men are gonna be over at Key Arena today and they may be hiring a few temporary workers. You know, just for the run in Seattle. So maybe I'll give that a whirl before I start hauling my resumé around again."

"The circus? Doing what, for goodness sake? A gofer for the clowns? They'll let you hang out in clown alley? Water the elephants, then? I thought only twelve-year-old boys did stuff like that."

"Why the fuck should twelve-year-old boys have all the fun? Times have changed."

"They sure have. When a decent middle-aged woman uses language like that." Bootsey opened the door and peered outside. "Cloudy," she announced. "And kind of chilly. Wouldn't it be adorable if this was the day when the leaves start to turn?"

Miss Ginger Sweetie, guiltily clutching a tip that she felt she hadn't earned, had scarcely exited the Green Spider than Dickie was dialing a number on the vintage black telephone. He spoke to the answering party in Lao. The answering party did not comprehend, even though Lao is linguistically quite similar to Thai. Believing, reluctantly, that his southern accent must be at least partly to blame, Dickie switched to the singsong Anglo baby talk that in that part of the world frequently passed for English.

"I want speak Xing."

"Uh?"

"Speak Xing. Xing!"

"Xing no here." The voice belonged to a mature woman, possibly the mother of one of his contact's confederates.

"Where Xing?"

"Uh?"

"Where? Where Xing? Very important."

"Today I no know."

"When? When he home?"

"I no know. Next day maybe."

That wasn't good enough. Dickie's throat was tightening like a paw around a peanut. As he anxiously considered his options, mama-san volunteered, "Tonight Xing go Patpong."

Okay! Great! Now they were making progress. "Where?" asked Dickie, cognizant all the while that Patpong was a large area, that there were actually three separate streets named Patpong, and that addresses there were about as useful as name tags on fruit flies. Before the answering party could say she no know, Dickie fired off another, perhaps equally futile, question. "What he do in Patpong?"

"Go see Elvisuit."

Dickie almost whooped. Joy rose up in him like a champagne reflux. "Elvisuit!" All he'd have to do was find where Bangkok's foremost Elvis Presley impersonator was performing that night, and, with any luck, Dickie would be on his way back into Laos to do . . . whatever at this point could possibly be done.

"Kaw roo nah," he thanked the woman in Faulknerian Thai. "May the buddhas sing in your chili paste."

The afternoon passed more slowly than a walnut-sized kidney stone. It was typically torrid and muggy, and the air conditioning in the Green Spider Hotel operated at less than maximum strength. Nude, perched on a rattan stool, Dickie tried to concentrate on his new guitar, keeping one ear tuned to the television audio. While CNN offered no further coverage of Dern's arrest, Dickie did learn that an unexpected typhoon-strength storm had closed the Philippine airports on the previous day, which would account for Manila-bound Dern landing on Guam. His flight must have bypassed Manila and made an unscheduled stop—on an island that remained under American control, which meant paranoid security, overzealous narcs, and sniffer dogs. Well, maybe Dern had been asking for it. Stubblefield, too.

The guitar Dickie had bought at one of those nighttime open-air markets where twenty-dollar "Rolex" watches and ten-dollar "Gucci" loafers were sold, and to the untrained eye, it looked exactly like a dandy Martin D-28, right down to the herringbone purfling.

"Is this decorative border made from real herring bones?" Dickie had asked the salesman.

The fellow had looked dumbfounded, but he quickly recovered. "Oh, yes! Real! Alla time bes' real hurreen bow. Hurreen bow number one!"

"Excellent," said Dickie. "But are the bones from virgin herrings?"

For a moment, the poor salesman appeared torn: was he ignorant in some area vital to the successful merchandising of knockoff guitars, or was his customer a dangerous lunatic? He hadn't stalled long, though. "Yes! Okay! Hurring bow number one cherry virgin bow. Okay. Alla time bes' 'Melican virgin. No problem!"

Remembering the exchange now, Dickie smiled that winning southern-boy smile. Then he went glum again. He thumped the purfled sound board. He caressed the inlaid peg head. He plucked each individual string. Eventually, stealing glances all the while at CNN, he attempted a Phil Ochs tune, but couldn't progress beyond the first verse. Same for Bob Dylan and Neil Young favorites. He couldn't even remember Cohen's "Suzanne," which he'd sung perfectly for that nice freelance girlie girl only the night before.

There was one song in his repertoire, however, whose lyrics no amount of anxiety would probably ever erase—and Dickie performed it, off and on, throughout the tic and trickle of that interminable afternoon.

> Meet me in Cognito, baby,
> We'll soon leave our pasts behind us.
> The present is always a mystery,
> As the future never fails to remind us.
>
> Once we're alone in Cognito,
> We'll remove all of our clothes very fast,

But though we be naked as jaybirds,
At no time will we take off our masks.

Cinderella went incognito,
And it's said that she had a ball.
It's always midnight in Cognito
By the black clock at the end of the hall.

We're destined to be clandestine,
Incognito is our very last hope.
I'll meet you where the sun don't shine,
With a fake I.D. and some dope.

So do join me in Cognito,
You know that I'll never tell.
We'll sneak in the back door of Heaven
And stroll unnoticed through Hell.

Incognito
Incognito
There, every day's a surprise.
Incognito
Incognito
Where truth tells all the best lies.

When socialism is pushed beyond a certain point, it becomes totalitarianism. Capitalism, on the other hand, if carried to *its* extreme, becomes anarchy. Anyone who doubts the accuracy of this last observation has never walked the streets of Bangkok.

It was for that very reason—capitalism run amok and the chaotic consequences thereof—that Stubblefield refused to travel to Bangkok (or so he professed); but the constant construction, deconstruction, and reconstruction, the ceaseless commerce, matter-eating pollution, brain-numbing noise, and twenty-four-hour-a-day traffic gridlock failed to deter Dern from the occasional risky visit; while for Dickie, the city held a strange appeal, all the more odd because Bangkok, the Big Bad Busy B, was in such dramatic contrast to the life he led and loved in Laos. It may have been the clamorous city's equanimous mixture of gentle, bright-eyed Buddhist benevolence and shameless smiley-faced sexual hucksterism that fascinated him, although he no more than sniffed around the edges of either element (as Miss Ginger Sweetie might affirm).

To call Bangkok a city of contradictions is worse than a cliché, it's a trite superfluity, not merely because it's so patently obvious but because there's a sense in which virtually *every* city is a city of contradictions. Are we not a contradictory species occupying a dichotomous planet wobbling about in what, from all indications, is a paradoxical universe? That said, Bangkok's contrasts are just too immense, too dramatic, to be easily dismissed as the norm.

Simultaneously a frantic, high-tech juggernaut and a timeless Asian dream, Bangkok straddles like no other metropolis the boundary between acrid and sweet, soft and hard, sacred and profane. It's a silk buzz saw, a lacquered jackhammer, a steel-belted seduction, a digital prayer. Its numerous temples and shrines are obscured by clouds of mephitic exhaust, its countless vices and crimes by smiles of tender delight; and through it all, Bangkok manages to maintain the most graceful balance, a grace no less genuine for being well-rehearsed and no less pure for being supported by con men and whores.

Well, okay, there's no sense going on and on about Bangkok and its incongruities, its commotional commingling of supplication and flash. For our purposes, it should suffice to report that approximately a half-hour after sunset, Dickie Goldwire, too agitated and impatient to wait a moment longer, locked his new guitar in his hotel room and ventured out into the aforementioned hubbub of dirty, mystic glamor.

Hot and heavy, the very air seemed to sprout fat red fingers, baker's fingers that kneaded pedestrians as if they were lumps of dough. It was probably not the sort of weather that Bootsey Foley would describe as "cute"—but you never know.

As usual, the streets were teeming. There seemed to be an equal number of entrepreneurs in linen suits, girlie girls in skimpy skirts, and monks in saffron robes. In addition, there was a liberal sprinkling of Caucasian males in khaki trousers and white bush shirts: the uniform of the expatriate. Dickie wore just such an outfit, for the purpose of blending in, although when he would near the Safari or one of the other bars favored by ex-pats, he would hurriedly cross the street, guarding against the possibility, remote as it was, of being recognized.

> (Those who travel in Cognito
> —Their very lives can depend on a hunch.
> They eat intuition for breakfast
> And sip cold paranoia at lunch.)

The quickest, most efficient way to travel around perpetually congested Bangkok was via water taxi, but since the Green Spider was equally as far from the river as it was from Patpong, Dickie took a *tuk-tuk* to his destination. Forty minutes passed before the three-wheeled contraption deposited him on the northern perimeter of the district. Patpong's roads had for years been closed to vehicular traffic, so Dickie was obliged to enter on foot, which was just as well because he had no clue in which of the district's many clubs Elvisuit might be playing.

The borders of Patpong were patrolled by the freelance prostitutes, the rare ones not employed by bars or enslaved by pimps (and thus frequently harassed and physically threatened by those who would own or control them). Dickie kept an eye out for Miss Ginger Sweetie and was both disappointed and relieved that he did not see her.

He'd walked only a few yards, however, before he encountered the Professor.

❀

Dickie called him "the Professor." Nobody else did, although they easily might have: the little old man had an aura of academia so thick it could cause the most liberated dropout to suffer frightening flashbacks of dream school.

Slight of build and tufted with rumpled gray hair, the fellow wore wire-rimmed glasses, a baggy blue suit dusted here and there with tobacco ash, a boring brown tie decorated with random stains of fish sauce and chili paste, brown shoes on which a kennel of rottweiler puppies might have been cutting their teeth, and an air of dignified seriousness, undermined somewhat by wandering expressions of utter distraction. It was easy to imagine him having tenure in the department of physics at Mahidol University.

For a dozen years, Dickie had been slipping into Bangkok two or three times a year, and on each and every one of those visits, he had been approached by the Professor within minutes after entering Patpong. In his masticated oxfords, the Professor would shuffle up to Dickie, as he shuffled up to all unattached males (and Western couples should they appear to be tourists), greet him politely, and then inquire—as earnestly and hopefully as if he were asking an esteemed colleague if he might wish to attend a conference on double-charged subatomic particles:

"Please, mister, you want to see a girl fuck a monkey?"

As usual, Dickie, with a manner as formal as the Professor's, respectfully declined. "Thank you, but I would not care to witness such an engagement, not even were it between Cheetah and Jane. King Kong and Fay Wray might make a more irresistible combination, due to the problems presented by their considerable differences in scale, although technically speaking, of course, neither King Kong nor Cheetah are monkeys." Usually, Dickie would babble something in this vein, award the Professor a few baht for his trouble, and continue on his way, scolding himself for having just sounded so much like Stubblefield. Now, however, he stayed on to ask a question of his own.

"Can you tell me where is Elvisuit?"

"Elvisuit?"

"Yes. You know. Elvisuit. Where he play tonight?"

The way the Professor scratched his brow, he might have been contemplating the strong-force interaction during which a pair of nucleons exchange electrical roles. "Tonight," he answered slowly, cautiously, "I think Elvisuit play Shay-ray-bom."

"*Where* you speak?"

"Shay-ray-bom."

"Sheraton?"

"Shay-ray-bom."

"Sheraton. You're saying the Royal Orchid Sheraton." Dickie swore under his breath. "Goddamn!" The Royal Orchid Sheraton was located in the riverside luxury hotel district, more than a mile—a steamy, gritty mile—away.

But the Professor shook his gray head impatiently, as if frustrated by a particularly dense student. "No! No Rora Orchid Sharaton. Elvisuit play at Shay-ray-bom. Patpong. Shay-ray-bom Club."

It was Dickie's turn to frown. Then, something clicked. "Oh. You mean Cherry Bomb. The Cherry Bomb Club?"

Smiling just long enough and wide enough to release a harsh hint of cheap Thai mouthwash, the Professor concurred. "Yes. Yes. Shay-ray-bom. No problem. Okay!" He accepted a crumple of baht bills with a dignified little bow and a Buddhist salute, then immediately began searching the street for another mister.

Skirting the Safari and King's Corner (the latter a haunt for those ex-pats who recognized it as, with the possible exception of the Vatican, the finest transsexual club in the world), Dickie jostled his way through the gradually thickening mob of hawkers and gawkers, to the Cherry Bomb. He stood at its entrance, listening hard for strains of "Hound Dog" or "Love Me Tender." No note of music wafted from the place, however, nor any ray of light. The Cherry Bomb was quiet and dark. Maybe the proper bribes had not been paid. Maybe some rowdy Australians had trashed it in a brawl. Whatever—the Cherry Bomb was closed.

There was no cause to fret. Was there? Wasn't Xing coming to Patpong specifically to see Elvisuit? Didn't that indicate that Elvisuit was performing that night in Patpong and not in one of the Silom Road riverside hotels, in Nana Plaza, Soi Cowboy, or any other district of Bangkok? One would assume so, yet what if Xing had been planning on catching Elvisuit at the Cherry Bomb, unaware that the club had closed? Xing had contacts in Bangkok, all right, but he resided in a distant village near the Lao border. What did *he* know?

Dickie began scouring the street in earnest, staring into each and every bar that looked as if it featured live music. Because the sex clubs offered only canned music, he passed them by without investigation, although as usual, he did pause briefly, uncontrollably, at that most infamous of Patpong signboards, the one that read:

PUSSY PLAY PING-PONG
PUSSY SMOKE CIGARETTE
PUSSY EAT WITH CHOPSTICKS
PUSSY OPEN BEER BOTTLE
PUSSY WRITE LETTER

If the purpose of advertising copy was to attract maximum interest, this was the most successful ad copy in the history of the medium. Even those passersby who'd rather fall down a flight of stairs than actually attend a genital stunt show were galvanized by the sign. Women were shocked by it, amused, intrigued, perhaps secretly inspired. Men were titillated, wonderstruck, maybe even piqued with a subliminal pang of vagina envy. Whether awed or disgusted, no one could ignore it—and, moreover, unlike 95 percent of Madison Avenue's handiwork, this ad was *truthful:* if you ventured inside (and Dickie had done so once or twice, back before he fell in love), you witnessed everything that was promised and more.

Still, Dickie was a bit disappointed to note that the wording on the sign hadn't changed in at least a decade. Not that he expected or wanted this sex show to start including live frogs on its program, as was currently the rage in Nana Plaza, yet considering how technophilic Thailand had recently become, he easily could envision an addition on the order of:

PUSSY ACCESS INTERNET

Imagine a city in which there are three streets running side by side, more or less parallel to one another, each with the same identical name. Such a city exists, and while one would think those repetitive avenues ought to be located in Pago Pago or Walla Walla (or more appropriately, Pago Pago Pago or Walla Walla Walla), that was not the case. The logic in whose face this peculiar redundancy flies cannot here be explained, but any municipality that flaunts so brazenly the conventions of city planning has got to be admired. The world's old pre-industrial towns, with their organically twisting and circuitous lanes, nurture the free spirit even as they confound the pragmatic mind, but few if any have ever wandered quite this far in the direction of happy abandon.

When told of the trio of parallel Patpong Roads, Stubblefield had remarked, "How refreshing! I've always been wary of the urban grid, Goldwire. It's a repudiation of nature, a barrier to spontaneity, and a cage for the soul. Maybe Bangkok's worth visiting after all."

But Mars Stubblefield had *not* visited Bangkok. Dickie Goldwire was there now—searching both sides of an artery that some city maps labeled "Patpong I": the most wildly active of the three Patpong Roads. But to no avail. Dickie was starting to feel that trying to find Elvisuit in Patpong was like trying to find Jonah's contact lens in the belly of the whale. Dickie also was feeling weak and dizzy—and he remembered that he'd had nothing to eat all day but a custard apple and a small bag of shrimp chips.

There was a little restaurant on Patpong III with a reputation for exceptionally delicious *yang kung*, and while he was no Tanuki when it came to food (nor any Stubblefield, either), the sudden thought of that dish (seafood was unavailable in the mountains of Laos) set Dickie to salivating.

Patpong III was a quieter street, not much more than an alley, really, although several lively gay clubs had sprung up there. Dickie's restaurant, he noted with some apprehension, had expanded to add a karaoke stage, but the stage was empty at the moment and the prawns were as good as he remembered. He washed them down with a couple of pints of beer and after dinner ordered a double whiskey. He thought (foolishly, of course) that the alcohol might calm his mind.

The immediate situation was not that complicated. He needed to track down Elvisuit so that he might hook up with Xing. He needed to connect with Xing so that he might be safely smuggled back into Laos. He needed to return to Laos in order to rush to Villa Incognito and warn Stubblefield of Dern Foley's arrest—and gather his own wits and possessions in preparation for his next move.

Dickie must have been brooding into his glass because he was startled when the restaurant owner spoke to him. Normally, his radar would have warned him of her approach, but the combination of worry and booze had obscured the blip.

"Whatsa matta? Whiskey no good?"

"Uh? What? Oh. No, no, whiskey good. Whiskey *sabai dee*. Whiskey *sanuk. Kaw roo nah.*"

The owner giggled. "You speak Thai very good," she lied. "Number one. But have Lao accent."

Dickie blanched. His spine tingled. He assumed an innocent expression (easy for an upperclass Carolina boy) and shrugged. "Thank you," he said. No more Thai.

"You no happy," the woman accused. Although heavyset and every inch middle-aged, she wore a tight blue dress, and her lips and nails were painted rocketship red. "Why you no happy? You want girl?"

"Girl? No. Me happy. No want girl. Me have girl."

"Where?" She made a show of glancing around the room. "Where you girl? You girl work now? Catch other man?"

Again, Dickie blanched. He sat upright, wishing he didn't feel so woozy. "My girl far away," he said weakly. She *had* gone away to work, though not as a bargirl. Yet for all he knew, she very well *could* be in bed with some other man.

"Ah. Girl far way. You need girl now. I have pretty girl. Number one. Make *sanuk*. Make happy."

"I no look for girl," he insisted. "I look for Elvisuit."

"Elvisuit?"

Dickie nodded pathetically. "I no can find where Elvisuit play. I want see him tonight."

The woman grinned. "No problem. Elvisuit my friend. I call Elvisuit, he come here. No problem."

"Yeah, right," muttered Dickie as his hostess bustled away. *No problem. It's always "no problem" with these Thai. Same with the Lao. Whether they're conning you, feting you, or saving your life, it's always no problem.* Mai pen rai. *No problem. Is it Buddhism, or what, that makes these people so much happier and more relaxed about life than Westerners? In the midst of Bangkok's relentless turmoil, they just smile on and say "no problem." If Jean-Paul Sartre had been Thai, existentialism would have been a sit-com. Jeeze!*

The diners at the adjacent table—two couples—were celebrating a birthday. They were drunker than Dickie and infinitely more festive, and just as he finished off his drink and went to signal for the check, they sent a second whiskey to his table. It was a single, and they were beaming at him. Oh, well. Hypocritically, he flashed them his sweet southern smile, lifted the new glass in their direction, and sipped.

He wasn't used to booze. In Laos, he rarely drank. As wasted as he was feeling, however, he remained aware of his limited options. He could stick to the original schedule, wait three more days, and then bus to Xing's village, as had been previously arranged. Or he could bus to the border in the morning and hope that Xing would show up there earlier than expected. Or he could. . . . No, sorry, that was the extent of the menu. Sure, he had a fake French passport just like Dern (though he'd never used it), but he lacked the money to fly to Vientiane. He'd been counting on the cash that Dern was to bring him from Manila, and now he was running dangerously low. After the dinner tonight, he'd be lucky to pay his hotel bill let alone return to Laos via jet.

There was nothing to do at that point but down his whiskey.

After that, head spinning, there was nothing to do but weave up to the karaoke stage, seize the microphone, and without waiting for musical accompaniment, launch into a rendition of "Blue Christmas."

He sounded nothing like Elvis Presley. In fact, he sounded nothing like Dickie Goldwire. He crooned the way a can of cheap dog food might croon if a can of cheap dog food had a voice. *Generic Puppy Chow Sings Holiday Favorites*. On the Skippy label. His delivery was so flat, so off-key and toneless and awful that his own ears felt violated. Ordinarily a pretty good amateur vocalist, he was astonished at how bad he sounded. The other diners listened politely, the birthday party smiled its encouragement, but it was all Dickie could do to keep a straight face. Giggles built up in him to the point where he felt like a bottle of champagne that had been vigorously shaken for about five minutes. If something had popped Dickie's glottal cork, the resulting laugh-blast would have blown out all the windows.

It was at that moment that he heard someone exclaim in a loud, southern American voice, "See ya later, alligator!"

Shielding his eyes, Dickie, still singing, squinted at the front door to see what fellow countryman his horrid rendition of "Blue Christmas" was driving from the premises—praying all the while that it was not a man who might have recognized him. As it turned out, the remark had issued not from someone departing the restaurant but from someone entering. Specifically, from a monk in a saffron robe, with a strange saffron silk scarf around his head.

With a theatrical gesture, the newcomer tore off the scarf, revealing long sideburns and a puffy black cumulus of pomaded hair. In a flash, he slipped out of the monk robe, beneath which he wore a tight-fitting jumpsuit as sparkly and white as frozen milk. (He left on his monk sandals, but they happened to have been painted silver.) The diners' murmurs escalated when a boy came through the door and handed over the guitar that, out in the streets, he'd been pretending was his.

No longer incognito, Elvisuit sprang onstage, nudged Dickie aside with a bony elbow (except for his hair and sideburns, the skinny little Thai resembled the late Mother Teresa as much as the late Mr. Presley), and bellowed out what was apparently his signature greeting: "See ya later, alligator!"

Then, as Dickie shambled back to his table, Elvisuit commenced crooning "Blue Christmas," taking up right where Dickie had left off. It was obvious that he was singing it phonetically, comprehending scarcely a word (for him as for the Buddhists in the audience, Christmas was one of the peculiar American preoccupations—such as handguns, lawn care, and psychoanalysis—about which the Thai maintained a minimum of curiosity), yet he sang it so flawlessly, so exactly, so note-perfect, one could close one's eyes and believe that the Memphis King, like his rival, the King of the Jews, had risen from the tomb.

Dickie's pent-up laughter evaporated without a single snicker. Did he feel chagrined? Somewhat, and embarrassed, as well. That, however, was not the worst of it. He noticed that Elvisuit kept a beeper attached to his guitar strap—so that he could be instantly summoned to the next gig.

This cat, thought Dickie, *must play ten venues a night. Hell, twenty!* As a means of locating Xing, Elvisuit was about as useful as a pocket road map of Venezuela.

No sooner had he suffered that realization than it occurred to Dickie that since he'd requested Elvisuit's performance there, the restaurant was probably going to charge him for it. Such a fee could easily run as high as a hundred dollars (or its equivalent), not including tip. And this on top of the dinner and the drinks. Should he object, management would call the police, and that would *never* do. It was then that he decided to bolt.

Waiting until the owner and the waiter had their backs turned, he rose unsteadily and made as if he were going to the toilet. Elvisuit had segued into "Blue Hawaii," and Dickie swayed unintentionally in time to the music. When he came alongside the front door, he rushed it. *Whump!* Unfortunately, he had run head-on into a customer who was entering.

For a moment, the two seemed entangled. Dickie tried to break free, but the man had grabbed hold of his bush shirt. Unable to pull away and complete his escape, the normally mild-tempered Dickie, in full panic now, drew back his arm to throw a punch. It was then that, for the first time, he looked at the man's grinning face.

It was his border guide. It was Xing.

Knock! Knock!

"Who's there?"

"It's me. I lost my key. Let me in quick! I have to tinkle."

Pru opened the door. *"Tinkle?"* Pru asked, scowling. "That's a preschool potty word."

"Who cares?" said Bootsey, brushing past her sister and heading for the bathroom, where she remained for what seemed an inordinately long time.

Knock! Knock!

"Who's there?"

"Now who you *think* would be knocking on our bathroom door? Edgar Allan Poe? What's taking you so long?"

"I've got other issues. Something I ate for lunch."

"Well, I've got some stuff to tell you. I got the job."

Through the door Bootsey asked, "What job?"

"At the circus. They called this morning. It doesn't pay much, and it's only for a few days, but it ought to be fun."

"That's great. Maybe you can get me a pass. I wouldn't mind seeing those adorable little animals, the funny ones with the snouts, those katoonies."

"I think they're called tazukies." Pru paused. "There's something else. A man stopped by. From the government, apparently. He wants us to come to San Francisco. Right away. I think it's about Dern."

On the other side of the door, there was silence. Then, finally, the familiar sound of water being strangled by a jealous lover. The old-fashioned flush.

Knock! Knock!

"Who's there?"

"It's me."

"Pardon?"

"Stub, it's *me*. It's Dickie."

"Ah, Goldwire. Back so soon from the numinous nexus of nirvanic nookie, Buddha's boisterous bordello?"

"I *had* to get back. There's a reason."

"Lan, unlatch the door for Monsieur Goldwire. You can come in, Dickie, but you'll have to be quiet. You're interrupting us here."

The door was heavy, fashioned from reddish tropical hardwood into which had been carved folk heroes and a procession of pachyderms, a reminder of the time when Laos was known as "The Land of a Million Elephants." On its huge brass hinges, the door opened slowly, gracefully, almost luxuriously, *gliding* open despite its weight, like a beefy dowager who hasn't forgotten her finishing-school drill.

Coming in from brilliant sunlight, Dickie was momentarily sightless in the dim, cavernous parlor. "This is important, Stub," he said, directing his words into darkness. "It's urgent."

"Now, Goldwire." Dickie couldn't see Stubblefield's serene, sagacious yet somehow ever ironic smile—but he could tell it was there. "You know well enough that nothing's ever urgent in our little green mousehole in the opium closet of the world. I'm just winding up my lecture. Go to my study and I'll be with you shortly."

If you had any idea what I went through to get here when I did, thought Dickie. On his behalf, let us list the highlights of his ordeal:

1. Xing had coerced him into returning to his table in the restaurant, where he drank more whiskey and did, indeed, end up paying a considerable amount of Elvisuit's command performance fee.

2. Riding to the Green Spider on the back of Xing's motorcycle, he spotted Miss Ginger Sweetie on a corner and made Xing pull over. She looked so pretty, so demure, so vulnerable, so tired—and drunkenly, he gave her the little that remained of his bankroll, bidding her to go home and sleep. Miss Ginger Sweetie threw her arms around him, nearly knocking the motorcycle over in the process. "Okay, Dickie, I go sleep. No problem. Thank you, darling. You sleep, too. Okay? No go dream school." He watched her until the bike carried him out of range.

3. Early morning, broke now, he crossed the lobby as nonchalantly as possible, his belongings stuffed in his guitar case, his backpack abandoned, aware that running out on the bill meant he could never stay at the Green Spider again.

4. With a hangover that could have been productively employed in the Inquisition, he spent the next fourteen hours aboard Xing's speeding Yamaha, a spine-chattering, hemorrhoid-inflating experience that, itself, might have been put to torturous use by a

Church with a novel interpretation of the Sixth Commandment.

5. Next to a water buffalo and her calf, he tried to nap for a few hours in a shed in Xing's village while waiting for the moon to set.

6. He handed over his prized new guitar to Xing when the irate smuggler refused to extend him credit for the border crossing.

7. Lying on his back beneath a blanket that smelled worse than the buffalos, he was rowed across the Mekong River and dropped off, wet and reeking, at a spot where he was assured there would be no border guards.

8. Jittery to the bone at the prospect of stepping on a cobra, he walked for two hours over marshy terrain to the place where he'd hidden his own small motorbike.

9. Having run out of gas after thirty or so miles, he pushed the bike for another five miles to a gas station—a "gas station" in rural Laos consisting of a low wooden table behind which a woman sat, watching over maybe a half-dozen plastic Evian bottles refilled with low-octane petrol. Dickie traded the woman his leather belt, his empty wallet, and his high-school graduation ring for two quart-bottles of fuel, then putted off on another long ride.

10. The last four miles to Fan Nan Nan (or "La Vallée du Cirque") had to be covered on foot, as the trail was too steep and rugged for even a motorbike. When at last he arrived at the lovely little hill town, he did not even stop by his house to wash, eat, or change clothes, but set out immediately for Villa Incognito, a matter of only a few hundred yards, yet, from Dickie's

perspective, the most harrowing part of the entire journey from Bangkok.

During the monsoon-enforced lull in the Southeast Asian circus season, many of the more famous or unusual acts, such as Madame Ko and her tumbling tanukis, had taken jobs with European or North American shows, but a few performers, primarily old-timers, had returned to the cooler, drier elevations of Fan Nan Nan to relax or work on their routines. It was one of those veteran aerialists who agreed to push Dickie in a wooden wheelbarrow across the slender cable that connected Fan Nan Nan with Villa Incognito.

In many respects, Dickie Goldwire was a devil-may-care sort of guy. Put him in a warplane in a combat zone and he was as cool as a popsicle. When his own base had come under attack, he had usually been the last to take shelter, and he almost always dove into the bunker with a song on his lips. Ah, but that wheelbarrow ride was quite another story.

The wire over which the primitive vehicle rolled was no wider than a child's wrist. Ratcheted as taut as physically possible under the circumstances, it nevertheless would sway gently in the wind. From wooded promontory to wooded promontory, the cable ran nearly the length of a football field—above a yawning chasm, a gorge so deep its bottom could scarcely be seen for the mist that rose from the rock-strewn torrent that coursed through it. There was said to be a plethora of cobras down in that gorge, and even a tiger or two, but incidence of wildlife would have been of no concern to anyone unlucky enough to topple off the wire. One unexpected gust, one misstep by the aerialist, and the passenger would spend his last seconds of life learning how it felt to freefall without a parachute.

The odd thing was, Dickie longed to experience that feeling. It wasn't any kind of death wish: there was not a suicidal cell in his body. Rather, it seemed that the very sensation, the inner force that made Dickie's scrotum tighten, his throat constrict, and his eyeballs swim in dizziness also made him want to tumble into the precipitous void. And ultimately, his fear of longing to fall was greater, more disturbing, than his fear of falling.

When there were no circus performers in Fan Nan Nan, no wirewalker available to pilot the gayly painted wheelbarrow, one either crossed the gulch hand over hand, commando style (Dickie had done it only once), or waited for Dern to get his old Russian helicopter running. Of the two reasons (three, if you counted his fiancée) that Dickie seldom visited Villa Incognito, the dread of traversing that chasm was decidedly paramount.

On this particular afternoon, though, he had no choice. He couldn't send a messenger, for both the gravity and sensitivity of the predicament demanded that he confer with Stubblefield promptly and in person. Their situation might very well be desperate. Thus, he climbed into the little red-and-yellow wheelbarrow and with his long legs and arms hanging out of its box and with his eyes squeezed shut like a six year old at his first horror movie, allowed himself to be wheeled along a swaying steel thread in the sky. Taking one short, deliberately measured step after another, never once wavering or altering her rhythm, the aerialist delivered him limp but alive to the opposite side of the abyss where, after a slow, grateful trot through the trees, he presented himself at the villa.

He presented himself in sorry condition. Filthy, smelly, unshaven, unsteady, red-eyed, and agurgle with hunger, Dickie looked like something the proverbial cat *refused* to drag in, looked worse than Tanuki at the end of a sake saga. Stubblefield took no notice—partly because of the insufficient light, partly because of the odor-camouflaging incense, but chiefly because he was preoccupied with furthering the education of his servants and concubines.

Now," said Stubblefield, "just before we were interrupted, I used an English term—*soul*—that neither those of you who are Buddhists nor those of you who are Hmong animists probably understand. That's perfectly okay because very few Westerners really understand it, either."

His audience was rapt. It consisted of six concubines (four were Stubblefield's, two Dern's), about ten male servants, and two or three village elders. Sipping tea, they squatted on opulent Oriental carpets, rare and expensive rugs stacked two or three deep in places. Over the years, Stubblefield had taught most of his "students" to speak English, and not the tenseless singsong baby-talk version, either. They might not comprehend a lot of what was said, but they were attentive—and so was Dickie, who stood in the doorway to the study, not about to leave the parlor. Dickie loved Stubblefield's pedantic discourses, always had, and were it not for the wire and certain business activities, would have attended the lectures at the villa on a regular basis.

"What are we talking about when we talk about the soul?" It was a rhetorical question, of course, but Stubblefield paused, as if he expected his cook or that night's designated bedmate to reply. The big room was shuttered against the sun as well as the incongruous mixture of daily-life village noises and shiny toot-toot-jingle-jingle circus music that periodically drifted across the gorge. As Dickie's eyes grew accustomed to the dimness, he had the impression that Stubblefield's bulk, already considerable, had increased since he saw him last.

For some time now, the perimeters of Stubblefield's silhouette had been steadily encroaching upon the world at large. His corpus had expanded to the degree where those who cherished the popular image of Buddha must have felt reverential in his presence, while the hill-tribe animists surely saw in his massively bushy beard and the hair (still mostly brown) that reached down below his shoulder blades, some reflection of the god—or the ogre—of the gorge. That impression doubtlessly was enhanced by the prowling tiger tattooed across his chest. He wore, without a shirt, a Western-style suit of glossy, lightweight purple silk. Save for the tattoo, his chest was bare, as were his feet, the toenails of which one of the girls had playfully painted scarlet. The nail polish, Dickie thought, made Stubblefield's long, meaty toes look like the nosecones of a lilliputian space agency.

"What are we talking about when we talk about the soul? Well, pop culture to the contrary, the soul is not an overweight nightclub singer having an unhappy love affair in Detroit. The soul doesn't hang out at a Memphis barbershop, fry catfish for supper, and keep a thirty-eight Special in its underwear drawer. Hard times and funky living can season the soul, true enough, but joy is the yeast that makes it rise.

"On the other hand," Stubblefield continued, "the soul is most definitely not some pale vapor wafting off a bucket of metaphysical dry ice. For all of its ectoplasmic associations, it steadfastly contradicts those who imagine it to be a billow of sacred flatulence or a shimmer of personal swamp gas.

"*Soul* is not even that Crackerjack prize that God and Satan scuffle over after the worms have all licked our bones. That's why, when we ponder—as sooner or later each of us must—exactly what we ought to be doing about our soul, religion is the wrong, if conventional, place to turn. Religion is little more than a transaction in which troubled people *trade* their souls for temporary and wholly illusionary psychological comfort—the old give-it-up-in-order-to-save-it routine. Religions lead us to believe that the soul is the ultimate family jewel and that in return for our mindless obedience, they can secure it for us in their vaults, or at least insure it against fire and theft. They are mistaken."

Stubblefield was pacing back and forth, striding now like that tiger in the tattoo, but his face was completely at ease. "If you need to visualize the soul, think of it as. . . ." He paused to ponder. "Think of it as a kind of train. Yes, a long, lonesome freight train rumbling from generation to generation on an eternally rainy morning: its boxcars are loaded with sighs and laughter, its hobos are angels, its engineer is the queen of spades—and the queen of spades is wild. *Whooo-whooo!* Hear that epiphanic whistle blow." The audience giggled at the sound effects. "The train's destination is the godhead, but it stops at the Big Bang, at the orgasm, and at that hole in the fence that the red fox sneaks through down behind the barn. It's simultaneously a local and an express, but it doesn't transport weaponry, and it certainly ain't no milk run."

If his students were bewildered by this, their expressions didn't betray it. Nevertheless, the big man said, "I may be waxing too fanciful here, and I apologize. I do. Let's look at it this way, friends: the soul is nothing more, probably, than the authentic vibration of the biosphere, registered and amplified within the human sensorium. Think of it as that somewhat lumpy cloud of indefinable energy that is generated when human emotion and human intelligence interface with the larger body of nature.

" 'How then does soul differ from spirit?' you're probably asking yourself," although he *must* have been reasonably sure nobody was. "Well, soul is darker of color, denser of volume, saltier of flavor, rougher of texture, and tends to be more maternalistic than paternalistic: soul is connected to Mother Earth just as spirit is connected to Father Sky. Of course, mothers and fathers are prone to copulation, and in their commingled state, soul and spirit often can be difficult to distinguish the one from the other. Generally, if spirit is the fresh air vent and ambient lighting in the house of consciousness, if spirit is the electrical system that illuminates that house, then soul is the smoky fireplace, the fragrant oven, the dusty wine cellar, the strange creaks we hear in the floorboards late at night.

"It's a bit of a cliché to say it, but when you think of soul, you should think of things that are authentic and things that are deep. Anything superficial is not soulful. Anything artificial, imitative, or overly refined is not soulful. Wood has a stronger connection to soul than does plastic, although, paradoxically, thanks to human interface, a funky wooden table or chair can sometimes exceed in soulfulness the soul that may be invoked by a living tree."

At this juncture the reader may be going, "Yeah, yeah, right, and Pinocchio's semen is the source of the best Italian furniture." Fair enough. Fair enough. We've quoted Stubblefield sufficiently here to establish that he was: (1) erudite, (2) verbal, and (3) a free-thinker—and apt to sail a bit over the top in all three departments. This particular display, for example, went on at length, until he rather abruptly stopped pacing and summed up his talk thusly:

"In the end, perhaps we should simply imagine a joke; a long joke that's being continually retold in an accent too thick and too strange to ever be completely understood. Life is that joke, my friends. The soul is its punch line."

For at least a full minute, Stubblefield stared at his feet, at the way his painted toenails stood out against the richer reds of the carpet. This was not for effect. He was thinking. The room was so quiet you could almost hear the incense smoldering. Finally, he lifted his beard off his torso and said, "Let's not chisel that last remark in stone. Okay? It may be high wisdom, it could be pure bullshit. There's often a thin line. I'll run it by Lisa Ko sometime and let you know what she says."

At the study door, Dickie blanched.

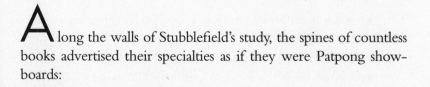

Along the walls of Stubblefield's study, the spines of countless books advertised their specialties as if they were Patpong show-boards:

BIOGRAPHY SMOKE CIGARETTE
POETRY EAT WITH CHOPSTICKS
PHILOSOPHY PLAY PING-PONG
Etc., Etc.

"How dear my pupils are," said Stubblefield, closing the door behind him. "They laughed at my train whistle, although not
one of them has ever been anywhere near a train. My God,
Goldwire, look at you! It would appear Bangkok has chewed
you up and spit you out. Your customary boyish charm could
use a good hosing down." Sensing that Dickie had been admir-
ing his library, he said, "Remember when we first met and you
asked to borrow my copy of *Ulysses*, believing it to be a biography of General Grant?"

"Yeah, but now, thanks to you, I know who's buried in
Grant's Tomb. It's James Joyce."

Stubblefield chuckled. "I sure hope Foley brings me some
readable new novels. None of that coming-of-age claptrap.
None of that dreary, cancer-ridden, lawyer-worshiping—"

"Dern's not going to be bringing you *anything*, Stub. Dern's
been busted."

"What?!"

"They nailed him on Guam. His flight was diverted. I saw
him on CNN. In handcuffs. They were hauling your stuff away.
It's been three or four days now." In Dickie's tone there was both
the pig iron of despair and the stained glass of hysteria.

Stubblefield whistled—and he didn't sound remotely like a
train. "Holy fucking moley!" he exclaimed softly. Then, when
he'd rebounded from the shock, "Foley won't sing, of course,
but they'll identify him sooner or later. Probably already have."

"And that means . . ."

"That means that the game is about to get very, very interesting."

"You needn't sound so damn cheerful about it."

There was, in fact, a kind of fresh sparkle in the older man's kelp-green eyes. He said, "It's rotten for Foley, naturally. But maybe it's what we all needed. We've been in an extended rut."

"Yeah, well, I liked my rut. Especially when I consider the alternatives. What the hell are we going to do, Stub? What? We've got to act fast. We're on the bubble here. I'm out of money. I'm—"

"Easy now, Goldwire. Don't panic on me. Pull yourself together. We've got decisions to make, obviously. But first let's try to look at the big picture. Let's put the situation in perspective." He settled a steak-sized hand on Dickie's shaky shoulder. His fingernails had been spared decoration. "Let's . . . let's remember your girlfriend's words."

At the mention of his girlfriend, Dickie blanched once more. He'd been wondering, wondering hard, if he'd ever lay eyes on that girlfriend again. It was, frankly, his greatest concern. (There was no way he could have known, of course, that Lisa Ko, after being held up for a couple of days in Vientiane, due to socialist bureaucracy and passport questions, was at that moment bearing down on Fan Nan Nan and would arrive there before the sun set.) Dickie stared at Stubblefield. "What words?" he asked.

"Oh, you know. You know." Stubblefield had concerns of his own and was becoming a trifle impatient. "Lisa's family motto."

Dickie closed his eyes then. And the words came back to him:

It is what it is.

You are what you it.

There are no mistakes.

Neither wholly believing nor completely rejecting that there was any salvation in that litany, Dickie repeated it for the Lisa that was in it—while deep in the gorge below Villa Incognito, below the singing circus wire, where the mist was so thick it felt like fur on the eyeballs, a pair of tanukis who had escaped Madame Ko's traps were barking wisecracks at the tiger who fancied them for lunch.

PART III

If you won't meet me in Cognito,
Baby, I'm apt to go out of my head.
But if you really can't handle incognito
Meet me in Absentia, instead.

San Francisco. The City by the Bay. Bootsey thought the fog was cute.

They weren't shown the prisoner right away. After cabbing to a nondescript federal office building in the downtown area and riding a silent elevator to the seventh floor, the Foley sisters were questioned for nearly an hour in one of those windowless rooms that used to give Franz Kafka the willies.

Their interrogators were a military intelligence officer—a tall African-American name-tagged Col. Patt Thomas—and a tweedy, bespectacled civilian introduced as Mayflower Cabot Fitzgerald, who, judging from his name and demeanor, must have been representing the Central Intelligence Agency. Handsome Colonel Thomas was genial to the point of being flirtatious, while the dour Fitzgerald was sort of a steel eel, speaking in one of those official governmental I'm-privy-to-things-you're-not-fit-to-know monotones that seem to rise, resentful all the way, from deep down inside a refrigerated silo.

There was nothing threatening nor accusatory about the questioning, but it was definitely thorough. And all the while, as Bootsey and Pru tried to call forth details about a brother they'd always worshiped but had not seen in nearly thirty years, they sat facing a row of two-foot-high, grainy photographs (obviously blow-ups) pinned to the phlegm-green wall behind the desk where one would have thought a window ought to be. There were three photos in all, head-and-shoulders shots of a trio of young men in U.S. Air Force uniforms, complete with visored caps. Beneath each portrait, in large, neat type, were lines identifying the man's rank, name, age, and hometown.

LEFT: Maj. Mars Albert Stubblefield, 30, Millard, Nebraska.

Major Stubblefield had a full, jovial, almost puffy face, whose ostensible softness was overridden and reversed by eyes that were like tracer bullets of piercing intelligence; and by a curl, a twist at the corners that gave an ironic, slightly mocking cast to an otherwise thoughtful smile. He made observers think of the young Orson Welles.

CENTER: Capt. Dern V. Foley, 25, Seattle, Washington.

One could guess from his neck, from his brow even, that Captain Foley was a burly man, not overly tall, probably, but giant of muscle; a fellow apt to sprout coarse whiskers and thick nails. Battered of nose, flat of mouth, there was both a roughness and an ephemeral quality about him, like a moth made from unmilled lumber. His expression seemed to say, "I couldn't be here in spirit, so I came in person," a detached expression his sisters had come across time and time again in their family albums. It unsettled them.

RIGHT: 1st Lt. Dickie Lee Goldwire, 23, Mount Airy, North Carolina.

Here, from all appearances, was a rangy, sweet-tempered, small-town heartthrob; a country-club party boy, a former homecoming king, perhaps, though not the sort to get all high-and-mighty about it. It was easy to imagine him cruising sorority row at UNC in a spirited little sports car, snapping his fingers to Sinatra, blithely enjoying the world, yet secretly, if vaguely, concerned that he might ought to be doing something to help those less privileged than he. There was a natural, easy aristocracy about him, in contrast to, say, the Ivy League haughtiness that Mayflower Fitzgerald wore like a one-size-too-small suit of armor. Pru found Lieutenant Goldwire rather appealing in his old photograph, while in Bootsey's view he was as adorable as, say, the year's first robin.

When the investigators were satisfied that Bootsey and Pru were, indeed, the siblings of Capt. Dern Foley, and willing to accept, for the moment at least, that they'd had no contact with him since before he and his fellow crewmen (whom the girls professed never to have met) were shot down over the Lao-Vietnamese border in the winter of 1973, the two men led the two women down a long gray corridor, near the end of which was a room with a wall of one-way glass. Behind the glass, a solitary figure sat on a bare cot, reading a Gideon Bible. Instantly and simultaneously, the sisters were struck by the fact that the man in the cell was as bald as a boiled potato, although it shouldn't have surprised them since even as a high school fullback, Dern's hairline had been inching arcticward.

Impatient with the sisters' silence, Mayflower Fitzgerald turned on them. *"Well?"*

Still they did not speak. "Well?" he repeated, staring at them over the top of his wire-rimmed glasses. "Is this or is this not your brother?"

Tears had been blistering Bootsey's eyes, and now she began to blubber in earnest. Colonel Thomas and his civilian counterpart nodded at each other, ready to take Bootsey's sobs as an affirmative answer. Pru, however, was not so forthcoming. Mayflower Fitzgerald, frankly, was getting on her nerves.

"Hmm," Pru said, pretending indecisiveness. "Hmm. He does have some of Dern's characteristics. I can see that. But . . . I'm not really sure. He kinda looks like Dern, all right, but he also looks like somebody else. Yeah, you know . . . he also looks a lot like Bozo. Bozo the Clown? I mean, without the honker nose and the sexy orange hair."

Pru smiled innocently, as if trying her best to be helpful. The CIA man emitted a purplish fume. Colonel Thomas fought to maintain cordiality. Even Bootsey regarded her sister with disdain.

The following afternoon there was a family reunion. Of sorts. How much reuniting can relatives really achieve when separated by three inches of shatterproof glass, whose density their voices can only breach with the aid of a closed-circuit telephone? No kissy-kissy huggy-huggy here. The warmth of reconnection was further diminished by the presence of Colonel Thomas and Operations Officer Fitzgerald, who sat together on a wooden bench at the rear of the small visitation room.

"Dern, Dern, Dern," said Bootsey. She said it over and over, as if the name was a mantra that had gotten stuck in a groove in her larynx. There was wonder and disbelief, grief and elation in her voice.

"Where the hell have you been?" asked Pru.

Into the phone on the opposite side of the glass, Foley said, "Southeast Asia, Sis. Keeping the world safe for democracy."

"Dern, Dern, Dern."

"Dern, the war's been over for a quarter of a goddamn century."

"Not for everybody. I got an extension."

"Dern, Dern."

"I've been on special assignment, Sis. Top secret and all that." He put a stubby finger to his lips.

"It's not so damn secret, brother dear. We saw you on television. We got us a good look at your 'special assignment.' "

"Now, now. You know better than to believe everything you see on TV."

"Oh, Dern, Dern. I don't give a darn what you've done. I don't care. Dern, Dern . . ."

"Shut up, Bootsey!" Pru snatched the receiver from her sister's hand.

"Why, Pru, I can remember the days when you were absolutely convinced that Howdy Doody was a real little boy."

In spite of herself, Pru smiled. Bootsey commenced to blubber.

"We thought you were dead," Pru said.

"O ye of little faith! I guess that explains why you haven't written."

"Boo-hoo-hoo."

"Everybody. Everybody thought you'd been killed."

Dern Foley shook his honeydew noggin. "As someone once put it, 'Only the survivors are dead.' How've you girls been? God, it's great to see you. You haven't changed one bit. Do I have any nieces and nephews? No kids? Poodles, then? Parakeets? White mice?"

"Boo-hoo-hoo."

"Shut up, Bootsey!"

And so it went. On their bench, Colonel Thomas and

Operations Officer Fitzgerald looked at each other as if in agreement that there were screws in the Foley family badly in need of tightening.

"When you accept an invitation to a war, you expect to get shot at."

That was the way Stubblefield saw it. To Stubblefield it was elementary. "You sign up to go to war, there's a clause in the contract that says, 'I agree to get shot at.' It's not hidden in the fine print, either. It's right up front. 'In consideration for engaging in combat against parties of the first part, the undersigned hereby assigns to parties of the first part the right to aim bullets, bombs, grenades, mortar shells, rockets, and heavy artillery at his miserable ass.' Land mines, booby traps, and bayonet charges are covered by a separate clause.

"So, what happens when you're shot at? You get hit or you get lucky. You're killed or you're wounded or you escape—either to go home or else to get shot at some more at a later date. Sometimes, of course, you may be captured. And sometimes, in the chaos of shooting, nobody is quite *certain* of your fate. You go missing. And you can go missing for a long, long, time. Maybe forever.

"Granted, for your spouse, your parents, siblings et cetera, it must be terrible not knowing the fate of a loved one, or, if resigned to his death, imagining his remains scattered in disrespect about some filthy foreign cow patch. But it's not appreciably more terrible than any of the other fruits of armed conflict. There's nothing deliberately personal, barbaric, unfair, cruel, or perverse about it. It's just a perfectly natural feature of the mad game of war, a possibility that should be weighed before you sign that contract or accept that invitation. Closure is no more guaranteed than survival. I fail to understand all this widespread public hand-wringing and continuous bellicose puffery regarding MIAs."

Needless to say, Stubblefield's view was not the popular one. It may have been logical, it may have had a ring of moral authority—considering that Major Stubblefield, himself, was Missing in Action—but it was not generally shared.

As late as the summer of 2001, it was common to see bumper stickers that read "Bring Home the MIAs"; Congress was still regularly lobbied by MIA relatives and support groups; while on the Internet the electrons piled up in burying drifts, a ceaseless MIA blizzard, some of it in the form of heartbreaking anguish and lament, some of it no more than chauvinistic posturing, the old don't-fuck-with-God's-republic yankee doodle strut. The MIA issue—1,966 of America's Vietnam combatants remained unaccounted for in August, 2001—was a potato that never entirely cooled, although with the establishment of the Joint Task Force-Full Accounting office in 1992, sincere efforts were being made by the U.S. government to comb every Southeast Asian battlefield and excavate every reported crash site. Teams of military forensic experts and civilian archaeologists searched for bone fragments, teeth, dog tags, class rings, faded letters, and so forth, and though most sites had been systematically scavenged by enterprising locals, they occasionally yielded definitive human remains and personal effects. As a result, the cries of bereaved relatives and professional patriots were becoming somewhat less shrill.

But now, Capt. Dern V. Foley, traveling incognito, carrying a small fortune in narcotics, had popped up like a jack from the MIA box. Boo! Suddenly, there was a new wrinkle in the folded flag, a disturbing wrinkle that Col. Patt Thomas and Mayflower Cabot Fitzgerald, on behalf of their respective agencies, had been assigned to iron out.

On the one hand, the appearance of Dern Foley was likely to ignite in families fresh—and doubtlessly false—hope that their long-missing loved ones might be alive. (Rumors periodically surfaced that American military men had been spotted in slave labor camps from Hanoi to Moscow.) On the other, the fact that Captain Foley had been arrested for drug trafficking was a black eye for everybody concerned, a buzzard that took the sky away from hawk and dove alike. The buzzard was so ugly, its droppings such a potential contaminant, that its possible extermination had been discussed by men who are paid to discuss such things.

But buzzards seldom travel alone. And, like even the tweetiest little songbirds, buzzards lay eggs. Who were Dern Foley's confederates? What was the source of the contraband he'd carried? How long had he been involved? Where were the other airmen who had gone down with him in his B-52? What else had Foley been involved in, what did he know that might drop a fetid plop of buzzard poop into the regal nest of the American eagle?

Foley refused to answer such questions. Foley refused to answer virtually every question he was asked. The single significant question he did answer only made matters worse. A lot worse. "I don't get it," an exasperated Colonel Thomas had complained. "Since the war was over, since you were healthy and no longer being held, why did you choose to stay over there in that gook shithole? For the drugs? The loot? The Commie politics? Or what?"

Dern had looked the colonel in the eye and smiled that flat, distant smile of his that had never been much of a smile at all, and said coldly, "Maybe I preferred that shithole to this shithole."

Oh, my! Oh, fine! Suppose the media got their grubby hands on *that*. An MIA who "preferred" to stay missing. An American hero who rejected America. And who hadn't denied that there might be others like him. Talk about your nasty buzzard omelet.

Under the circumstances, then, it shouldn't be surprising that Bootsey and Pru were warned to tell no one of Dern's reappearance, nor that those warnings were emphatically repeated and had ominous overtones. As far as the public was concerned—and the public had already forgotten the incident—the drug smuggler arrested on Guam was precisely who he'd said he was: a French missionary, Father Arnaud Gorodish. For the foreseeable future, any information to the contrary would be vigorously denied, the source of such information would be vigorously dealt with. And who besides Pru and Bootsey could have provided that information? Dern had had few friends, and both Foley parents had died in a boating accident soon after he entered the air force.

When, on the third day, as the sisters boarded an Alaska Airlines jet bound for Seattle, they were in shock. The jolt of finding Dern alive (there were those who suggested that the reason the Foley girls had never married was due to their attachment to their vanished brother) was compounded by the situation in which they'd found him and by the government's threats, none too subtle, to themselves.

Although she kept professing that everything would turn out well in the end, Bootsey was in such a state that the flight attendant had to fasten her seatbelt for her—and she, Bootsey, from an aviation family! Embarrassed by her sister, and suspecting that they were being watched by one of Fitzgerald's joes, Pru immersed herself in the *San Francisco Chronicle*, almost wearing it like a mask. "Ink is the blood of language," Stubblefield had said in defense of his preference for the page over the screen. "Paper is its flesh." Pru made herself a newspaper face. Her frown was the crossword puzzle, her blinks the baseball scores. You could have wrapped a fish in her.

It was in the middle pages of the *Chronicle*, near the mouth of the mask, that she chanced upon a short article about the derailment of the circus train in the Oregon hills between San Francisco and Portland. There were no serious injuries, the report said, but several animals were thought to have escaped.

Exterminating Captain Foley was a definite option. Both Colonel Thomas and Operations Officer Fitzgerald knew how easy it would be to arrange for him to have a "heart attack" in his cell. The current administration certainly had no problem with prejudicial terminations of that sort.

Of course, they could simply paint him as a pro-Marxist deserter and see to it that he was sentenced to death or to life imprisonment. That, however, would necessitate a trial, and who could guess what he might say in court, or to fellow inmates were it a closed hearing, or to journalists covering his execution? The same problems would arise were they to charge him as an international drug trafficker, which, in point of fact, he was. Yet did it really matter what Foley said? Neither the public nor the mainstream press would take seriously for a moment the twisted statements of a drug-smuggling traitor.

Still, there was a fly swimming laps in whichever ointment they uncorked; a backstroking, belly-flopping, splish-splashing fly in the person of Maj. Mars Albert Stubblefield and 1st Lt. Dickie Lee Goldwire. For any number of reasons, nothing of consequence could be done about Foley until the whereabouts, condition, and involvement of those particular two MIAs were clearly determined.

Parting, Colonel Thomas and Operations Officer Fitzgerald (usually called Mayflower) agreed to concentrate on making that determination as quickly as possible. "By the way," Mayflower said, as they left the building, "how did your cousin's kids enjoy the circus the other night?"

"Oh, they liked it fine. Enjoyed the hell out of it. Too bad, though, that that clown got drunk and messed up the animal act."

A knowing, insider smile razored across Mayflower's lips.

Leaning close to the colonel's ear, he hissed through the mineral gleam of his all-too-perfect teeth, "That was no clown. That was a *dyke*."

Knock! Knock!

"Who's there?"

No one replied. The village was at its evening meal, and the only sound Dickie could hear was the bamboo grove, rustling in the dusk like so much Zen gossip.

Knock! Knock!

"*Sabbaii dji? Sabbaii dji?* Who's there? Who hava yes?"

Still no response. Dickie was reasonably certain that even if Dern had given them up it was too soon to expect the authorities. Nevertheless, he stiffened. He was standing on the woven matting in the middle of his hut, stark naked, having just bathed and washed his clothes in the narrow stream that rushed past the village on the side opposite from the gorge. Before the knocking interrupted him, he'd been searching for a clean pair of khaki shorts, his normal attire in Fan Nan Nan.

As he stared, barely breathing, the flimsy rattan door opened a few inches, and a hand sent a cylindrical object rolling across the matting toward his feet. Instinctively, automatically, Dickie looked for a place to dive, but while his hut was spacious by Fan Nan Nan standards, there was no heavy furniture to duck behind nor any alcove in which to escape the blast.

Blast? Yes, Dickie was so convinced that it was a grenade rolling toward him that his whole life flickered past his eyes. His sixth-grade teacher flickered past, demanding to know where his math assignment was (for a millisecond he was back in dream school); his ruddy daddy zoomed past in one of the convertibles he flogged at the Goldwire car dealership, his mother zipped by on her golf cart; his older sister sashayed by, flashing her bare breasts as she'd done so many times just to fluster him; his wealthy old grandparents, his alcoholic guitar instructor, a gang of UNC fraternity brothers, the psychopathic commanding officer of his B-52 squadron: a whole parade of supporting actors popped in and out of the major scenes that Dickie Goldwire's brain rightly or wrongly believed had defined his life; and he was wondering of all the places and all the ways that that life might have ended, why in a hut in Laos, naked, fifty-one, blown to bacon bits by an assassin's . . .

But the blast didn't come. And the "grenade," when it stopped rolling, looked suspiciously like a glass jar with a familiar blue and yellow label on it. This was no flashback. This was not a spectral artifact summoned by his psyche to remind him that he had squandered his life, just as most of us, by refusing to wake up, squander ours. No, it was no more a hallucinatory relic of personal shame—or triumph—than it was a bomb.

What it was . . . was a jar of mayonnaise. Best Foods mayonnaise (marketed as Hellmann's east of the Mississippi). And while he was gaping at it, all agog, the door opened a little wider, and someone flung a loaf of Wonder Bread across the room and bounced it off his penis.

Dickie fixed sandwiches. Not right away, of course. First, they embraced. Next, they discussed Dern's arrest (Lisa Ko was amazed that he already knew about it; was, though she concealed it, more than a little annoyed that he knew, after she'd traveled halfway around the world, walking out on the circus, leaving her tanukis in the care of an unstable individual, to bring the news). They talked about what the arrest might portend for

Dickie, for them as a couple, and for Stubblefield. Then, she got as naked as he, and they made love.

They made love as fast and furious and noisily as an illegal drag race, each of them climaxing in less time than it would have taken Daniel Boone to skin a teddy bear. Dickie was packed tight as a fist with the pent-up desire left over from his abstinent night with Miss Ginger Sweetie (if the truth be known, he thought of Miss Ginger Sweetie once or twice during his prolonged orgasm), while the only sex Lisa Ko had had in three months had been with Bardo Boppie-Bip, and though that had been new, exciting, and plenty enjoyable, it was different, very different. (Since it was with another woman, it couldn't be counted against her vows of betrothal, she reasoned, although for Bardo Boppie-Bip, it seemed to have counted for *something*.)

By then it was quite dark, and Dickie made sandwiches by candlelight. He'd once told Lisa Ko that what he missed most about America was sliced bread and mayonnaise. Now, she'd brought those things to him, which in his mind signaled that she loved him more than he sometimes thought she did.

All Carolina folk are crazy for mayonnaise, mayonnaise is as ambrosia to them, the food of their tarheeled gods. Mayonnaise comforts them, causes the vowels to slide more musically along their slow tongues, appeasing their grease-conditioned taste buds while transporting those buds to a plane higher than lard could ever hope to fly. Yellow as summer sunlight, soft as young thighs, smooth as a Baptist preacher's rant, falsely innocent as a magician's handkerchief, mayonnaise will cloak a lettuce leaf, some shreds of cabbage, a few hunks of cold potato in the simplest splendor, restyling their dull character, making them lively and attractive again, granting them the capacity to delight the gullet if not the heart. Fried oysters, leftover roast, peanut butter: rare are the rations that fail to become instantly more scintillating from contact with this inanimate seductress, this goopy glory-monger, this alchemist in a jar.

The mystery of mayonnaise—and others besides Dickie Goldwire have surely puzzled over this—is how egg yolks, vegetable oil, vinegar (wine's angry brother), salt, sugar (earth's primal grin-energy), lemon juice, water, and, naturally, a pinch of the ol' calcium disodium EDTA could be combined in such a way as to produce a condiment so versatile, satisfying, and outright majestic that mustard, ketchup, and their ilk must bow down before it (though, at two bucks a jar, mayonnaise certainly doesn't put on airs) or else slink away in disgrace. Who but the French could have wrought this gastronomic miracle? Mayonnaise is France's gift to the New World's muddled palate, a boon that combines humanity's ancient instinctive craving for the cellular warmth of pure fat with the modern, romantic fondness for complex flavors: mayo (as the lazy call it) may appear mild and prosaic, but behind its creamy veil it fairly seethes with tangy disposition. Cholesterol aside, it projects the luster that we astro-orphans have identified with well-being ever since we fell from the stars.

Okay, maybe that's sailing a ways over the top, yet even its detractors must admit to mayo's sheen. And nowhere, under no condition, does it shine more brightly than when lathered upon an ordinary slice of bread.

Wonder Bread was Dickie's favorite. Lisa Ko opened it for him, the antic spray of red, blue, and yellow dots on its wrapper reminding her, to her guilty dismay, of the circus. She laid out the slices. With a blade more bayonet than kitchen knife, he spread the silky dressing from crust to crust, careful to leave no speck, however minute, of surface uncovered. Dickie, you see, understood the true beauty of the well-made sandwich. Those who allow dry, bare patches to show on their bread, who neglect to plaster the mayonnaise liberally to every edge, are triflers, artless hacks unworthy of the name of "sandwich maker."

As for the filling, that was somewhat problematic. The usual suspects—canned tuna, cheese, pastrami, ripe tomato, et al—were absent from Dickie's Fan Nan Nan larder. He experimented with a boiled rice sandwich, adding chili peppers, garlic, and *màak kàwk* (a sour, olivelike fruit) for flavor, but while it tasted better than it sounds—thanks to the mayonnaise, no doubt—it landed somewhat short of expectation. A sandwich of *nàam phàk-kàat* (fermented lettuce paste), mint, and *nàng khwái hàeng* (dried skin of water buffalo) proved even less gratifying.

In the end, then, while Lisa Ko shook her head in disbelief, Dickie contented himself with plain mayonnaise sandwiches, the basic kind that he'd fixed for himself as a small boy when his mother was away golfing, his daddy was holding court at the skeet club or the car lot, and it was the cook's day off. Mmm-mmm! Even after days of international travel, the Wonder Bread was wonderfully squishy; the mayonnaise, for all the aforementioned reasons, a jubilant justification of the trouble to which Mother Nature had gone to embed an oval cluster of sensory cells in the epithelium of the tongue. Mmm-mmm!

Soon he'd had his fill of sandwiches, though apparently not of nostalgia, for he commenced to take slices of the pliant bread and fold them, twist them, and mash them into shapes as he'd done as a child. Dickie made little animals. Little barnyard animals. He made a pig, a goat, and a goose. Unmindful of Lisa Ko's guilt about the circus, he sculpted an elephant and a giraffe. Guilt-ridden or not, Lisa was fascinated. She'd never seen anything like it, not even her granny's origami. However, while he was struggling to make her a tanuki—he experienced difficulty with both its belly and its scrotum—she decided she'd reached her limit of appreciation.

She kissed him hard enough to get his attention. Then, she crossed to the bed and lay down. She raised her knees and spread her legs. Her glossy black pubis parted like the curtain at a theater, gradually revealing a stage set—architectonic, kind of surrealistic, and as rosy as a classical dawn. Mysterious, apertural, glistening, and crimped, the set semed to be awaiting the entrance of an actor to make its meaning clear.

Well, having already successfully auditioned for the role,

Dickie entered at once, not from the wings but the footlights, and no Laurence Olivier, no James Dean, ever put more of himself into a performance. Lisa Ko gave as good as she got. This time, they made love slowly, thoughtfully, painstakingly, although with the occasional spontaneous flourish. They went at it that way for the better part of two hours, and when at last they uncoupled, they lay panting in a veritable pond of perspiration and sundry other moistures.

The aftertaste of mayonnaise sandwiches mingled in Dickie's mouth with the brine of Lisa Ko. He brushed a bread crumb from his stubble, plucked a hair from between his front teeth, and—the uncertainty of his future notwithstanding—fell asleep a glad and happy man.

When he awoke at daybreak, however, he saw that Lisa was already up and dressed and dabbing perfume behind her pretty, ever so slightly pointed ears. Without asking, he knew that she'd be off in a minute or two to find an aerialist to take her to Villa Incognito. And though that came as no surprise, Dickie's heart felt suddenly like an iron piano with barbwire strings and scorpions for keys.

Someone who knew him might ask: in what direction exactly did the green music of Dickie's jealousy flow? Toward Stubblefield or toward Madame Ko? For the truth is, he loved the man very nearly as much as he loved the woman. He'd loved Stubblefield almost from the moment they met.

That meeting had occurred in the day room of the officers' quarters at an American air base on the southernmost island of Japan. It might be useful at this juncture to scroll back just far enough to glimpse the spray of events that had brought Dickie to the air base and that disposed him to be so immediately impressed by Maj. Mars Albert Stubblefield. It's best called a *spray* because events are seldom as linearly linked as those who tout "history" would prefer to believe, although in this case, the trail is rather easy to sniff.

Early in the autumn of his sophomore year at the University of North Carolina, Dickie had been playing his guitar and singing folk songs at a fraternity picnic. He wasn't entertaining an audience really, just strumming and crooning beside the bonfire, more or less entertaining himself, although four or five students had gathered around him and were joining in on the choruses. At one point, following a rendition of "On Top of Old Smoky," a young woman, a girl he'd never seen before, stepped out of the shadows and took his hand. "Man, you're too good to waste your pipes on these ignorant frat rats. I'm gonna take you to a more appreciative audience. Come on, now," she insisted when he made to resist, "this is a command performance."

Well, the audience at the Rhinoceros Coffeehouse in downtown Chapel Hill, though quieter, proved to be only marginally more appreciative than the raucous Pi Kappa Phi picnickers, yet his hesitant debut upon the Rhino stage was to be a turning point in Dickie's life.

The girl's name was Charlene, and while she, with her frizzed brown hair, combat boots, and barbarically kohled eyes, wasn't as attractive as the cheerleaders he'd dated back in Mount Airy or the coeds who usually caught his eye on campus, she had . . . well, a *voltage*, a grit, a mystery not one of those others could approximate. In addition, Charlene was both more generous and more expert with her sexual favors than any girl he'd ever encountered, and before that night was through, he realized that he'd been blindly operating in a state tantamount to virginity. Sure, he'd long had an iron in the fire, but prior to Charlene he'd only been toasting marshmallows.

If Charlene pussy was the metaphoric mayonnaise in his life

that year, the ham, the tomato, the bread itself was more cerebral in nature. Dickie, with little effort, had always made good grades in school, but the best of grades are no indication whatsoever that the student is awake. Had you suggested to Dickie before he entered UNC that the Civil War was not fought over slavery; that it wasn't Columbus who discovered America; that Jesus Christ had never been a Christian; that *unique* was not a synonym for *unusual*; or that a screwed-over inventor named Nikola Tesla was the father of both electrical and electronic technology in the U.S., with accomplishments that made Thomas Edison's look like the putterings of a neighborhood handyman, had you imparted even such elementary bits of knowledge as those, he, like almost everyone else in Mount Airy, "educated" or not, would have regarded you as a lunatic spouting heresy. Now, here he was in a coffeehouse (he'd taken to performing almost nightly at the Rhino, despite the fact that no one, himself included, thought his Bob Dylan covers appreciably superior to those a well-trained Mexican parrot might produce), here he was listening to Charlene and her friends gab about existentialism, assassination conspiracies, Jungian UFO theory, Tibetan death manuals, Gandhian pacifism, and the triple aspects of the Mother Goddess in universal art forms; listening attentively and hardly batting a lash.

Moreover, because he didn't want to just sit there like a pimple on a pumpkin, because for some mysterious reason he longed to be accepted by these campus freaks, because he wanted to impress Charlene, and because a lot of this new information genuinely intrigued him, he commenced to spend afternoons in the library researching all manner of esoteric subjects. He managed to keep up his grades in automotive engineering (daddy's idea), but his heart wasn't in it. He was happier reading Buckminster Fuller, unorthodox reassessments of the Civil War, and biographies of Tesla and the Compassionate Buddha. The horizon of his world view was stretching like string cheese on a pizza.

At the Rhino, he'd always been liked well enough. The girls

liked him because he was cute, gentlemanly, and kind of innocent (even the bohemian female is not immune to maternal instincts). Guys liked him because he let them drive his Fiat Spider and lent them money to score marijuana. His musical talents, minor as they were, lent him at least a modicum of hipness, and both sexes were secretly impressed by Charlene's veiled allusions to the measure of his masculine endowment. Now that he could occasionally contribute something of real interest to coffeehouse conversations, he achieved his goal of fitting in with the misfits. However, any danger that his expanding persona might be getting too big for its shoes disappeared when on the first warm day in April, spring shooting out of the tender Carolina sod like goat genes out of a hose, Charlene split for Berkeley with an itinerant acid dealer named Gypsy, taking her peacock feathers, astrology charts, and Colette novels, leaving behind nothing but a patchouli-and-pussy-scented vacuum: not even a note.

Dickie's heart was not so much broken as it was dehydrated. He felt like a potted plant in a haunted house. For seven months, he'd been diving into the waters of life—and now the finance company had repossessed the irrigation pump.

There was still a trickle in the ditch, still all those new areas of thought to investigate, but conditions were no longer right for diving. With the defection of his "coach" and the loss of any interest in conventional curricula, he felt the world had left him high and dry. Sensing that he easily could wither away in that state, and too happy-go-lucky by nature to succumb to paralysis, he forced himself to act. As soon as final exams were done, Dickie, over strenuous parental objection, enlisted in the air force.

"You'll be shipped to Vietnam!" they squawked.

"I hope so," murmured Dickie, and he meant it, though he was not exactly clear why—especially after all the convincing anti-war rhetoric to which he'd been exposed at the Rhinoceros.

In an introspective mood, he recalled the last night he and Charlene had slept together. They'd been lying on her narrow mattress, the sleeping bag that served as its duvet tossed aside, the better to facilitate their postcoital cool-down. He was going on and on about how the principles that govern the universe are not ones of matter but design, or some such business he'd gleaned from Buckminster Fuller, just going to town on it, when Charlene regarded him with a strange light in her eyes.

Years later he would see that same eye-light in Lisa Ko time and time again and would always wonder at it, wonder at how it seemed to seep from a distant, ancient, exclusively *feminine* place. It was a barely perceptible gleam that had, believe it or not (and cynics are free to jeer), a sacred quality—yet no pope or holy guru or actor playing a pope or holy guru could ever hope to project it. A vixen could project it to her kits, perhaps, but it was as absent as lactation in the province of the male. For that matter, it was rare in women, and Dickie might only have imagined its distant, arcane origins, though the World of the Animal Ancestors was probably beyond his powers of imagination.

At any rate, he perceived *some* sort of different expression in Charlene when she'd turned to him that night, shushed him, and said, "Just remember, man, that the head bone's connected to the heart bone."

"Huh?"

"You know, when I met you, man, you were really in touch with your feelings. That's what turned me on about you, I guess. You were living in your heart. Now, you've packed up your khaki pants and polo shirts and moved into your head." She propped herself up on one elbow. "It's gotta be *both*, man. It don't matter how sensitive you are or how damn smart and educated you are, if you're not both at the same time, if your heart and your brain aren't connected, aren't working together harmoniously, well, man, you're just hopping through life on one leg. You may think you're walking, you may think you're running a damn marathon, but you're only on a hop trip, man. You're a hopper. The connection's gotta be maintained."

Charlene yawned, kissed him, yawned again, and fell asleep.

When he looked back on it, as he was flying to Texas for basic training, he supposed she'd left him a note after all.

And he supposed that Vietnam was as good a place as any to hook up one's head to one's heart.

Knock! Knock!

"Who's there?"

"The All-Controlling Agent of Destiny and Change."

"Are you really the All-Controlling Agent of Destiny and Change?"

"Of course not, you ninny. There's no such thing. I'm the Mindless Tosspot of Random Chance. If you detect patterns in my swath, in my wake, that's your prerogative, I guess, but should you base important decisions on those 'patterns,' you could be in for a surprise."

Well, whatever the terms upon which fortune is predicated—whether the storybook of our lives is authored by divine fate, pure chance, or force of will—it's obvious that one thing does lead, however circuitously, to another; and in the narrative of Dickie Goldwire, the wheels of the future were gathering speed.

Dickie's grandmother, who came from old tobacco money and had bankrolled the careers of several Carolina congressmen, pulled strings to have him accepted for Officers Candidate School. Dickie hadn't sought a commission, he hadn't really thought about it, but no stranger to privilege, he nonchalantly accepted rank as his due. Emerging from OCS a second lieutenant, he was then funneled into navigation school. "Okay," he reasoned, "it's good to know the smoothest way to get to where you're going," though suspecting all the while that Buckminster Fuller mightn't necessarily agree. Upon completion of the course, near the top of his class, he was rewarded by being shipped off to war.

He'd stayed in Vietnam less than six months. Typical military illogic had him assigned to a ground air-control post, where, like so many other victims of Pentagon inefficiency, he was forced to function far below the summit of his potential. About the time he'd become acclimated to the steam and the rot, to the boom and the bugs, to the itchy white rashes that kept erupting under his skin and the red lightning that kicked like neon frog legs in the jukebox sky; about the time that he'd resigned himself to never hearing another discussion that didn't revolve around gooks and doom on the one hand, cars, baseball, and girlfriends (real or fantasized) on the other, somebody somewhere woke up long enough to reassign him to a B-52 squadron in Japan. From then on, he'd only see Vietnam from up in the red-lit Wurlitzer.

After reporting to the squadron commander, he was escorted to his quarters by an orderly. The orderly helped him unpack, then pointed out the officers' club and the day room. It was too early for a drink, so he ventured into the day room, at one end of which two rather unkempt individuals in rumpled Hawaiian shirts were arguing loudly but articulately over which was worse, conspicuous consumption or conspicuous non-consumption. They were visibly annoying a table of poker players and a solitary captain trying to write a letter home—and they didn't seem to care. Dickie drew near the pair with a flicker of hope.

Both of the men were large, but one was tall, soft-faced, arrow-eyed, and crowned by a bush of hair whose length dangerously exceeded air force regulations; while his companion was short and burly, with sullen features that might have been hammered into his face, the hands of a stockyard skinner, and a broad forehead that seemed to shout, "Mush, you huskies!" to the hairs it was driving onward, onward toward the backslope of his skull. By the time Dickie had settled into a leather armchair adjacent to their own, they had entered the finer points of their

discussion. Specifically, they were debating the distinctions between: (1) nouveau-riche ostentation; (2) the compensating ac-
quisitiveness of an adult who'd been deprived as a child; and (3)
the extreme displays of the American Indian potlatch in which
consumption transcended mere greed to become sport and surrogate warfare.

Without missing a beat, the taller man handed Dickie a beer
(apparently it was *not* too early to drink), and began challenging
his opponent to distinguish between the genuine ascetic and
what he termed the conspicuously nonconsuming "poverty
snob." Foley (for that's who he was) obliged, though he became
evasive when Stubblefield (obviously) interrupted to ask on
which side of the fence Christ would fall. Was Jesus an enlight-
ened being who understood *maya* (the illusionary nature of the
material world) and the folly of seeking happiness through
wealth, or was he merely a humorless, undersexed, masochistic
proto-communist with an olive branch up his butt?

At this point, the letter-writing captain turned scarlet.
"Enough!" he bellowed, slamming down his pen. "I'm not going to sit here and listen to you blaspheme my Lord!"

Stubblefield smiled benevolently. "I'm sorry, Seward," he
said. "Forgive me. I hadn't realized you were British."

"What're you talking about? I'm no Brit, and you damn well
know it." Captain Seward was fuming. The poker players were
losing track of their aces.

"But, Seward . . ." Stubblefield's voice was as mild as baby
shampoo. "Didn't you just say you had a lord? I thought a *lord*
was a titled nobleman who exercises authority as a result of
hereditary property rights. So if you have a *lord*—"

"Try reading the Bible sometime!"

"*I've* read the Bible," put in Dern Foley. His voice was flatter,
colder than Stubblefield's. "I've read it in English, Hebrew, and
Greek." Everybody in the day room except the newcomer knew
this to be true. "And Major Stubblefield's right. The word *lord*
didn't exist in biblical times. It's a British political term forced into

the scriptures by King James's chauvinistic translators." He paused. "Interestingly enough, in Old English, *lord* meant 'loaf ward.' That is, 'guardian of the loaf.' Shows you how important bread—the food not the cash—has been in human society, I guess."

Closing his eyes, Dickie saw a long white wrapper enlivened by blue, red, and yellow dots. Next to it sat a jar of mayonnaise.

"There you have it," Stubblefield said. "So, you're accusing me of insulting the guardian of your loaf. Well, Seward, I wasn't aware there was a loaf keeper in your—"

"Oh, stuff it!" snarled Seward. "You're so damn sophomoric. We're talking equivalents here. How else could the English translators have referred to—?"

"They didn't much refer to Jesus as *lord*," Foley corrected him. "That's a more modern thing, it's not even from the King James Bible, where *Lord* almost always meant Jehovah. As for you, Seward, I suppose you could call Jesus your *commander-in-chief*, undercutting that oaf in the White House, but what Jesus was, actually, was an itinerant rabbi."

"Exactly," agreed Stubblefield. "A homeless Jewish peace activist. Tell me, Seward, knowing that, would you allow your sister to marry Jesus? How about your daughter? How would you like him moving in next door to you? Whores and publicans and sinners dropping by at all hours, him expecting your wife to come over and wash his dirty peacenik tootsies?"

Redder than ever, Seward had had all he could bear. He scooped up his writing material and headed for the door. Two of the poker players folded their cards (the other two were stifling chuckles) and made to follow him out.

"Oh, don't go away mad," Stubblefield pleaded. He sounded sincere.

Seward whirled on him. "I don't get mad," he said, "I get even."

"Even, eh? Not me. I get odd." With that, he stood, let his

copy of Joyce's *Ulysses* tumble to the floor and twirling his arms above his bushy head, commenced to dance the most bizarre little dance Dickie had ever seen. Stubblefield jumped around like a monkey with its tail in a grinder, occasionally becoming clinically spastic, complete with drool, only to suddenly execute a slow, controlled, entirely graceful waltz turn; and all this erratic movement miraculously in time with a Beach Boys tune that was playing at low volume in the background.

Foley, on the surface at least, more reserved, more introverted than the major, rose slowly and joined in, imitating Stubblefield's gyrations in a lumbering fashion, like a circus bear following the lead of its trainer.

Seward slammed the door behind him. The card players, even the two who'd been offended by Stubblefield's irreverence, shook their heads and burst out laughing. And Dickie fell in love.

Around Seattle, it's said that summer begins on the fifth of July. That's an imprecise observation, of course, yet not without general validity. It's common for Seattle's Junes to be chilly and wet, and its Independence Days are famous for soggy firecrackers and canceled barbecues. Yet, interestingly, inexplicably, maybe even unpatriotically, the sun often will abruptly break out the very next day, and like a wallflower gone accidentally drunk at the punchbowl, carry on brazenly for a couple of months thereafter.

The carrying on isn't necessarily consistent, however. Sometimes, even after its motor is running, the long-awaited Pacific Northwest summer will proceed in fits and starts, as if driving in meteorological midtown traffic. There'll be days in August when, with the "kiss of fall" in the air, sweaters are pulled over a million heads and shorts are packed away for the season. Then, a few days later, the pale gasbag of a sun will flare like a cosmic Molotov cocktail, and every top of every convertible will come down again in raggy unison.

In this particular year, for example, Bootsey's cheery salutation to autumn proved almost embarrassingly premature. Summer was definitely out of retirement and back on the job on the end-of-August afternoon when Bootsey came home late from the post office (there'd been a union meeting) and dragged her shiny, panting body through the door as if she were lugging the Statue of Liberty in a plutonium suitcase. In point of fact, all she really carried was her purse, her Winnie the Pooh lunchbox, and a rolled-up newspaper.

"Whew!" she exclaimed, fanning herself with the paper. She stood in the doorway, waiting, perhaps, for Pru to ask, "Hot enough for you?"—a question posed to Bootsey, much to her delight, at least thirty times that day. Pru said only, "Hi, Sis," and turned back to the six o'clock news, which was practically over.

Joining her sister on the sofa, Bootsey made an announcement. "It's a warm one!" she said triumphantly. Receiving neither argument nor affirmation, she, disappointed, went on to inquire, "Any word?"

"If you mean word from our friends in Frisco, no, nothing. My sense is that Dern isn't telling the Feds any more than he told us. And until something breaks. . . ." She shrugged. "Who knows? Maybe he's protecting an international drug cartel—or maybe he's just being Dern."

Silently, slowly, distractedly, Bootsey loosened the top two buttons of her damp blouse. She gave herself one last fan with the newspaper and then unrolled it. "Okay," she seemed to say, though it was more a sigh than a word. "Anyway, there's a tidbit in here you might find interesting. I read it on the bus."

Indeed, Pru did take some interest in the article to which Bootsey referred. It concerned the aftermath of the circus train derailment near Grants Pass, Oregon. According to the report, several apes and a lion had been recaptured unharmed and without difficulty, but the entire troupe of rare tanukis had escaped into the hills and simply vanished.

❖

The Fan Nan Nan gorge: laden with space and mist, dizzy with emptiness, a wound in the green wind, a vault where tigers store peacock bones and the shadows of ancient elephants are stacked. A solitary wire spans the chasm like a string of spittle linking smooching deities. Two women, one in a wheelbarrow, teeter on the strand like ants negotiating a broomstraw between fire and honey.

Unlike her fiancé, Lisa Ko never failed to be thrilled by the wire walk. She was a circus girl, after all, and though no aerialist herself, she'd long rubbed spangled shoulders with those who embraced the Karl Wallenda creed: "On the wire is living, everything else is only waiting." She didn't look down, even Wallenda wouldn't have looked, but she didn't need to. The height, the abyss, the jealous throb of gravity, the audacity of the act, those things made themselves quite apparent, and precariously aloft in the morning ether, she felt a delirium of defiant freedom that no gull or falcon, protected by wings and instinct, could ever know.

Midway in the crossing, a smallish bird, neither falcon nor gull, swooped by and plucked a long black hair from Lisa Ko's head. Wisely, Lisa managed to postpone exclaiming or flinching until they'd reached the bamboo platform on the opposite side. As for the aerialist, she parked her void taxi gingerly and refrained from so much as mentioning that she thought she'd seen the hair turn into a glowing noodle in the cuckoo's beak.

L an (or was it Khap?) admitted her to Villa Incognito and showed her to Stubblefield's study. Bare-chested, his tiger resplendent, the big man sat in a pair of knockoff Armani trousers, sipping Roederer Cristal champagne, reading Baudelaire. Upon seeing her, he faked a cough to conceal his gasp and lowered his eyelids so he wouldn't show surprise.

"*Bonjour*, maestro," said Lisa Ko. There was no mayonnaise hand grenade, no flying loaf. "Your little protégée has returned."

"You've got that backward, sweetheart. *I'm* the protégé. The only thing I ever taught *you* we can't do anymore because you're practically a married woman."

She laughed. "You're incorrigible. And humbug modesty doesn't become you. Nor does bad manners. This is your statue speaking, Pygmalion, and you'd better get up and kiss her hand."

Slowly, Stubblefield rose. "My God, look at you! What're you doing back here so soon? My guess is the puritanical Americans deported you for arousing widespread prurient interest. It's a good thing the yahoos couldn't read your mind." He took her hand as if to buss it, then pulled her to him. Her resistance was slight. "Did they figure out that you were a threat to subvert their good ol' way of life?"

"No, and never mind the flattery. *You're* the subversive. My hand-me-down ideas couldn't corrupt a flea."

They argued for a while about who was the more radical and who exactly had influenced whom. Could the reader have overheard them, he or she would have quickly noticed that the woman arguing with Stubblefield sounded nothing like the woman who spoke with Bardo Boppie-Bip. Was it the same Madame Ko? Oh, yes. Whether it was a quirky accident of mind or an intentional ruse (a ploy to be incognito), it was only in America and to certain foreigners that Lisa Ko talked like a

nineteenth-century Chinatown laundry woman. In Laos, her broken English miraculously mended, and she conversed fluently in
the nearly immaculate syntax that Stubblefield had taught her before he taught her . . . the lascivious stuff. (On second thought, it's
unlikely that anybody can *teach* another to excel in bed. Rather,
what they might do is *awaken* in the other her or his predisposition
for copulative excellence. Not everyone is so disposed. Apparently, young Lisa was. In her, it was as innate and inevitable as
the accumulation of nectar in a mellowing mango. Fortunately,
though, she had possessed other predispositions, other gifts, that
had prevented her libido from defining her life.)

Arguing thus, articulately and with amusement, the pair remained in a near embrace. Neither conceded anything, and eventually Lisa said, "I'm not here to stay. I have to get back to the show
right away. I took an unauthorized absence to come warn you and
Dickie about Dern's arrest. But it appears that's old news to you."

"Not that old. I learned of it yesterday. Our boy Goldwire's
pretty worried."

"And you're not?"

He shrugged his fleshy shoulders. The tiger shrugged, too.
"Hey, it is what it is. There are no mistakes."

"You dog!" she cried, but she couldn't hide her grin. "So?
What are you going to do?"

"Oh, maybe get me to the pleasure domes of Europe. Take
the waters. Submit to cosmetic surgery. Have a sex-change operation. Become a TV repairman. I've got fake papers and a Hong
Kong bank account." He gestured then at the carpets, French
Colonial furniture, sumi scrolls, Meiji-era bronze okimonos,
Thai and Burmese wooden buddhas, Shojo Noh masks, porno-
graphic netsukes (*shunga*), and shelves of fine books. "And I
could always hold a garage sale to pick up some extra change."

"Yes, you have so many valuables. But how could dealers
possibly get to them or you get them out? There won't be the
luxury to take them out one or two at a time the way you had
them brought in."

"Maybe not, but the U.S. government's slower to move than a constipated tortoise—and they'd be more successful extracting information from a tortoise than from the likes of Dern Foley. Odds are they're unlikely to trace us to La Vallée du Cirque on their own. And I doubt that it would even occur to anyone around here to give us up."

"You can't be sure. Suppose there's a publicized manhunt? What if there's a reward? I understand there's been an American search team up on Phou Louang for months now, excavating an old crash site. That's not fifty kilometers from here."

"Yeah, I know. A little too close for comfort. But comfort's a form of paralysis. It's stupefying. I don't want to waste my golden years in a goddamn cocoon. I'd always planned to burst out of here someday, become at large in the world, further loosen the bolts in my cannon." He paused to stare into her eyes. "Of course, I'd hoped I'd be taking you with me. Back then, I mean."

Only a few inches separated their faces, but so dense was the tension in that narrow space that a neutrino with overhead cams scarcely could have breached it. As if greased and self-propelled, her lips moved toward his, his toward hers. There was a swift grazing of lip meat—before each of them rocked back on their heels.

"Enough of that," he said. He took a deep breath. He dropped his arms.

"Quite," she agreed. Her eyes were damp, her panties as well, but she'd never have acknowledged it.

"Let me pour you some bubbly, baby. I want to hear your views on America. Obviously, the ol' homeland is still hiding behind its mask of lipstick democracy and mascara faith, but what bouncy, enterprising weirdness is leaking out around the edges of its disguise? *That's* the real America. That's what justifies its existence." Stubblefield moved toward the bronze urn in which the champagne bottle was iced. Then he stopped and slowly, almost shyly, returned to her. "Forgive me," he said. "I just have to know."

With his fat thumb, callused from turning the pages of so many books, he parted her lips. Lisa Ko relaxed her jaw muscles and admitted his finger. Gently, he probed the roof of her mouth. Her palate was warm to his touch, and slippery and wet. He found what he was searching for. It was hardly the size of a buckshot. A tiny zap zinged through her when he pressed it. He withdrew his finger.

"Still there," he concluded.

"Yes," she said, and smiled, but there was something in her voice and in that smile that gave him cause to wonder.

On the tinny, gray desk of Col. Patt Thomas—it looked like an old Spam can turned inside out—there lay amidst the clutter two crisp manila folders. One of these, he handed to Mayflower Cabot Fitzgerald, who had just entered the office, looking a trifle peaked. "Don't want to Tom Clancy you here, Mayflower," the colonel said, freeing a cigar from the clamp of his molars, "but these are the specs on the H-model B-fifty-two that Foley's squadron was flying back then. Say, you feeling okay? Maybe I shouldn't of fed you that barbeque last night." Colonel Thomas, a native of Louisiana, was suspicious of the gastronomical fortitude of certain white men when confronted with the kind of eats that really counted.

Mayflower winced. He was clearly uncomfortable about discussing personal matters with his military colleague. Perhaps his reticence was a natural byproduct of his CIA training, perhaps it was due to a difference in class and race. At last he mumbled, "I've been experiencing a touch of . . . distress. I underwent a test this morning. That's why I'm late."

"Oh? What kinda test?"

"Uh. Umm. Ultrasound."

"Yeah? Well, what showed up?"

Again, the civilian winced. "Very little." He was hesitant to continue, but the colonel was staring, so he added, "Three stones in my gallbladder."

"Three stones is all? Hell, long as one of 'em ain't Keith Richards, you'll be fine."

Mayflower looked rather puzzled and did not smile. *Man,* thought Thomas, *this cat ain't even hip to* white *musicians!* "Just don't try rolling 'em up a hill," Thomas advised. Surely the reference to Sisyphus was not lost on the Langley man (he'd attended both Yale and Princeton), yet he exhibited no sign of mirth. Giving up, Thomas blew a smoke ring and returned his attention to the first folder. "Nothin' in the specs that could shed any light on the case, really. Only question is, why were there only three crewmen aboard Foley's aircraft the day it went down? B–Fifty-two normally carries a crew of five."

"Let me remind you that this was 1973. The war was winding to a close. Personnel were being rotated home at a higher rate than replacements were being shipped overseas. Foley's squadron was shorthanded. It was certainly not S.O.P., but an experienced crew of three could manage the aircraft safely and efficiently unless . . ."

"Unless something went wrong. Which it did. Was every plane in the squadron flying undermanned?"

"No. Just the one. The former C.O. is in a nursing home in Wisconsin, but he's reasonably cogent. He claims that Foley, Stubblefield, and Goldwire *volunteered* to undertake the mission without a full complement. However, the fellow Seward whom we interviewed in Virginia remembers it differently. He says the C.O. chose their plane to be the undermanned one because nobody particularly liked flying with them. They were *intellectuals.*" Mayflower pronounced the word in a manner that suggested he'd just bitten into a worm.

"Meaning what?"

"Meaning they were constantly engaging in *intellectual* conversations. Ranting about things no normal, rational man could care about or understand. They got on people's nerves. Men trying to win a war and get home safely to their loved ones, and there those snobs were, just blathering on and on about some effete European. . . . You know, Seward had once been their weapons officer. He's an upright, God-fearing man. Well, it seems Stubblefield was always baiting him. Asking him things like, 'What exactly has Jesus been doing with himself the past two thousand years?' Asking, 'Are there toilets in Heaven, Seward; are there plastic sewer pipes beneath those streets-paved-with-gold?' "

As Mayflower grimaced in undisguised contempt, Thomas said, "Hmm. That's an interesting question. I never thought about that. Up in Heaven, would a guy still have to pull his pants down and take a—"

"Forget it!" Mayflower ground his steely little teeth. Had he been the one smoking, the cigar would be lying in two pieces, experiencing false memories of Havana and fighting for its life.

"I assume," Thomas continued thoughtfully, "that folks'll be eating in Heaven. So, even if it's only milk and honey—and I can't imagine *my* people being content for eternity with such truck as that—it'd still have to be digested, wouldn't it? So . . ."

"Please! Let us not waste time here, Colonel. We're under the gun, and I may be facing an interruptive infirmity." Mayflower bit his thin lower lip. He was wondering if he was going to have to contact the chief of air force intelligence and request that Thomas be replaced.

"Okay, so we know that Major Stubblefield was sacrilegious. . . ."

"It's pronounced sacra-*lee*-gous."

"No, it isn't."

"Oh, but it is. It's re-*lij*-ous, but it's sacra-*lee*-gous."

Thomas coughed out a hairball of smoke. "That doesn't

make a goddamn lick of sense! Is this some British deal? Why when you stick a . . . a prefix on re-*lij*-ous would you start pronouncing it . . . ?"

"Consult your dictionary. It's recently become acceptable, actually, to say sacra-*lij*-ous, but sacra-*lee*-gous has always been preferred."

"Not by me it hasn't."

"Very well, Colonel. That's your prerogative. Now please, let's get on with it."

No wonder this square's got rocks in his bile box, Thomas thought, but he said, "Okay, we've ascertained that Stubblefield was a fuckin' heathen, but what about our boy Foley, who was studying to be an Episcopal priest and who, even as we speak, is sitting down the hall there poring over the Bible like it was a menu and he can't make his mind up if he wants the fried chicken or the milk and honey. And what about Lieutenant Goldilocks? And—this is the important point—did their smart-ass, pseudo-intellectual attitude toward Christianity carry over into their politics? I mean, were they pinkos, were they disloyal?"

Mayflower frowned. "No. And yes." He paused. "You see, even Seward, who despised them, admits they were skilled airmen who performed their duties efficiently and bravely. Foley and Stubblefield were eligible to be rotated stateside months earlier, but because replacements were slow in coming, they voluntarily extended their tour of duty. They were flying dangerous missions when they easily could have been home." He paused again. "On the other hand, their C.O. calls them the most insubordinate officers he ever commanded, and Seward remembers them continually making sarcastic and derisory comments about the U.S. government and the war effort. Does that in itself classify them as unpatriotic pinkos? Not necessarily. Again, I remind you that this was 1973."

Across the desk (and Mayflower considered Thomas's battered, messy desk distasteful, compared to his sleek, spare, mahogany workstation at Langley), the two men locked eyes. The colonel knew what Mayflower meant, and Mayflower knew he knew. By 1973, only a few terminally ignorant grunts, gung-ho true believers such as Captain Seward, and that gullible, malleable, pusillanimous segment of the civilian public that seems ever eager to swallow any outrageous institutional lie, only those naive nonthinkers could any longer regard the Vietnam War as anything but a shameful example of political posturing gone horrifically awry.

For a minute or two, they were silent. At intervals, Thomas blew out puffs of smoke that, until they melted, resembled the clenched fists of angry snowmen. He could see the silver eagle on his right epaulet reflected in the left lens of Mayflower's assiduously polished spectacles. Eventually, he said, "I'm gettin' a classic picture here of good soldiers who questioned their orders but, however reluctantly, went on dutifully obeying them."

"That mightn't be the case, either," Mayflower cautioned. "Seward says that on its last mission, Foley's aircraft had separated itself from formation while crossing the South China Sea. It veered off into a cloud bank for ten minutes or so before rejoining formation. Seward has reason to suspect it might have secretly dumped its bombs in the ocean."

"Uh-huh." Thomas nodded. "So's they wouldn't have to drop 'em on the Ho Chi Minh Trail, where there were almost always collateral casualties."

"True. Villages on both sides of the border—Laos and Vietnam—occasionally took hits."

"Hey, man, that's war."

"Exactly," Mayflower agreed. He disliked being referred to as "man," but what could one expect from an individual who had attempted to coax him into eating something called collard greens? "It seems that Stubblefield's crew was outspokenly uncomfortable with inflicting collateral damage. They even objected to the prospect of their ordnance killing wildlife . . ."

"We talking *vegetarians*?"

". . . not that there would have been much wildlife left by then. The trail was bombed heavily between 1966 and 1971. Our raids never fully achieved their objectives—NVA troops, supplies, and ordnance continued to flow down the trail—and after seventy-one, as you know, we bombed it only sporadically. So, I suppose a few bamboo rats and leaf monkeys might have survived or returned to the area." He sneered.

"Or tanukis," put in Thomas.

"I beg your pardon?"

"Tanukis. Them funny little animals at the circus. They're supposed to be indigenous to Southeast Asia. Man, was that bippie boppie clown snockered or *what*?! First I thought it was part of the act."

Mayflower scowled, and it wasn't from gallbladder pain. His wife and eleven-year-old son were visiting from D.C., and he had been pressured into finally accompanying them to the circus. Mayflower didn't like circuses. Mayflower didn't like being pressured.

"Saw on TV," Thomas said, "that there was a train wreck and the damn tanukis got away. Up in Oregon or—"

"The environmentalists will be howling over *that*." Though his voice lost none of its monotone, Mayflower sounded almost gleeful. "At any rate, their last mission: it seems Stubblefield was aircraft commander and flying the plane, Foley doubled as co-pilot and electronic weapons officer, and Goldwire was both regular navigator and radar navigator. There was unexpectedly heavy anti-aircraft fire, but the B-fifty-twos were at an altitude where they shouldn't have been vulnerable. Nevertheless, something—a rocket or something—caught Foley's plane. Seward saw it lose altitude, but it disappeared into clouds and he was unable to ascertain whether or not the crew ejected. They were listed as MIA."

Thomas stubbed out his cigar. "So, that was that. Until 'Father Smack' turns up on Guam nearly thirty years later. Say—you don't reckon Captain Seward might have shot 'em down himself?"

"Ridiculous!"

"There was a lot of fraggin' going on in Nam."

"Seward is a devout Christian . . ."

"So were the Inquisition popes."

". . . and a loyal American. To frag an insufferable platoon leader is one thing, this was a sixty-four-million-dollar piece of government property."

"Yeah. Cost more than that these days. You know, I've never been able to figure out why them things are so blessed expensive. For sixty-four mil, you could buy my entire hometown, including the catfish farm, and have enough left over for a secondhand Cadillac and a weekend in Vegas. I've flown in B-fifty-twos, Mayflower. Where does all that money *go*?"

If Mayflower Cabot Fitzgerald had an inkling of where so much money went—and he probably did—he wasn't inclined to share. Instead, he stood, straightened his mauve bowtie, and reached for the other folder on the colonel's desk. "This isn't classified, so if you don't mind, I'll fetch it with me. I have an early lunch with an associate from Washington. Sorry I can't invite you along, but. . . ."

"No problem. See you at the three o'clock interrogation. *Bon appétit*. But better not eat any more of them greasy ribs."

In the midst of locking the folder in his attaché case, Mayflower froze. A cold, dry chuckle found its way through his clenched teeth. "You needn't worry about that."

The instant the company man left the office, Thomas grabbed a cell phone and buzzed one of his own men. He ordered a tail be put on Mayflower and his every move monitored until after lunch. Not for any particular reason, apparently. Just for the sport of it. Just to steal his crown.

The One Who Is Missing is missing,
He can't run but He certainly can hide.
His ghost car is parked in Cognito,
Do you think He might give us a ride?

Like Jesus, Tanuki is here and not here. He is always with us,
yet conspicuously absent. On some glorious day in the future,
will he come back to stay? No. He is perpetually coming back—
and perpetually leaving. Over and over again. Every time we
breathe. Such is the rhythm of the Two Worlds.

As a species, *Nyctereutes procyonoides* may or may not have
originated in what is now Japan. It's possible that it evolved in
eastern China, crossing to the Japanese islands many thousands
of years ago. Some believe it may have developed in Siberia.
What is indisputable is that Tanuki's reputation, his legend, his
legacy, was made in Japan. And it is to Japan that he is ever returning and from which he continually departs. Thanks to the
God of Nooks and Crannies, his movements are even more
stealthy than those of Christ.

Technically, Col. Patt Thomas was incorrect when he mentioned that tanukis are indigenous to Southeast Asia (Thomas
gleaned that information from his circus program). This is not a
point to quibble about, however, for tanukis have resided in the
mountains of Thailand, Vietnam, Laos, and Cambodia for a century or more. When and how they arrived there is not known.
What we do know is that in the last half of the twentieth century,
N. procyonoides spread into Central Asia, the old republics of the
USSR, and has been occasionally sighted as far west as Russia
and Finland. There have even been one or two reports of
tanukis in the French Alps!

At a time when many species of wildlife are being driven

into extinction by the grandiose arrogance and prolific bad habits of the human race, tanukis seem to be . . . well, if not actually multiplying, at least fanning out. What this portends, or if it portends anything at all, is not a matter for immediate speculation. If the reader is not in a rush, however, she or he might take a moment to imagine tanukis in France.

Imagine the faux badgers in the pine woods of the alpine foothills. Picture a tiny contingent of them actually taking clandestine residence among the shrubs and rocks of Paris's Bois de Boulogne. Picture Himself, late at night, scampering on all fours like one of those chubby little mutts Parisians adore, scooting down Boulevard Saint-Germain, weaving in and out among the legs of shadows, snatching *pommes frites* off the tables of sidewalk cafés, maybe even darting into Les Deux Magots to yank a freshly decorked bottle of Hermitage Côte du Rhône from the grasp of some literary luminary such as Gérard Oberlé or Jean Echenoz; draining it behind a clump of rose bushes in the darkened Jardin Luxembourg. . . . No. No.

No, it's impossible, really, to form a mental image of Tanuki in such a setting. It's just too incongruous to compute. Upon a will-o'-the-wisp, one's mind can set a snowflake derby, even a crown of thorns; but a top hat or beret is quite another matter. It is, in fact, not easy to picture Himself at all. When one dwells for very long on Tanuki, the folds of one's thoughts grow as slippery as frog skins, the pen in the hand becomes a stalactite, the screen shines green like owl piss, the keyboard sprouts a greasy mustache. As if an audio wrench has been tossed into the cognitive machinery, a faint but persistent sound attacks the inner ear: the drumming sound, one intuits, that the heart used to make before the heart was domesticated and yoked; the thump of pure *appetite* (so pure it is almost holy); the pounding pulse of some sweet and terrible unnamed joy. *Pla-bonga pla-bonga pla-bonga.*

As Dickie Goldwire chewed mayonnaise sandwiches and paced the floor of his hut, Mars Stubblefield and Lisa Ko lounged on brocade cushions and sipped champagne at the big house across the divide. Between sips they talked about America.

The Asian woman described, to the best of her ability, hip-hop and Harry Potter, election fraud and Plymouth Cruisers, body piercing, reality TV, Britney Spears, glass art, working-class golf, kiddie obesity, and something called "political correctness"; and after she had reported on current fads, styles, and preoccupations, she briefly addressed the state of the union. Shaking her head, she said, "Your country seems to have everything and yet has almost nothing. It's unbelievable. In that vast, beautiful, powerful land of unprecedented abundance live some of the most unhappy people on earth. Oh, generally speaking, they complement all that affluence by being generous and energetic and, except for their ruling class—which is wormy with evil like ruling classes everywhere—rather decent. But they're chronically depressed and dissatisfied. Chronically. Have you heard of Prozac?"

Stubblefield nodded. Thanks to the periodic reports that Dern and Dickie brought back from Bangkok, he was somewhat aware of the astonishing rate at which his countrymen gobbled antidepressants. That knowledge, in fact, permitted him to justify, however spuriously, his own participation in the pharmaceutical business. (Incidentally, thanks to his venturesome comrades, he was also vaguely cognizant of some of the aforementioned fashions, pop icons, etc. That he wasn't considerably more informed was due to the fact that he'd long ago forbidden the presence of a shortwave radio, satellite dish, computer, or telephone in Villa Incognito. The villa had its own small hydroelectric generator, but the power it produced was used primarily for spinning jazz on an old turntable, and, of course, for refrigeration: no one, not even in La Vallée du Cirque, liked warm champagne.) "In our

Declaration of Independence," he said, "we consecrate ourselves as a nation to the pursuit of happiness. That in itself is an admission of habitual discontent. One needn't *pursue* what one already possesses."

"It's actually kind of touching," Lisa said, "how Americans can be so proud, so full of adolescent bravado, and on the other hand be so transparently insecure."

"Self-importance and self-doubt are usually interchangeable. They're two sides of the same coin. But you know all that. You've always known it." He refilled her glass. "So tell me, my dear," he said, making an effort to sound facetious, "how many of my miserable brethren have you awakened from their medicated trance?"

She scoffed, as he knew she would. She waved her free hand. "Don't be silly. That's not remotely in my domain. The tanukis and I, we travel from city to city and put on our little act. Hip-hip, hoo-hoo, pla-bonga pla-bonga. People do get a certain delight out of it, but nobody's inspired to rush home and flush their Prozac down the toilet."

No, he didn't suppose anybody was. And yet he'd never been able to entirely divest himself of the notion, the suspicion, that there was something below the surface of Madame Ko's circus act (indeed, of most of Lisa's actions), something obliquely instructive, a physical if subtle manifestation of an arcane philosophical system. Aside from the fact that she'd shared with him a curious assortment of Zen-like pronouncements that she'd inherited from her mother and whose impact on her worldview, while persistent, was not always easy to categorize, there was precious little evidence to support such a notion. Obviously, the presence in her mouth of that alleged transgenerational implant, to which she gave such ominous if unspecified importance, amplified the dimensions of her mystique, yet an oral bump was hardly the foundation on which a civilized man built his opinions.

Stubblefield was well aware that, justified or not, he'd

always been a bit in awe of Lisa, and that any expression of that awe usually ended up embarrassing them both; he because it put him at an intellectual disadvantage, she because . . . well, perhaps she was just being coy. In any case, he was not on that occasion inclined to press the issue further. He'd take her at face value, as if she was what she was—and possibly she was.

"Only a show," she said, as if reading his mind. "And now I've got to hurry back to it."

"So soon? Ow, did you hear that? My poor heart is rupturing."

"That was a belch!" She wagged a finger at him and laughed. "If I can reach Vientiane tonight, I can get a flight out in the morning. But what about you and Dickie? My plan was to be back in Laos by late October. . . ."

"That's right. For the wedding. Well, as best man, at least I'll get to kiss the bride."

For a moment they stared at each other, and one needn't have been a detective or a psychiatrist to deduce from that stare that there was not a place on that bride-to-be's body he hadn't kissed a hundred times. Fighting back a blush, she went on, "Well, those plans are up in the air for now. Sooner or later somebody's bound to come looking for you. You seem to be taking it lightly, but you must know you're in danger."

"Shame on the man who isn't."

"I'm leaving you my cell phone number. Call me when or if you run. I'm unsure where Dickie could even run to. He may not be able to market his rubies anymore, and obviously Dern never brought him the money for the last batch. He—"

"Stop fretting. I'll take care of him. Personally, I think the U.S. government is the least of Goldwire's problems."

Lisa had been smoothing the wrinkles out of her dress. She stopped abruptly. "What do you mean?"

Stubblefield didn't answer, his face revealed nothing, but

they both were well aware that he was referring to her "implant."

The folder that had lain on Colonel Thomas's desk, the second folder, now rested on a linen-clothed table in an old-line San Francisco restaurant, an oak-paneled dining room noted for its crab louie salads and sourdough bread, the fare at which Operations Officer Mayflower Cabot Fitzgerald cautiously nibbled that lunch hour, as if encouraging his stones to gather moss.

Inside the folder were the FBI background compilations on three American MIAs whose B-52 Stratofortress (dubbed "Smarty Pants" and "The Think Tank" by fellow airmen) had gone down on the western side of the Lao-Vietnamese border in 1973. The files on the trio were detailed and thorough, but for our purposes (whatever, exactly, our purposes might be), we need list only a few salient facts.

DERN V. FOLEY

Scholar athlete at Roosevelt High School.

Dreamed of playing fullback for University of Washington. When UW failed to recruit him, turned down scholarship offers from numerous smaller colleges. Said to have become angry and withdrawn.

Worked minimum-wage jobs (Pizza Haven, Dick's Drive-in), took flying lessons from father, a Boeing engineer. Earned pilot's license. Experimented with drugs.

Encouraged by mother, enrolled in Union Theological Seminary, intent on earning a doctorate of divinity.

During third year of study for priesthood, arrested for selling controlled substances. Two kilos of marijuana, fifty hits of LSD in his possession.

Due to clean record and high academic achievements (honor-roll student, president of Latin Club at the seminary), judge offered to drop charges if he would join the military.

Enlisted in air force. Accepted for flight training. Earned wings. Assigned to bomber group in Asia. Excellent combat record, but twice cited for insubordination.

Known interests: biblical history, dead languages, aviation, altered states of consciousness.

MARS ALBERT STUBBLEFIELD

Father was professor of astronomy at University of Nebraska. Early in life, sent to school for gifted children in Lincoln.

At age sixteen, enrolled at University of Chicago. Three years later, graduated with double degree in anthropology and philosophy.

Studied at Sorbonne in Paris, and Trinity College, Dublin. Specialized in analysis of folk tales. Bummed around Europe. Impregnated daughter of high-ranking Belgian diplomat. Employed for six months as waiter at Village Vanguard in Greenwich Village, New York City.

Taught at junior colleges in Illinois and Nebraska. Reprimanded at both schools for unacceptable behavior (unorthodox dress, rants at faculty meetings, suspected sexual misconduct with female students). Published papers and essays dealing with traditional Asian influences on modern Western thought.

Married Lisa Szaborska, his former student and runner-up in Miss Nebraska contest.

Enlisted in air force, apparently on a whim. Accepted for flight training. Earned wings. Assigned to bomber group in Asia. Excellent combat record, though cited for insubordination and conduct unbecoming an officer.

Adept at talking his way out of trouble.

Known interests: art, literature, jazz, epistemology, food, wine, women.

DICKIE LEE GOLDWIRE

About him, we are already sufficiently informed.

At the Fan Nan Nan landing platform, Madame Phom dumped Madame Ko out of the wheelbarrow as though she were a sack of rice. Shrieking, Lisa grabbed the other's wrist and pulled her down on top of her, and the two circus performers were rolling and giggling like a couple of rowdy schoolgirls when Dickie rounded the corner, carrying wildflowers.

Risking the deadly venom of bamboo vipers and foot-long centipedes, Dickie had picked the flowers on the slopes above the village. *My Dickie*, thought Lisa. *Always so romantic, so tender.* Then, noticing the several wild chrysanthemums in the bouquet, added, *And so clueless.* Although he'd been in her mouth nearly as many times as Stubblefield, he'd either never noticed or hadn't thought to ask, unable to imagine that a polyp on her palate might possess the potential to sabotage his heart's agenda. Her mood darkened as she wondered which would be most cruel of her, to jilt him or become his wife.

Well, there are no mistakes—and she had to start making her way to Vientiane. When he helped her to her feet, she kissed him, feeling him flinch slightly at the taste of Stubblefield's champagne. She kissed Madame Phom as well, then followed Dickie back to his hut. While she packed, they spoke of the future, weighing their prospects on scales so scientifically imprecise they could counterbalance a watermelon with a toothbrush or, say, a wedding bell with a chrysanthemum seed.

"If I end up in prison, will you come visit me?"

"Probably not," she said, not wishing to deceive him. Then, not wishing to distress him, either, she added, "But I'll have my manager send you bread and mayonnaise."

Sometime after 1971, pro-Hanoi forces in Laos, fearing an American invasion, began moving prisoners of war farther away from the Vietnamese border, onto the western side of the frontier-defining Annam Mountains. One such ragtag group of POWs included the crew of the Smarty Pants. They moved slowly, for the terrain was rugged, unexploded bombs haunted the jungle like inert assassins, and Captain Foley limped on an ankle severely sprained when his parachute landed.

The soldiers who escorted the prisoners grew impatient. They were needed back at the border, and it was a long march to the in-terior camps. After several days, they hit upon the idea of turning over a few POWs at a time to local policemen for internment in village jails. They could be collected at a later date.

Stubblefield, Foley, and Goldwire were left in an open-air stockade located in the foothills a hundred kilometers or more from the U.S. bombardment zone. Villagers there, while fairly sympathetic to the leftist Pathet Lao and fairly disdainful of the right-wing National Union government that had won power in 1960 in an election rigged by the CIA, were less than fervently political. They farmed their rice and vegetables, fished their ponds, raised their families, held their festivals, practiced their unrefined brand of Buddhism. Once the novelty wore off, they paid scant attention to the trio of funny Americans in the town stockade, considering them just three more mouths to feed. Se-curity was lax.

One cloudy April night, after Dern's ankle had finally

healed, the Smarty Pants crew broke out of its rickety hoosegow and reasoning that they would be more easily recaptured in the flats, headed upland to wilder territory. For a week the men slept by day, traveled nocturnally, often circuitously, gaining elevation but ever spooked by snakes, centipedes, and unidentifiable shapes and sounds. Did that purring rumble issue from the salivating chops of a menu-planning tiger? Was that drumming *pla-bonga* noise the happy host of Hell hammering the lids of their coffins? The moon bloomed like a radiation sore, every tree was ajitter with swinging intestines.

They came upon Fan Nan Nan by chance, and a lucky chance it was. Emerging from the canopied forest, the sky above them in a sudden fit of astronomy, they instantly liked the look of the place, trusted its vibe, we might say, trusted it to the extent that at daybreak they strolled—hungry, thirsty, dirty, fatigued—into the village center, where they stood brimming with fake confidence and genuine good will. Astonished villagers took them into custody but treated them hospitably right from the start. Stubblefield's intuition had been correct: there was something special about Fan Nan Nan. It was to become even more special in a couple of years. Fan Nan Nan and Villa Incognito were made for each other.

Knock! Knock!

Who's there?

James Michener.

Liar! You're not James Michener.

You're right. And you're probably not a typical Michener reader. Nevertheless, if you don't object, we're going to wax Micheneresque very briefly, very lightly, in order to impart herewith at least a modicum of background detail.

Certainly, there's no good reason to heap upon the reader's plate the fossilized fruits of geological research. As for those who require geographical orientation, let them consult an atlas. Historically, we might note that the original Lao Kingdom congealed in the porous soup bowl of Southeast Asian tribalism in 1353 and endured centuries of successive invasions by neighboring powers, followed by French and Japanese occupation, before finally being toppled in 1975 by the drab fist of communism. However, since this report is not about Laos in the way that Michener's *Hawaii, Poland*, and *Texas* were about those places, any wider historical perspective is probably irrelevant. The little nation's enduring rural traditions, its strong spiritual flavor, its relatively sparse population, have already been implied. Beyond that, what's left for our beneficial consideration is the *composition* of the population, inasmuch as it affected Fan Nan Nan.

The interesting thing about that population is not so much that it's a mix of four separate major cultural groups, but rather— ignoring such ethnic differences as language, dress, religion, customs, and points of origin—that the groups are classified according to the altitude at which they've chosen to reside.

In Laos, the concept of upward mobility has been turned upside down and inside out. For example, the group that has dominated government and society for centuries—the Lao Lum—is a lowland culture. The Lao Lum live just above sea level, tending rice paddies along the Mekong River and its tributaries, and minding the country's official business from the capital, Vientiane. The former aristocracy and what remains of the middle class are members of this group. They are followers of the Theravada school of Buddhism.

Moving upland, we next encounter the Lao Thai, a name as appropriate as it is confusing, since the hereditary line between Lao and Thai is generally a very fine line, indeed. The Lao Thai cultivate both wet rice (paddy grown) and dry rice (mountain grown), and likewise practice both spirit-cult animism and their own primitive variation on Buddhism. The stockade where our three Americans were temporarily imprisoned (more temporary than their captors had intended) was located in a Lao Thai foothills village.

Should we keep climbing, eventually reaching the high mountain valleys, we'd find ourselves among the Lao Theung, an impoverished, animist society descended from slaves and servants of the nobility. The Lao Theung farm dry rice, cotton, and tobacco, employing only wooden tools and bamboo implements; settle near mountain streams in huts with dirt floors; and believe that the human body is host to somewhere between 30 and 130 spirits (to what degree obesity or anorexia determines the size of the spirit habitancy is unclear).

At last, continuing upward, we reach the distant, cloud-hatted mountaintops, where live those tribes known collectively as Lao Sung (High Lao). The Lao Sung tribes—which include the Lisu, the Mien, and, most predominantly, the Hmong—are the most recent immigrants in Laos, having migrated from China, Burma, and Tibet probably no earlier than the end of the nineteenth century. Even though conditions for agricultural success are poorer at those lofty altitudes, the Lao Sung (particularly the Hmong) are much better off than the Lao Theung, with their wider and deeper deposits of topsoil. Why? Because Hmong farmers concentrate on one cash crop and one cash crop alone: the opium poppy.

(There was a Hmong village not much more than an hour's climb above Fan Nan Nan, and with the horticulturalists of that village, Stubblefield and Foley were to establish a mutually rewarding relationship. We'll touch on that later.)

Okay, we have just passed through the Michener zone, and, assuming that narcolepsy hasn't leadened our lids, that we've not been Lao-this'd and Lao-that'ed into a comatose state, we're now in a position, as we rejoin the narrative flow, to conclude that Fan Nan Nan was a Lao Theung community. Are we not? Rest assured that the government in Vientiane, even the inhabitants of surrounding villages, would support us in that conclusion. Ah, but we'd all be wrong.

At this juncture, the curious are fated to be told a little story: not much more than an anecdote, really, but as steeped in romance as a Krispy Kreme doughnut in grease.

It seems that around the turn of the last century, say 1900 or 1899, perhaps a few years earlier, when Fan Nan Nan was, indeed, a tiny Lao Theung outpost, several young men from the hamlet were conscripted into the royal army. Due to the Lao Theung history of indentured servitude and reputation for industriousness, it's not surprising that their draftees were spared the battlefield and instead billeted at a garrison adjacent to the palace in Vientiane, where their propensity for manual labor would be at the easy disposal of the court.

At a Pii Mai Lao festival to celebrate the new year, one of the soldiers met a young woman from a prosperous village near the outskirts of the capital. Shyly, they held hands during the elephant parade, cheered together as the full moon rose, and threw water on each other, as is the custom during Pii Mai Lao. By the end of the three-day festival, some inaudible, inexplicable chemical dialogue between hormonal transmitters, male specific and female specific, had caused them to fall hopelessly in love.

Although they would have much preferred she marry another Lao Lum, the girl's parents declined to forbid the union. The soldier was well-spoken and handsome, strong and honest: they could understand their daughter's attraction, and as she was stubbornly determined, they gave their consent. A few days after his discharge from military service, a wedding was celebrated at the girl's home.

Now, the groom had been sorely missing the pure mountain air of Lao Theung country, missing the abundant wildlife, missing the waterfalls and rocks (and spirits that inhabited them), missing even more the affection of his own family. He was tired of slapping mosquitoes. He knew nothing of farming wet rice, and the paddy stink was offensive to his nose. When he announced that he was taking his bride upcountry, her parents were overcome with regret and woe. You see, they were innocent of blind parental bias when they boasted that their daughter was no ordinary girl. She was pretty (perhaps as pretty as Miss Ginger Sweetie); she was dignified (maybe as dignified as Lisa Ko); she was the best dancer, the best singer, the best seamstress in the town; and, on top of that, no one had ever heard her break wind. Her father and mother and sisters and brothers couldn't bear to be separated from her—so, about a month after her new husband took her away, they sold their water buffalo, packed up, and followed her to Fan Nan Nan.

A few months later, everyone of the bride's relatives, including even distant cousins, decided that life was meaningless without that most talented, most delightful girl, not to mention her pious and generous family, and so the relatives, as well, set off for the hills and Fan Nan Nan. Their departure tore a hole in the fabric of the community; there was an abiding emptiness there. "They were our finest citizens," the villagers lamented. "And that pretty girl, she was the best dancer, the best singer, the best seamstress in town. And never in her life has anybody heard her break wind." Within a year and a half, the whole damn population had abandoned its native village on the fertile plain and resettled many, many kilometers away in a high-valley hamlet nestled between a turbulent stream and a daunting abyss.

Well, by this time Fan Nan Nan had become severely overcrowded. Some new homes had been built, but space for new construction was limited by natural obstacles. Three or four families were forced to occupy houses intended for one. Sufficient rice could not be grown on the hillsides to adequately satisfy demand, and the infrastructure, such as it was, was under considerable strain.

Eventually, one of the Lao Theung elders thought to inquire of one of the Lao Lum elders what had become of the houses and paddies the group had left behind in the lowlands. "Oh, they stand empty," replied the Lao Lum. "We abandoned everything we couldn't strap to our backs." The idea of those nice unoccupied dwellings, those fertile fields left fallow, began to play on the Lao Theung imagination. When they factored in the proximity of the deserted village to Vientiane, with its wealth, employment opportunities, entertainment, and prestige, temptation proved irresistible. One dawn, the new Lao Lum residents of Fan Nan Nan awoke to see every last Lao Theung household (save one, the mixed one) filing down the path with their belongings strapped to their backs.

The two villages had swapped places. It resembled a game of municipal musical chairs.

Pure mountain air whistled in the ex-soldier's receptive nostrils. His ears registered contentedly the familiar pounding of waterfalls, the shrieks of wild peafowl, the husky coughs of leopards, the squeakings of half a hundred species of bats. In the marriage bed, his bride's dignified facade gave way to growls and squeals of her own, to raw demonstrations that rattled the crockery and caused chili paste in comparison to seem as mild as porridge. Life appeared to be good. Yet, the young man's heart had a warp in it. He felt isolated, alien, dissatisfied.

The day he informed his bride that he was leaving to rejoin his clan (now firmly established in *her* former village), she was not surprised. Nor should we be surprised to learn that she supported his decision, telling him without hesitation that she would accompany him there. "No," he said. "You cannot. If you accompany me, your family will again be distraught, and in no time at all they will move back down to their old town to be near you. Then your other kinfolk—and soon everybody else—will follow them, leaving Fan Nan Nan deserted. Our living conditions will again become miserably cramped, prompting my people to return to this place, compelling me to sooner or later go along, and starting the whole shuttling mess all over again. This is madness. It cannot continue. You must stay where you are. I love you. Good-bye."

After she watched his figure disappear down the mountainside, the girl—swollen with child—walked with dignity and determination to the edge of the chasm. There was no wire across it in those days, no big house on the other side; nothing but the open yap of the planet, yawning as if bored by the pace of evolution. Wistfully, she gazed once more at the path her husband had taken, then threw herself over the brink.

The horrified (and later awestruck) firewood gatherers who witnessed her leap agreed on this strange fact: midway in its plunge into the gorge's interminable bird-drilled void, the girl's body suddenly ceased falling, reversed direction, and rose in the air almost back to the lip of the canyon. Then, just as abruptly, it lost its lift and went hurtling downward into the final mists of oblivion.

Some thought that a crosscurrent, a powerful updraft, had momentarily caught her and carried her skyward. Others believed that the love of the Lao Lum girl for the Lao Theung boy was so strong that it actually interfered with the force of gravity. There were a couple of less sentimental onlookers, however, who, claiming they heard a loud report just before she began her short-lived ascent, reasoned that the girl, after a lifetime of holding it in, had finally farted—and the built-up pressure had been so great as to blow her three hundred feet in the air.

Whatever happened, if anything beyond an ordinary suicide leap happened at all (the girl's levitation might have been a mirage), the truth is that Fan Nan Nan was from that day forward a Lao Lum village pretending to be a Lao Theung village. The national census counted it as Lao Theung, it was listed as Lao Theung on taxation rolls. Villagers dressed and spoke as if Lao Theung. They maintained their Buddhist shrines but concealed them behind closed doors, paying at least token homage to magic gods who lived in tree trunks and to those spirits (30 to 130, though they usually went for the low number) who supposedly were conducting spirit business in various parts of their bodies. After two or three generations, their very features became Lao Theunglike. Yet, it was all a masquerade, a ruse adopted in shame and sorrow, and perpetuated—who knows?—maybe just for the fun of it.

In any event, it is probably not far-fetched to characterize Fan Nan Nan as a tribe of imposters, a burg behind a mask, a village gone incognito.

If Fan Nan Nan's eccentric identity fraud influenced the Smarty Pants crew's decision to linger for a while in Laos once the war was over; if, indeed, the airmen were even aware of the deception, it was not alluded to when they—almost unintentionally—confessed to one another their vague intentions to tarry.

By the autumn of 1973, very few American troops remained in Vietnam. Despite a succession of cease-fire agreements, however, the conflict between the North and the South raged on, with the U.S.-backed South getting by far the worst of it; and finally, in April, 1975, Saigon was overrun, the U.S. hurriedly evacuated the last of its military and civilian personnel, and the South surrendered unconditionally. A mighty superpower slunk home with its red-white-and-blue tail between its legs; this most needless of needless wars had ended. News of the surrender took more than a week to reach Fan Nan Nan.

At that point, Foley, Stubblefield, and Goldwire had been in the mountain village for two years. Although technically prisoners, they'd had the run of the place for most of their time there, moving about freely, helping with planting and harvesting; sharing meals, rice whiskey, and the occasional opium pipe with their wardens; engaging the elders in lively discussion; giving English lessons (even to some who didn't request them), participating in bird hunts and festivals, enjoying regular sexual intercourse with any number of compliant girls and women. Their original captors had long since lost track of them, and the Fan Nannies, as Stubblefield had dubbed them, lacked any motivation to report them to responsible authorities.

The peace news from Saigon elicited an all-night celebration in Fan Nan Nan, a whiskey, cannabis, and flesh-flavored dance party in which both natives and Americans participated merrily, though it was never quite clear who was celebrating what. Early in the evening, Stubblefield—who, thanks to his size, intellect, and verbosity, had become a prominent, even dominant, figure in the community—delivered a long oration, the tenor of which nobody, least of all he, could afterward recall. In any case, the mayor seized the opportunity to officially grant his prisoners their freedom, and it was generally accepted that they would be leaving without delay.

The next day, however, none of the foreigners so much as packed a button. Dickie assumed Dern and Stub were too hung over to pack, they assumed the same of him and of each other. All three were right: they were in a mutual state of dehydration and gastro-neurological shock. But then a second day passed, and a third, and not one of the trio, though healthy enough by then, cleaned out his hut. Each seemed preoccupied, just noodling around, performing unnecessary chores, basking in the sunshine, avoiding eye contact with his countrymen.

On day four, Stubblefield, as ranking officer and aircraft commander, called a meeting. Seeking privacy, the men assembled at the edge of the gorge, not far from the spot where decades earlier the young wife, propelled by heartache (and perhaps repressed flatulence) had ejected into nothingness. Recognized by everyone who'd ever met them as relentless practitioners of combative discourse, they were at this meeting oddly reticent. For a long time, they made only small talk and admired the clouds. Uncharacteristically, it was Dern Foley, the most introverted of the three, who broke the ice.

"For a while now," Dern said, squirming nervously on his rock, "I've been having a kind of hankering to crack open the, uh, the giant mysterious pearl of Asia. You know. To find out if there's anything besides an oyster's itchy morbidity inside. Is this Eastern wisdom we've always heard so much about just another more esoteric and equally fruitless attempt to explain the unexplainable, to hang a bell on the God of Smoke and Mirrors, or is there something ultimately more . . . well, ultimately more effective, ultimately more profound, ultimately more, uh, *ultimate* about it?

"For example, this so-called animism that not so much the Fan Nannies but everybody else around here subscribes to. Can we really just write it off as primitive superstition run amok? Do only human beings have souls, or is that a narcissistic, chauvinistic piece of self-flattery? I mean, can't we look at that great old teak tree over there or at this gulch, and see as much of the divine in them as in some ol' anthropomorphic Sunday school Boom Daddy with imaginary long gray whiskers and a platinum bathrobe? Are we capable of entertaining the possibility that there may have been a holy entity *in* the cross as well as *on* it?

"Lately, I've been getting more and more fascinated by these notions of a multitudinous deity, of spirits and demons and inorganic intelligence and non-human souls, all that stuff, and . . . I don't know . . . just when I'm starting to connect with it, to penetrate it a little bit, it seems a shame to have to *leave*. You hear what I'm saying? There's some open-minded, scholarly work to be done in this area. Before the shills of monotheism come back and try again to turn the whole rich and juicy and vibrant extravaganza into a tight-assed little one-man show."

Foley stared at the grass around his feet, as if, indeed, monitoring sentient activity in its stalks and blades. Then, Dickie spoke up. "Well, Dern," he said brightly, "if you want to hang around for a while longer and pursue your scholarship, I'd be willing to stay with you for a time. I miss North Carolina, obviously, but when I get home, I'll just have to go back and finish school and then go to work at my daddy's car dealership. I'm in no hurry for that, I'll freely admit." Dickie glanced in the direction of the village. He smiled anxiously. He shrugged. "It's a pretty sweet life around here."

Dickie and Dern looked at Stubblefield. It was his turn, and they expected nothing less than a torrent of verbiage from the man who frequently spoke as if his brain was a rodeo champion and his tongue a bucking bronco. To their surprise, Stubblefield merely shook his large, voluptuous head and mumbled something. They thought they heard him say, "Vine ripe tomatoes."

"What was that?" In Dickie's mind there was a rush of images: Wonder Bread and Best Foods mayonnaise. Was Stubblefield dreaming of those fine things, as well?

"Vine ripe tomatoes." He pronounced it more clearly. "You'll see that sign—which, grammatically, ought to say 'vine-ripened'—in every produce department in every supermarket in America. You'll see it in the winter when the vines are under a foot of snow. Yet even in July and August, the tomatoes in the bin aren't really ripe. They're pinkish and hard and bereft of flavor. Not only did they not ripen on the vine, they've never ripened at all. But does anybody object? Does anybody shout, 'Who are you kidding—these fucking tasteless tomatoes were picked when they were *green*!'? Or do they rip their menu in half when it says 'farm fresh eggs,' knowing, as even the dimmest ignoramus must, that the eggs in that restaurant have been in cold storage for weeks and that they've never been anywhere near an actual farm? A country that practices and condones such blatant, systematic fakery is a country capable of anything—even of nominating Henry Kissinger for the Nobel Peace Prize." He sighed, and it was a thick, wet sigh. "Those who willingly accept being conned are as corrupt as those who con them. Umm. Yes. Just as my wife was as culpable as I when I mouthed my counterfeit vows. She was my accomplice."

Though they didn't quite know what to say to that, Dickie and Dern were getting the impression that their major might not be inclined to make a speedy beeline for Nebraska. Sensing their discomfort, Stubblefield grinned and gestured toward the French Colonial–style edifice whose roof peaks were visible on the opposite side of the chasm. "Before I get me back to the land of the falsified egg and the betrayed tomato, I want to have a closer look at that deserted house over there. That is, if I can find a way to do it without either breaking my neck or becoming a temporary and gratuitous link in the food chain of indigenous fauna."

Within weeks of that inconclusive but inferential conversation, during which time the airmen continued to enjoy the hospitality of Fan Nan Nan and to follow their nebulous pursuits, the Hanoi-backed Pathet Lao had seized control of most of Laos. On August 23, the Lao People's Revolutionary Party (the merchants of Marxism employ the term "people's" with a veracity every bit as sincere as "vine ripe" and "farm fresh"), declared itself the ruling party of the newly formed Lao People's Democratic Republic. A policy of "accelerated socialism" was embarked upon, and among other vine-ripened reforms, the people's practice of Buddhism was severely curtailed.

Now presumably, the new Communist government would have been obliged to turn over the American airmen to the International Red Cross for repatriation, but the hard-liners were drunk with victory and vengeance, and should the Smarty Pantsers, undocumented as they were, be discovered or give themselves up, there was a definite chance they'd be shot as spies. Of course, if they were shrewd and careful and lucky, they might sneak across the Mekong into Thailand, where—glory hallelujah!—they'd be debriefed by U.S. agents for days on end and then paraded down Main Street America as heroes of a war everybody would have preferred to forget. "If they brought us to the Rose Garden to pin medals on us," Stubblefield suggested, "we could suddenly jump on the President and bite off his ears"—but they never followed up on the idea.

No further meetings were called. In fact, they never had another conversation—not one—about whether they ought or ought not to head home. Sentimentalists might say they *were* home, but it wasn't as simple as that. Cynics might deride them for wallowing in the romance of exile, but it wasn't that simple, either. The door to novelty is always slightly ajar: many pass it by with barely a glance, some peek inside but choose not to enter, others dash in and dash out again; while a few, drawn by curiosity, boredom, rebellion, or circumstance, venture in so deep or wander around in there so long that they can never find their way back out.

By October of '75, the time for talk of homecoming—of bright futures, mature aspirations, and the ties that bind—apparently had passed. By then, Dern and Stubblefield had gone into business in Fan Nan Nan. Dickie had acquired a handful of rubies and a cheesy guitar. And the circus had come to town.

In Vientiane, Lisa Ko checked into the Novotel Belvedere, the most expensive hotel in the capital but one from which she knew she stood a chance of making a trouble-free international call. Even before washing off the dust of the road, she rang up the circus production office in Tampa, Florida, and got Abe Altman on the line. Abe was the talent scout who'd "discovered" the beautiful trainer of unusual animals, then twenty-nine, in Singapore the previous year, and who functioned as her North American manager.

"Herro. This Madame Ko."

"Madame Ko," acknowledged Abe. "Where are you? They've been concerned about you."

"In Vientiane. In Laos. I come U.S. tomorrow."

"Is everything okay over there? Your family's okay?"

"Everything okay. So sorry they concern. I come back tomorrow. Show now is in Porkland?"

"Portland. Yeah. But tomorrow they're moving to Seattle."

"I come Seattle."

"Okay." Abe hesitated. "Of course, your . . . your little animals won't be there."

"*What?* What you say?"

"Damn. I guess you haven't heard. Your, uh, your natook-ies . . ."

"Tanukis!" She almost shouted it.

"Tanukis. They're gone. All of 'em. The train derailed between Frisco and Portland. That clown, that Bardo Boppie-Bip, I guess she was supposed to be looking after 'em . . ."

"What she do?!" Lisa demanded.

"Well, what I heard is that she was drunk and didn't lock 'em up properly, and when the car derailed, the door flew open and they escaped. They took off up in the hills and nobody could round 'em up. Tried everything. Show hired professional trackers even. Hell, they went in there with dogs, but the only two tanukis they flushed, well, the tanukis led the hounds into a river or a pond or something and then turned on 'em and drowned 'em. Drowned both hounds right there."

Picturing this, Lisa couldn't help but smile—but the smile quickly faded. "They . . . they no find?"

"No. They've pretty much quit trying. They're hoping that when you get back you can maybe go in there and recapture the things. But it's all thick woods, you know. And I guess the tanukis have spread out. Trackers say they hear 'em making weird noises from all different parts of the mountains."

Lisa moaned. "I come tomorrow," she said softly.

"Good, honey. But I have to tell you, even if you do round up your pets, your act is probably done for *this* year. We'll see what the future holds. You got a pretty popular schtick. That damn clown, they're letting her finish out the season, and then I'll bet it's back to the oddball channel for her and her red nose. Circuses don't tolerate boozers like they used to. Well, good luck, Madame Ko. Have a safe flight."

After hanging up, Lisa sat on the bed for a while. Then she drew a hot bath and slumped in the perfumed water up to her small but perfectly sculpted breasts. She pinned up her hair, but as she relaxed, it got wet anyway.

Outside, beyond the open shutters, a monsoon wind played the palm fronds as if they were musical saws. Somewhere below the window, cicadas were holding a political rally, Morse-coding their single slogan—*Live and let live!*—over and over to the four indifferent directions. A flesh-colored moon, as ripe as any "vine ripe" tomato, was skinny-dipping in a lake of its own light. Leaning back, Lisa watched it slowly swim out of sight, languid, naked, and unashamed. The occasional stars were like inflamed eyeballs, spying on the swimmer—and the bather—through peepholes in an anthracite curtain. Due to the lateness of the hour, the city's acrid charcoal cookfires had long since cooled, and as it lumbered through the bathroom window now, the air sagged under the weight of the sweetness it carried: jasmine, lemongrass, sandalwood, frangipani, and olfactory reminders of the afternoon's explosive rain.

The sounds, aromas, and colors of the natural world calmed her heart in a way the bath could not. As she gave herself over to them, they made her feel as though she were some sort of *creature*. She made faint, unconscious creature noises as she toweled off the tubwater. Her movements were as fluid as the tail of a beast.

Dry, Lisa draped the damp white towel over the television set. From her bag she produced a tattered square of silk—a scrap from an antique kimono—and centered it on top of the towel. To the left of the square, she placed a tiny folded-paper figurine, not a buddha exactly but close enough. On the right, she laid the ruby ring that Dickie had had made for her to signal their nuptial intentions. She searched for something suitable to complete the arrangement, thinking how a fresh chrysanthemum would have been perfect, it would have matched the one embroidered on the silk, but, of course, Vientiane was too tropical for 'mums. Finally, she settled on one of her black patent-leather boots, the shiny bad-ass show boots she wore when she performed. "Isn't that what I am in this life: a performer?" Then she smiled. "Isn't everyone?"

She stood the boot atop the square. And, still naked, she knelt in front of the makeshift shrine.

At first the words were slow in forming. "Mother." A long pause. "Mother? Mother, I need your guidance. Grandmother Kazu, I call on you, as well. Help me, please. Great-grandmother Miho, you gave us our character, our direction, our knowledge, if it can be considered knowledge; you bound us to something outside the realm of normal expectations, and although my earthly connection to you has been limited to this scrap of old kimono, I feel entitled to call on you, to beg for your light upon my path. Mother, grandmother, great-grandmother, please visit me tonight. In my dream mind, a door will be left open for you. I will leave tea on this foolish shrine here, or sake if you prefer. I am your daughter, youngest of your line. I need you. I need you. Please. Please come."

Did Miho or Kazu or Lisa's mother, O-Ko, contact her in her sleep that night? Maybe, maybe not. She couldn't quite get a handle on it. The clock radio blared on at 5:00 A.M. (preset: she had an early flight), jarring her into wakefulness so abruptly, so violently (it was a news broadcast and the U.S. President was ineptly biting sound) that any dream she might have hosted, any memory of dreaming, was crushed instantly to dust. There seemed to be a shadowy residue right behind her eyes, a trace of ectoplasm on the pillowcase, yet try as she might she could reconstruct nothing.

Knock! Knock!

"Who's there?"

No answer. If, indeed, there had been any knocking at all.

At that moment, however, she unthinkingly touched her

tongue to the roof of her mouth—and a walloping jolt shot through her. She gasped. She sat partway up in bed.

The thing had doubled in size. More than doubled. Small still, but growing. Swelling, actually. Quivering, too. Roundish. Hard yet spongy. Hot to the tongue. Moist to the finger. One could imagine the prostate of Lawrence of Arabia. A radioactive gooseberry. Frida Kahlo's clitoris. Or maybe not. Maybe just a cyst or a boil. Yet, its throb was anything but pathological. It was not the red throb of affliction but the blue throb of conception, the blue pulse of fate.

"It's happening," Lisa Ko whispered. "Isn't it? It's starting to happen now. It's happening to *me*."

PART IV

The true believer can believe in a political system, in a religious doctrine, or in some social movement that combines elements of the two, but the true believer cannot truly believe in life.

A true believer may worship Jehovah, Allah, or Brahma, the supernatural beings who allegedly *created* all life; a true believer may slavishly adhere to a dogma designed theoretically to *improve* life; yet for life itself—its pleasures, wonders, and delights—he or she holds minimal regard.

Music, chess, wine, card games, attractive clothing, dancing, meditation, kites, perfume, marijuana, flirting, soccer, cheeseburgers, any expression of beauty, and any recognition of genius or individual excellence: each of those things has been severely condemned and even outlawed by one cadre of true believers or another in modern times. Thus, it should come as no surprise that when the communists seized control of Laos in 1975, they shut down the National Circus in Vientiane. A circus was a frivolous distraction from the serious business of socialist reform, was it not?

Immediately following the closing, the managing director of the circus (he also functioned as what in America would be called a ringmaster) assembled all performers. "Our brave young commissars, in their excitement and patriotic zeal, have neglected to take into account that this very arena was built with Soviet money or that it was modeled after the renowned Moscow Circus. From the European example, we know that circuses have never been considered at odds with the aspirations of the Marxist state. Sooner or later, our brave young commissars will be made aware of their error, and the National Circus of Laos will be revived. In the meantime, however, our brave young commissars are in a bit of a frenzy and tend to be somewhat indiscriminate in their hunt for deviants to imprison or shoot dead. It is best that we go into hiding."

Suddenly, everyone was talking at once, but the ringmaster shushed them. "Since a day will come when our abilities will be considered not only nonthreatening to the revolution but excellent for the people's morale, we need to stay prepared. We need to hide together so that we can rehearse and practice together."

The ringmaster knew just the place. He had been born in Fan Nan Nan and lived there until the age of fourteen when his parents (secretly Lao Lum, of course) sent him to live with a family friend in Vientiane so that he might get a formal education. Thus, under his direction, the circus performers—one by one, in pairs, or in small groups—made their way to the isolated village on the rim of the gorge, where they reassembled as an invisible circus, giving name (shhh!) to La Vallée du Cirque.

Because of its French and Russian influences, the National Circus of Laos was somewhat more varied than the circuses of China and Japan, which have always consisted almost exclusively of acrobats, tumblers, and jugglers. Still, it had very few animal acts, so except for the problem of concealing costumes and rigging, the moving piecemeal to Fan Nan Nan, once the elephants had been appropriated by a nationalized logging operation, was not extremely difficult. Among the showfolk who turned up in the village was a four-year-old girl named Ko Ko.

At that tender age, Ko Ko's sole "job" with the circus had consisted of donning an ersatz Wild West cowgirl costume and sitting amidst the antlers of a stag, while its trainer provoked it into galloping around the ring. The stag, tough as its steaks must have been, was eaten by hungry revolutionaries and never made it to Fan Nan Nan. Little Ko Ko was carried there by her foster parents. Her biological mother, a gaminelike tumbler called O-Ko, had abandoned her only a year after her birth.

Perhaps "abandoned" is too strong a word. O-Ko had suckled her baby daughter almost to the time of her departure, caring for her with obvious devotion. Then, she'd deliberately left her in the care of the most tenderhearted couple in the circus. (O-Ko had slept with any number of showmen, but none was ever identified as the father.) There was a note with a few instructions and many expressions of love and regret, but absolutely no explanation of why she, O-Ko, had taken it upon herself to simply walk off into the forest one night and never reappear. Some blamed it on her Japanese ancestry. And most seemed content to believe that eventually everything would be explained in the other note that O-Ko had left behind: the sealed one that was supposed to be opened by Ko Ko on the day of her first menstruation.

There was one other thing. Baby Ko Ko had a sore bump in the roof of her mouth. Under no conditions, O-Ko instructed, was it to be incised, compressed, or medicated in any way. "Leave it alone," the fleeing mother wrote. "It will be fine, I promise you. Someday my daughter will understand."

As the fugitive circus was settling into Fan Nan Nan, our MIAs were in the process of weighing an opportunity that would enable them to more comfortably remain missing—if to remain missing was their intent, and in retrospect it appears that, subconsciously at least, it was. In his effort to fully comprehend animism, Dern, ever the religious scholar, had paid an up-mountain visit to the area's largest Hmong settlement. Stubble-field, who, with no library at hand, was waxing restless; and Dickie, who, though he'd taken to Lao village life like a duct to tape, was always eager for new experiences, went along for the climb. What they found up there that day served to further deepen the trough of novelty into which they'd descended.

In comparatively gentle Laos, Hmong tribesmen are consid-ered aggressive and warlike by nature. When the CIA went look-ing for resistance fighters to help guard the right-wing royal government against leftist insurgents, the Hmong were ideal can-didates. U.S. spooks covertly armed them, trained them, bribed them, conned them, and sent them out to fight and die for America's "national interests." Their efforts failed, the red revolu-tion succeeded. By late 1975, Hmong refugees were pouring into Thailand by the thousands, seeking haven there or petitioning for free passage to California. While the vast majority of Hmong had neither served as U.S. mercenaries nor actively supported them, they all shared in the stigma, and it was fear of reprisals that sparked the mass exodus. Those Hmong who remained in Laos were obliged to keep a low profile, the result being that they were afraid to take their opium crop ('75 was a banner year for poppies) to market.

When our American airmen—pretending to be representa-tives of a United Nations relief organization—saw that dusty grainery crammed with teddy-bear-colored dream paste, they began to entertain romantic and dangerous ideas.

Those ideas grew larger, more lurid, after they shared a few pipes with the local gentry. (*Ahhh.* "The smoke of paradise," opium has been called, although, technically, opium produces chemical vapors rather than smoke: it bubbles and melts when heated but does not actually burn.) And the ideas ballooned and sprouted crazy legs when the hosts threw aside a pile of grass mats at the far end of the hamlet to reveal an intact if immobilized helicopter.

Soviet-built, the small chopper had belonged to the Pathet Lao's elite troops. Sometime in 1972, it had run out of fuel—the Lao were careless with machinery—and made an emergency landing on a ledge just below the village. The Hmong wasted no time in killing all aboard. Then they spent grunting weeks with ropes and skid planks, muscling the craft up to the chief's personal poppy patch, where, camouflaged, it had sat ever since. Dern Foley's pupils, already dilated, commenced to resemble something at the end of Stephen Hawking's telescope.

A deal was struck. Dern moved in with the Hmong. Eventually, he managed to get the whirlybird whirling. Fuel was obtained. He took the chief and two of the prettiest girls in town up for a spin. There was a celebration. More fuel was soon procured from black marketeers down-mountain. The helicopter was loaded with bricks and loaves of the sweet-smelling caramel God dough. "You're a lord now, Foley," Stubblefield proclaimed, as his friend got behind the controls. "Guardian of the loaves."

Only Dickie Goldwire felt a sick maggoty squirm in his innards when the chopper lifted off for Thailand.

At the Foley bungalow, that year's Labor Day observance brought about a reversal in roles. Bootsey had the Monday off, the post office being closed for the holiday, while Pru, so long unemployed, was beginning her temporary job with the circus: the big show, having just trained into Seattle, was scheduled to commence its week-long run on Wednesday.

"There's something so . . . so *manly* about Labor Day," said Bootsey. "It's cute."

In the midst of slipping into a pair of baggy polyester slacks, Pru paused and snorted. "Explain this to me then," she demanded. "If Labor Day is a day set aside to honor the working stiff, you know, to honor honest toil, why then do people celebrate it by staying home and goofing off? I mean, if work is so noble and good for us, wouldn't you think we'd choose to honor it by working twice as long and hard on its special day?"

Although her sister was regarding her with disbelief, Pru continued. "It strikes me that if the way people celebrate work is by not working, then what they're really celebrating is leisure. They're admitting that they'd a whole lot rather be having fun day in and day out than have their nose to the fucking grindstone."

"Pru, if you really don't want to pay your own way, then—"

"You're missing my point." Pru zipped up her pants with a flourish. "It's like celebrating Valentine's Day by acting hateful and sending rude notes to your loved ones. Don't you get it? Would you pour me another glass of tomato juice? Thanks. The fact is, I'm excited about today. I'm looking forward to it. But in general, workers *do* hate to go to work. That's why so many heart attacks occur on Monday mornings—which, now that I think of it, may be why they decided to put Labor Day on a Monday."

Speechless in the teeth of such logic, Bootsey let a minute or two pass before saying, "Well, then, I guess we won't be hearing anything today from San Francisco."

"Hardly!" Pru finished off her juice. "You know, Sis," she said more quietly as she headed for the door, "I've been thinking that maybe we should go out and get Dern a lawyer. You know, some famous, high-profile defense attorney. There's obviously something going on here besides a routine drug bust, something the feds want to keep hushed up, and a hot-shot attorney might take the case just for the publicity it would bring him."

Bootsey frowned. "Oh my. Colonel Thomas and those government agents wouldn't like that one bit."

"Who cares if they like it or not? It might force the feds to treat Dern more fairly, more openly, and with a star like Johnnie Cochran hovering over 'em, they'll think twice before pulling any strong-arm stuff on me and you. Anyway, let's mull it over." She took one last look at herself in the mirror and, satisfied, raised her voice. "Ladies and gentlemen, boys and girls, children of all ages! Hi ho! Prudence Victoria Foley is off to join the goddamn circus!"

In Vientiane, Lisa Ko walked the broad old Indochine avenues in her jade green cheongsam, brooding, mumbling, gliding a tongue tip over the object—the *event*—in her mouth, stopping occasionally in the shade of one of the sandalwood trees (there was no Zen in the crumbling temples) to pray for guidance. She had a dilemma and wanted something more specific than her ancestral "it is what it is" routine.

Lisa had canceled her original flight to the States. In the days since, she'd several times been on the verge of rebooking, only to change her mind in the middle of dialing the airline office.

To be sure, she felt some urgency to hasten to Oregon to try to retrieve her troupe, yet when she prayed she kept hearing—or imagined she was hearing—a distant, very faint yet insistent voice that counseled against it. To whom did the voice belong? It was too masculine to come from Miho or Kazu or her mother, and it lacked the compassionate tone of a buddha. It had a slick, sly, oily quality; not precisely a hustler's voice, a pimp's voice, but there was something foxy about it.

"The tanukis are fine, little darling," she thought she heard the voice purr in her ear. "You've had your fun together, you and them, your fling in the illusory arena. Now allow them to be true animals again, free of hoops and the drug of applause. Let them do what they will in the New World, wild and free. It's what Tanuki's been needing. It may be what America needs, as well."

Oddly, Lisa was starting to become convinced that the voice was somehow correct. She was resigning herself to the possibility of life without her usual act. Letting go wasn't easy, however. She'd come to regard those silly badgers almost as her surrogate children. But that shouldn't matter anymore, should it? Now that she apparently was going to have a child of her own?

> You play the game incognito,
> You risk paying a very stiff price.
> You'll bet the ranch on Number 13,
> Though that number is not on the dice.

For several years, Dern, sometimes accompanied by Stubblefield, flew loaves of raw Hmong opium over the mountain range to a drop-off base operated by Thai smugglers. For that service, the three MIAs shared in the profits (Dickie was at that point reluctantly involved). Those profits were fairly modest, even after Stubblefield demanded and eventually received a higher price from the Thai. The boys soon learned that raw opium per se is a pretty crappy substance, naturally sullied by vegetable matter, gums, resins, and dirt, to which the Hmong might add powdered aspirin, molasses, tobacco chaff, and so forth to increase its weight on the buyer's scales. The stuff was barely fit for a peasant's pipe unless purified and turned into the paste called *chandoo*.

"We're a bunch of lugs shoveling ore while the ironmongers make all the money," Stubblefield observed. "We're going into the chandoo business."

By this time, thanks to the helicopter, the Americans had

claimed squatters' rights to the large house across the chasm, and in the midst of renovating the place, they set up a processing kitchen there where they removed the contaminants from the raw material and distilled a more valuable product. They began buying the opium themselves from the Hmong farmers, who were uninterested in any processing operation, and reselling it in Thailand. As cash flow increased, they purchased the helicopter from the farmers as well. (The chopper still bore the Pathet Lao insignia, so even when it was spotted, which was infrequently, it was never challenged. They christened it, incidentally, Smarty Pants II.)

Now as anybody but a full-time cretin must know, smoking opium is to shooting heroin what figure skating is to Russian roulette. Yet for reasons that cast grave doubts on the mental and emotional stability of modern man, happy opium-smokers have all but disappeared from the planet while nihilistic junkies abound. Thus, while chandoo might be a more profitable commodity than raw poppy bricks, the big bucks were in the dangerous and stupid stuff.

"We're a pack of lowly ironmongers," said Stubblefield, "while the steelworkers make all the money. No, no, we're not going to start manufacturing smack, but our end of the stick is destined to be as short as the Hmong's if we refuse to take the next step."

The next step was the refinement of the chandoo paste into a powder that was a hop and a skip away from morphine, morphine being a jump away from heroin. When Stubblefield and Foley voted to take that step, Dickie, with a heart like a fallen grape beneath a satyr's hoof, moved out of Villa Incognito and, there being no alternative, navigated hand over hand the high wire that now crossed the gorge, his palms bloody, fingers blistered, shoulders throbbing, head spinning, flip-flops falling off and fluttering into the abyss, arms almost pulled from their sockets, and—when he finally reached the opposite side—spewing breakfast like a gargoyle in a Gothic fountain.

Although he wouldn't try to stop him, Stubblefield was by no means pleased to see Dickie go. He found the sunny Carolina boy a refreshing counterpoint to the moody, often sardonic Dern; and as his erudition and confidence grew, Dickie had contributed more and more to the wide-ranging, roughhouse discussions that dominated social life at the villa. The conversation just prior to Dickie's exodus, however, was less boisterous than tense.

"What you're about to do now is criminal."

"Goldwire, *everything* we've been doing for years is criminal! We're deserters. Our very presence here is a crime."

"Okay, then, *immoral.*"

"From a semantic standpoint, 'immoral' is probably a more accurate word. From the standpoint of ethics, however, it's a sanctimonious exaggeration and a prejudicial judgment."

"It's not either one. You're going to be pushing morphine, for God's sake!"

Wearily, Stubblefield shook his big head. "Ah, Goldwire, you do carry that Southern Baptist gene for inflammatory rhetoric. We're not *pushing* anything. There's a demand so great that the pittance we can supply wouldn't begin to fulfill a finite fraction of it. Moreover, we're not, strictly speaking, making morphine. Yeah, yeah, I know, that's a technicality—but what if we *were* selling morphine? Morphine, in its proper place, is humanity's friend."

"It's named after Morpheus, the Greek god of dreams," Dern Foley quietly interjected.

"Foley's right. Many a poor soul racked with disease has gotten a blessed night's sleep thanks to—"

"Come on, Stub! A bunch of Filipino quacks are gonna be turning your . . . your semi-morphine, your virtual morphine, into heroin!"

Stubblefield made a show of clucking his long tongue. "My

goodness, Goldwire. With what *power* your righteous hysteria invests that simple word." He clucked some more, like a myopic hen scolding an omelet. "Heroin. The chemical archdemon. The crystalline Satan. A drug equally as addictive and almost as dangerous as nicotine."

"Nicotine," mused Foley. "Named after Jacques Nicot, the French god of lung cancer." The man knew his deities.

"That's sophistry," charged Dickie. "You can't compare them."

"No," Stubblefield conceded. "I suppose not. Were we supplying the Filipino 'quacks' with nicotine instead of our opiate, I'd be as uneasy as you in the morality department. Of course, there's scant medical benefit to be derived from Monsieur Nicot's lethal namesake. Whereas our criminal elixir, our immoral tonic . . . well, let me shush before I wax unseemingly altruistic. Profit *is* an issue here, after all. It's going to take a fair amount of moolah to restore this old house to grandeur."

Stubblefield's defense was not by any means a total rationalization. Heroin, we must note, is by far the most effective analgesic known to medical science. It has the unique capacity to relieve the pain that even morphine cannot dull; the relentless, excruciating torture that is many a cancer victim's fate. Over the decades, numerous compassionate American physicians have petitioned for permission to administer heroin to their terminally ill patients, only to be curtly dismissed by politicians, on grounds of the drug's addictiveness. Why it would matter one iota whether or not a doomed patient with only weeks to live became addicted, the wise men have never explained. A few congressmen have cited concern that if heroin was present in hospitals, it might be stolen and sold on the street or else secretly used by nurses and staff (such is Washington's conviction of the white powder's irresistible allure); while others fret that it would set a bad example for children, the logic of that excuse being beyond the comprehension of the ordinary mind.

Whatever the politicians' real reasons—pressure from the Mafia, perhaps, in whose financial interest it is to keep drugs

illegal and therefore expensive; or pressure from religious con-
servatives, whose rabid superstitions cancel out any tenderness
they might harbor in their "Christian" breasts—thousands of
terminally ill human beings are made to spend their last days in
wrenching agony, when relief, dignity, and a meaningful parting
from their loved ones, is only a syringe away.

In any case, toward the end of the 1970s, a laboratory on the
outskirts of Manila began refining medical-grade heroin from
unlicensed opiate sources (U.S. authorities have never hesitated
to impose their puritanical values on other, less uptight, cultures)
and providing it to a clandestine clinic in the Philippines and two
others in India. At those clinics—hospices, actually—moribund
patients were given the injections necessary to ease their great
suffering, and many died smiling when they would have died
screaming. By 2001, there were thirteen such facilities operating
secretly in Asia, Latin America, and the South Pacific.

The Manila lab remained a principal supplier for the Asian
hospices. A buyer from that lab, a biochemist scouting for
new sources, happened to arrive at the Thai outpost just as
Smarty Pants II was landing there with a cargo of chandoo. Stubblefield and Foley struck up a conversation with the Filipino
(he spoke good English, whereas the Thai smugglers had only
the most basic vocabulary) and learned of his mission. Within
an hour, thanks to Stubblefield's XXL personality and the
demonstrable quality of the Fan Nan Nan chandoo, they made a
deal.

As has been chronicled, Dickie Goldwire objected to the
arrangement. He'd been comfortable neither with the raw O nor
the chandoo, and now he took a stand. "You can't be sure," he
told his comrades, "that at least some of this heroin isn't going to
end up in an inner city shooting gallery or a rock star's veins."

Dern glanced up from his bottle of Beer Lao, at which he'd
been staring so intently one might have imagined him in com-
munion with the tiger head on its label. He had, after all, a fasci-

nation with animism. "You're starting to sound a lot like the government you've run away from," he said.

Stubblefield was more civil. "No," he admitted, "the white river of poppy sap is a meandering stream with many tributaries, few that flow above ground. We can't be a hundred percent certain that some portion of our contribution won't overflow its intended channel. We can only be trusting and hopeful."

"Right. Hopeful some downtrodden kid doesn't OD on the stuff you may be putting in circulation."

"There are reckless people who can—and will—die from the cars your father sells every day. Anything can be misused. Furthermore, every individual has to assume responsibility for his or her own actions, even the poor and the young. A social system that decrees otherwise is inviting intellectual atrophy and spiritual stagnation."

The night before, Dickie had endured an especially embarrassing session of dream school, one with endless missed assignments and lost classrooms, and now his lingering frustration was compounded. There was some truth in Stubblefield's views, he felt, but not enough to obscure the bleating of the Goldwire conscience. So, he gathered his meager belongings, including the piece-of-trash Ukrainian guitar on which he, for better or worse, would compose "Meet Me in Cognito," and piled them neatly in a corner for Dern at some point to ferry over to the village in the chopper. He shook hands with Dern, grunted audibly from the compression of Stubblefield's bear hug, and headed for the door and the terrifying wire across the chasm.

Before he was halfway to the exit, the other two had resumed their debate about the relative popularity of drugs such as heroin when common sense dictated that the use of those substances was self-destructive. Stubblefield contended that as long as methods were available that allowed people to dissolve the ego and kill time—not while away the time, not pass it, but *annihilate* it—they would seek out those methods regardless of the risks involved. The ecstasy of living completely in the present moment, which almost everyone experiences briefly in sexual orgasm, mystics access during deep meditation, shamans savor as a reward for their psychedelic ordeals, and some artists stumble upon gratuitously when they lose themselves in their work, that egoless euphoria was, according to Stubblefield, at the core of transcendence, the liberated state of elevated innocence for which every human animal unwittingly hungers. Transcendence was, quite literally, heaven on earth, and any narcotic that punched a ticket to paradise was going to be consumed, even if there might be hell at the end of the ride.

Dern, citing Buddhist texts and an obscure passage from Genesis, countered that the barriers that blocked our entrance into earthly paradise were not time and ego but, rather, fear and desire. The only problem with man's notion of time, Dern argued, was that it called constant attention to his mortality, as well as to the always uncertain future, thereby accentuating his fear of death and the unknown. Then, after a gulp of Beer Lao, the balding pilot asserted that the ego, when divorced from its weighty, neurotic burden of ambition and greed, was actually more of a boon than a hurdle. Could we but jettison our fears and desires, our relaxed egos would serve to keep us well-centered in a permanent, portable Eden. The hophead nodding on smack neither quakes nor covets, neither cringes nor grasps, and it's for that supreme equanimity, rather than to escape social squalor or personal responsibility, that he jabs his artery with the spike. So said Dern.

Subjected to this dialogue as he packed and, after farewells, as he made his unhappy way to the door, Dickie muttered upon exiting, "Jeeze! I wonder which god it is that's the God of Bullshit?" He didn't really mean it, of course: under normal conditions he would have loved to have taken part in the discourse, and, furthermore, he hadn't thought the others could possibly have overheard. Alas, the ever alert Stubblefield called after him:

"All of them, Goldwire. All of them. No particular god gets to preside over bullshit, or else they'd fight among themselves for the privilege. The gods tolerate the human race for no other reason than our talent for bullshit. It's the only thing about us that doesn't bore them to tears."

"What about love?" Dickie thought to yell back. "What about our capacity for love?" But by then the door had swung shut behind him.

For several years the MIA entrepreneurs relied on a "mule" to transport their product from northern Thailand to the Philippines. The mule was recommended by the lab and seemed reliable, always returning in a timely fashion with the previously specified amount of cash in the previously specified currencies: Thai baht, Lao kip, and U.S. dollars. Sometime in the mid-eighties, however, Dern Foley began to make runs to Manila two or three times a year. Dern had already ventured twice into Bangkok, and on his second foray there, had had fake French passports made for himself and his confederates. He had also managed to acquire the official garments of a Roman Catholic priest, breaking out, the first time he donned the habit, in what was undoubtedly the biggest smile of his adult life. "I thought I would expire of geriatric infirmities before seeing you actually grin," said Stubblefield.

On each and every visit to Manila, Dern did the best he could to ascertain that the heroin produced from the Villa Incognito narcotic was going exclusively to hospices and not onto the street. By the time of his third round trip, he and Stubblefield were "reasonably convinced" that they were providing a purely humanitarian service. So assured of this was Stubblefield that he would sometimes put on his favorite concubine's dressing gown, bind a dishcloth about his head, and prance around the villa, pretending to be Mother Teresa. (The champagne that Dern was bringing back to Fan Nan Nan in large quantities played no small role in the display.)

Though greatly encouraged by Dern's reports, and friendly with his fellow deserters, Dickie's suspicions failed to vanish to the point where, with a smooth conscience, he could rejoin the operation. Snug in his hut, he enjoyed the rhythms of village life, especially when the circus folk were in town. Moreover, he had established a modestly successful business of his own.

Up in the Hmong village, a woman had developed a severe crush on our Dickie. She was a middle-aged widow, who, in addition to losing her husband, had suffered such dental shortfall as to be seriously in the path of oral bankruptcy. The widow was as impoverished in the area of both central and lateral incisors as the object of her affection was reputed to be overprivileged in the area of the primary masculine faculty. Some, in fact, claimed that it was after coming upon Dickie bathing in a stream that she, galvanized by the priapic splendor, became enamored of him, but that story likely grew out of Stubblefield's teasing and cannot be trusted. At any rate, though Dickie was nothing if not egalitarian, the attraction was by no means mutual, and he politely spurned her advances. One day, while in the thrall of infatuation, she presented the American with a handful of small, rough rubies.

It would have been bad manners to refuse a gift, so Dickie accepted the stones and employing sand as an abrasive, cleaned them up to the best of his ability. He then sent them to Thailand aboard Smarty Pants II, whereupon they were purchased by the smugglers for considerably less than they were worth. Dickie gave 50 percent of the proceeds to his admirer, which, of course, only increased her ardor. He encouraged the widow to bring him additional stones, which she did as fast as she could dig them out of the dry riverbeds, mountain washes, and gullies. That was not at all fast, but it proved adequate.

Most of the rubies she unearthed were of the more common yellowish red variety, although about once every three or four years she'd luck upon one of the highly valued deep bluish red gems known as "pigeon blood." Such rubies, along with all larger specimens, were usually reserved for village elders, but Dickie persuaded the woman to sell them to him. It was rumored that she did so in return for the favor of being allowed to perform fellatio on him, an act for which, due to her lack of interfering nibs, she may have possessed uncommon talent—but the reader should be warned that that story, too, is very probably apocryphal.

When he could at last afford it, Dickie purchased a hand-cranked lapidary. Thereafter, the rubies in his inventory were more presentable. This paid off handsomely when the time came when he would send the gems to Manila with Dern (aka the good Father Gorodish), and Dickie might have become nearly as affluent as the occupants of Villa Incognito had not he shared his profits with the needy citizens of Fan Nan Nan. Thanks to the lanky American, no village in the Lao mountains had such a sufficiency of medical or school supplies. This was kept quiet, for who could guess what the bureaucrats in Vientiane would make of it?

W hen we think of a ruby, we may think of the sinister apple plugging the umbilical cavity of some greasy pagan idol; we may think of the fiery rays shooting from the eyes of an ornamental dragon; we may think of the jewel that put Burma on the map (never dreaming that Laos's guilty neighbor would one day change its name to Myanmar in an attempt to hide its shame: Myanmar is Burma incognito), or we may, if we are connoisseurs, think of fat drops of pigeon blood. Ordinarily, however, we would not think of aluminum, which, when excited by a lewd trace of chromium oxide, is what a ruby is; nor do we think rubies to be more highly prized in the marketplace than diamonds, which, in fact, they are. Had his gems been larger and of better quality, and had he received a fairer price, Dickie would have been wealthy indeed. As it was, he did okay for a Goldwire without a Ford dealership to call his own.

Ruby money or no ruby money, the contrast between Dickie's hut and Villa Incognito only increased as the years went by.

The big, French Colonial-style house had been built as a summer retreat by an official close to the royal family. At the time of its construction, circa 1950, there was a narrow dirt road leading up to the site on the opposite side of the ridge from the gorge, making it accessible by buffalo cart if not motor vehicle. Scarcely a dozen years passed, however, before a mammoth landslide obliterated the road and sheared off the ridge side, rendering access to the house virtually impossible. A few hardy scavengers did labor their way up the precipice to loot the contents of the building, but once it was emptied, it was left to rot.

Actually, it rotted very little. Preserved, perhaps, by the dry mountain air, its structure and foundation remained quite sound. Indoors, the primary task facing Stubblefield and Foley was to chase out the bamboo rats and kill all the spiders and snakes. Dern, conditioned, no doubt, by his fascination with animism, felt uneasy about this carnage, but the Lao helpers, closet Buddhists every one, slew left and right without a qualm. Once the house had been depopulated, Dern and a bevy of the finest local carpenters set about restoring the teak wainscoting and refinishing the mahogany floors. Stubblefield supervised from a big leather chair, the first of many luxurious items with which he would, over time, fill the villa.

Was it really a villa? Yes, even by European standards it would probably qualify. Hardly had he stepped out of the helicopter than Stubblefield christened the place Villa Incognito. Then, he changed his mind. "*Villa*," he said, "is a feminine noun, whereas *incognito* is a masculine modifier. I must apologize for the clumsy error in gender agreement." Upon his venerable Latin steed, Dern rode to the rescue. Were Stubblefield speaking one of the Romance languages, he said, it might well have verged on a linguistic faux pas, but since both *villa* and *incognito* had long since been incorporated into English, and since English had never burdened itself with gender endings, Dern decreed the name grammatically immaculate. Thus, Villa Incognito it was.

By the 1990s, the villa, despite its isolation, was a bit of a cultural hive, the countless hours that Stubblefield spent with his books and Dern with his tools (the aging whirlybird was in almost constant need of repair) in serene contrast to the giggling, jabbering, and sexual wailing of the concubines; the flitting about of housekeepers as they beat carpets and dusted champagne bottles, cigar humidors, and objets d'art; not to mention the aromatic bustle in the kitchen, where lemongrass, turmeric, tamarind, coconut chunks, and coriander leaves were being ceaselessly pounded with mortar and pestle, and shallots, hot chilies, ginger, mint, mangoes, and garlic cloves endlessly diced and chopped. They ate well at Villa Incognito. They fucked well. They strived to improve their minds. With time out to whip up a little virtual morphine for purposes of income, they lived like funky potentates in the former Land of a Million Elephants.

This is not to say that they gave nothing back to the adjacent community. Aside from hiring cooks, housekeepers, and carpenters from the area and paying them decent wages, aside from selecting a number of local beauties to live in luxury as their extralegal wives, they occasionally made monetary donations to the village coffers, although not nearly in the amounts given by the less advantaged Dickie. The villa's major contribution to Fan Nan Nan may have been Stubblefield's pedagogy. He forced half the villagers to become fluent in English, improved their rudimentary French, instructed them lightly in history, astronomy, geography, quantum physics, and the literary arts, and exhaustively in philosophy (largely his own), inspiring in the process an appreciation among them both for learning and for that bullshit that the gods are purported to find so redeemably entertaining.

It was in his capacity as a teacher that he got to know Lisa Ko.

Amidst the picturesque confusion that resulted when the National Circus of Laos unexpectedly reassembled itself in remote little Fan Nan Nan, it is surprising that a four-year-old child would attract any notice. Young Ko Ko, nevertheless, was frequently exclaimed over by those who glimpsed her among the jugglers, acrobats, and clowns. Despite almost imperceptibly pointed ears and a nose that lopped slightly to the side, she was remarkably pretty, albeit in the Japanese mode, about which many Lao (frankly, not among the planet's most handsome inhabitants) were inclined to be envious or snide. She carried herself with an uncommon dignity, though less like a princess destined to inherit a throne—there was nothing haughty or spoiled about her—than like a kind of rare animal, unaccustomed to the neurotic vagaries of men. She possessed an animal's self-containment and an animal's wary grace. There was always something furtive about her, and always just a bit of a faraway look in her shiny black eyes, giving the impression of a connection to distant elements she did not or could not understand.

On the other hand, she seemed grounded, present in the moment, and wise beyond her years, though one could never quite put one's finger on why she gave that impression. She seldom spoke, but just when an observer thought her as solemn as an idiot savant, she would erupt in such unguardedly sweet and silly laughter that others had to laugh along with her. Dickie had been delighted by her from the start. Stubblefield noticed her for the first time on the day when the cable was strung across the gorge.

Of all the performers exiled in Fan Nan Nan, the aerialists felt the most out of place. Aware that these daredevils, who thrived on risk and applause, were in need of excitement lest they strike out for Bangkok or return to Vientiane, the ringmaster challenged them to string a wire over the misty chasm and walk it if they dared. "Karl Wallenda would do it in an instant," he said, "Philippe Petit before breakfast and twice on Friday." After a week of hesitation and debate, during which they sat every day on the canyon's terrible lip, they announced that this feat, unprecedented in the history of Southeast Asia, was the feat they were born to perform.

Led by the Phom Troupe, the equilibrists hammered together a sturdy platform on the village side of the gorge. To a piling at the center of the platform, they fastened with metal clamps a rope of clear, clean, ungreased steel, composed of eight compressed strands, each seventeen millimeters in diameter, around a core of hemp. At the tip of the other end of the cable, they made a spliced loop with a thimble inside it. They hooked a heavy-duty turnbuckle to the loop, then had it and the attached cable flown across the chasm in Smarty Pants II. On the villa side, they built an identical platform, and with the aid of the turnbuckle and a pulley block, stretched the cable tight and secured it to a second post. Limited by the steep sides of the gorge, they steadied the cable to the extent they could manage with a tripod of guy wires on either side. This paucity of guys meant that the cable would have some slack toward its middle, a condition that heightened the challenge—and greatly stimulated the aerialists by making their sphincters wrinkle and their pulses race.

Everyone, circus folk and natives alike, gathered for the first walk on the wire. That honor fell to Papa Phom, the seventy-year-old patriarch of Lao wire-walkers. It was nearly dusk when, in baby-blue tights and a silk jacket adorned with silver stars, the elder Phom climbed onto the platform, offered prayers to the four winds, and slowly placed his balancing foot, shod in a light blue slipper, onto the cable. His leg fixed, he stood that way for several minutes, as if feeling the music of the wire in his body.

Then, gripping the balancing pole that is essential for any crossing of that length, he arched his back and with small, regimented but graceful steps moved forward. The villagers started to applaud. The circus people hushed them.

Halfway across the gorge, at the point where the wire commenced to sag, Papa Phom stopped, carefully turned around, bowed deeply, and saluted the crowd. Everybody smiled. He turned again and resumed his crossing. At that moment, Ko Ko began to weep. The child was quite agitated, and since no one else attempted to comfort her, Stubblefield picked her up. He was in the process of slipping a piece of nutmeg candy into her small, quivering mouth when there was a gasp from the throng. Papa Phom was teetering. Some thought it was just part of the act, a trick to scare and thrill the audience, but the wire-walkers recognized trouble.

A gust of wind? A heart attack or stroke? A bat that flitted too close to his head? A summons from the dead bride at the bottom of the abyss? Nobody would ever know. But they all watched in horror as the old man's legs splayed, one foot lost the wire, then the second, and, never letting go of his pole (as no professional ever would), he capsized. Down, down, down he fell in the twilight, his celestial jacket billowing like a sail; down, down until he vanished in the toothless mist that rose to swallow him; down, down until he flattened, as he must have, the bride's lonely ghost.

In the night of grief that followed, many thoughts were expressed, two of which may bear repeating. "He died as he lived," observed his sister, "doing that thing that made him most come alive. No man can ask for more than that." The other thought was spoken as an unusually pale sun, maybe a tad ashamed of its cheerfulness, peeked over the ridge. "The wire-walker who does not walk today will never truly walk a wire again."

Scarcely had the dew evaporated from the wild chrysanthemum petals than the equilibrists were lining up at the platform, each one clad not in practice duds but in his or her most colorful hippodrome finery.

Out of respect, the Phom Troupe was ushered to the head of the line. Papa Phom's eldest son had the honor. Wearing his father's spare jacket, the one whose sleeves were a little frayed and whose stars had lost their luster, he took up his pole and set his balancing foot firmly on the cable, letting his toes listen until they had memorized every note, every nuance of tempo, in the wire's hard, ethereal hum. He thanked the winds from four directions, including a special prayer to the God of Sudden Gusts, and began to glide along the wire as if he were on ice. That glide was his personal style, and it seemed to serve him well.

As the walker approached midpoint, where the wire was disposed to sag, Stubblefield kept a watchful eye on the small girl, Ko Ko. She remained calm, composed, almost hypnotized. When the son at last reached the opposite platform, she quietly nodded her approval. As for Stubblefield and everyone else, they released such a huge, collective sigh that had it occurred a minute earlier, it surely would have blown the man off the strand.

Next, it was the mother's turn. Old Madame Phom, so freshly widowed, allowed her red eyes to take in the full length of the cable. Then she set out in short, mincing steps like a geisha with a full pot of tea. However, at the precise spot where her husband had turned, bowed, and saluted the crowd, she did the very same thing, adding as a flourish, a drop to one knee. No longer able to contain themselves, the onlookers cheered. And the other aerialists began to jostle one another in their eagerness to pit their balance and breath against that thin thread that would stand between them and the vertiginous void.

Once Madame was safely across, the rest of the Phoms, the siblings, nieces, nephews, and cousins, each walked. Papa's seven-year-old granddaughter, Lisa Ko's lifelong playmate, cried and stamped her slippers because she was refused a turn. Then, all five members of the Anou Family (only two of whom were actually related) walked the wire. After that came the Paris-trained trio that billed itself as the Flying Yellow Devils. They crossed together, three on the cable at once, egging one another on. Finally, it was the Grand Kai's turn. Kai, whose name in Lao means *chicken*, wore greasepaint, a pointy hat, and baggy plaid trousers. Pru Foley might have loved him, especially when, mid-wire, he dropped his pants and treated the cheering crowd to a spectacularly sunlit view of his naked derrière.

In the months that followed, there was seldom a calm, dry day when there were no walkers on the cable. In addition to the sheer phenomenon of it, Stubblefield appreciated the wire for the auxiliary, though obviously restricted, route it provided to and from the villa: Smarty Pants II was destined to become increasingly unreliable, and fuel needed to be conserved for business trips into Thailand. The wire would serve as a passageway only when absolutely necessary, but it was satisfying to have it as an option. Incidentally, the first American to submit to being pushed across it in a wheelbarrow was Dern Foley, the quintessential aviator, a lover of heights. There were counterweights hanging from the wheelbarrow to insure its stability (and to free the pusher from the need to carry a pole), but it was still a daring proposition, and Dern's adrenal glands took full advantage of it.

The MIAs' concern that news of the high-wire performances would attract rubberneckers to the gorge was short-lived. The circus, being itself on the lam, paid a couple of Fan Nan Nan's toughest men to station themselves a full kilometer down the only path leading to the village, and curious strangers were summarily turned away. And since the Hmong, too, had reason to avoid publicity, there was nothing to fear from farther up the mountain.

Everyone was rather in hiding and no one seemed terribly to mind.

There is no activity in the cosmos more unvarying, more predictable than the rate at which uranium turns into lead. That's a good thing. If the universal clock was based on the rate at which novelty turns into routine, we might *never* show up at the dentist on time. Yet, sooner or later, however capriciously and imprecisely, the "oh wow" does decay into the "ho-hum," so it isn't surprising that before a year had passed, a man or woman merely walking a treacherous wire hundreds of feet above an abysmal gorge failed to divert Fan Nannies from their everyday chores. Moreover, since the circus equilibrists could just as easily practice their acts on a cable strung between tree trunks, three feet off the ground, there was no logical reason to brave the height, the vapors, or the gusts. And yet some did.

Of course, as Stubblefield observed, there was no logical reason to ever walk a high wire in the first place. That was what he liked about it.

"Look at him up there," said Stubblefield, directing Dern's attention to the silhouetted figure who appeared to be dancing alone in empty space out over the canyon. "He's feeding the angels." The Americans were sipping Cristal on the veranda, after a day that the one had spent adding brush to the crude canopy that camouflaged the helicopter, and the other, reading Oscar Wilde.

"Just look at him," Stubblefield went on, as in the distance the solitary figure jumped through a hoop and landed back on the nearly invisible wire. "What you're seeing is the perfection of a conscious act of craziness. What you're seeing is pinpoint focus combined with mad abandon in such a way as to cause the specters of death and the exaltations of life to collide at some kind of crossroads. The sparks that fly from that collision are like little shards of God. If you can hold them in your mind for more than five seconds, you can understand everything that ever was or will ever be."

"Well, now, I suspect you may be overstating the case," drawled Dern, his thick, rough fingers circling like barbarians the elegant contours of the champagne glass. "In fact, you're drifting into deep hyperbole, ol' Stub. But I must admit there's something Zen about those fools on a wire, something beautiful beyond our ordinary, uh, understanding of beauty."

"Yes, yes, you're quite right. But, Foley, my lad, it isn't beauty per se that makes wire-walking Zen or makes it art. It's the extremity of the risks that are assumed by each exquisite gesture, each impossible somersault. Here's a more extreme version of the dangerous beauty bullfights used to possess before the matadors became preening cowards and stacked the deck against the beasts. We only rise above mediocrity when there's something at stake, and I mean something more consequential than money or reputation. The great value of a high-wire act is that it *has* no practical value. The fact that so much skill and effort and courage can be directed into something so ostensibly useless is what makes it useful. That's what affords it the power to lift us out of context and carry us—elsewhere."

Dern gulped Cristal and made a face. Frankly, he would have preferred a beer. Dern was thinking that Stubblefield need not ever worry about boring the gods. Of course, as a result of his, Dern's, personal investigation of animism, he was no longer prepared to write off the notion of an "elsewhere," a "world behind this world" as strictly bullshit, even when floridly expressed. He took another unsatisfying swallow and said, "It's true there aren't many wire-walkers showing up on the covers of *People* or *Fortune*, but you can bet the crazy fools are getting something out of it aside from the aesthetic and the metaphysical. What about the spotlight? What about applause? I mean, every slack-jawed rube in the bleachers is sitting there wonderstruck while you do your stuff, and when you take your bows they're clapping their sticky palms together and imagining how they're gonna make the folks at home believe the near-suicidal display that some superhuman maniac put on just to give them a thrill. Come on. Any way you slice it, it's still show biz. There's gotta be a lot of ego gratification involved."

"Granted," said his prodigious friend. "Artists soon expire in a vacuum. On the other hand, look at that lonesome genius frolicking in the ether over there. Whose hosannas is he risking *his* neck for? This ain't no arena. There's nobody watching him at all. Aside from us and the birds—and that child beside the platform."

Dern squinted. "You've got better eyes than me, ol' horse."

In truth, Stubblefield couldn't see the child, either. But he knew she was probably there. She always was. Either there or else at the tanuki cage.

Knock! Knock!

"Who's there?"

"Lisa Ko."

"We thought your name was Ko Ko."

"In the beginning. Ko Ko was given to me at birth. But at sixteen, when Stubblefield became more to me than a teacher of English, he said he couldn't possibly have sex with me under my baby name, my little girl name, my student name. He started calling me *Lisa*. And I guess it stuck."

"But wasn't Lisa his . . . his *wife's* name?"

"Weird, isn't it? Maybe even a bit, how do you say, *kinky*. Of course, Stub has never pretended to be a normal guy. When we made love he—"

"Let's not get into that. Tell us how you got interested in the badgers."

"Yes, the tanukis. They really aren't badgers, you know, they're a species of wild dog, although they certainly neither look nor behave like dogs. Well, you see, after Papa Phom fell off the wire, a search party climbed down into the gorge to recover his body. Apparently, Papa Phom had landed on a mother tanuki and squashed her. Her two pups were hanging around the corpses, so the men caught them and brought them back to the village."

"As pets."

"Ha-ha. No, I think they planned to fatten them up and eat them. The Lao are notoriously unsentimental when it comes to animals. Anyway, they put the little creatures in a wire cage. A small cage, very cramped. Beside the ringmaster's house. Most people ignored them, and with good reason. They'd pretend to be docile, just cute and cuddly, but then when you got too close, they'd suddenly hiss and lunge and bite a hunk out of you if you weren't careful. Because they were so devious about their viciousness, Stubblefield nicknamed them 'Nixon' and 'Kissinger.'"

"That's appropriate. But you evidently liked them."

"Oh, yes. Probably a kid thing. Or an orphan thing. I brought them fried bananas and fried rice cakes whenever I could. Tanukis are good eaters, and they love fried food. Eventually, I won them over. They'd lick my fingers or sleep in my lap. Even follow me around. Later, I got them to do a few tricks."

"You had a natural rapport. Had you ever been around tanukis before?"

"Not that I know of, although I seemed to have had a vague memory of them."

"Hmm? Yes, well, we've been given the impression here that you're . . . that you may actually have tanuki blood in your veins. That you—"

"What are you talking about? That's the dumbest thing I've ever heard! Obvious nonsense. How could anyone in this day and age believe . . . ? Well, on second thought, when you consider that the two fastest growing religions in the world today are based, in one case, on an Arab flying up to Heaven on the back of a horse, and in the other, on a teenager meeting an angel named

Moroni in the woods who hands him a set of gold tablets, then I suppose you'd have to conclude that even in the twenty-first century, millions are driven to embrace miraculous tales and go so far as to give their lives over to primitive magical narratives. It's lovely in an absurd way, but tanuki genes in a human being? Get real!"

"Uh, okay. But speaking of instructive gold tablets, uh, we don't mean to pry, but your mother left you an envelope that you opened when you reached puberty. Wasn't there reference to tanukis in that . . . ?"

"No. None. Ha-ha. Pardon me for laughing, but you really are barking up a most unlikely tree."

"Then, if you don't mind us asking, what *was* in that envelope?"

"Mother-daughter stuff, mainly. Personal sentiments. Words of advice, which I believe came originally from some obscure Zen monk and which, incidentally, have served me extremely well. Family heirlooms. Family history. How my great-grandmother emigrated from Japan and my Grandmother Kazu made her way into Laos. And then she told me about my . . . my 'implant.' What to expect and when to expect it."

"Aha! Speaking of the intrusion of archaic magic into the twenty-first century! So what's with the chrysanthemum seed in your mouth?"

"I do hope you understand that this is a metaphor. There's no archaic magic involved, for goodness sake—and there isn't any chrysanthemum seed. That was simply my mother's fanciful way of describing a physical condition that's affected the women in my family for three generations. A hereditary disease. Well, no, it's more a 'condition,' as I said, than a disease. Although it definitely has medical consequences."

"Are you going to be okay? Have you seen a doctor?"

"Mother emphatically cautioned against physicians. But yes, sure, I'll be okay. We'll *all* be okay."

"There are no mistakes?"

"Ha-ha. That's one way to look at it. Well, I've got to be going now. I've enjoyed our little chat. If it cleared up some things, then I'm glad I knocked. *Sayonara*."

"*Sayonara*, Madame Ko. We'll be seeing you."

The scowl on Mayflower Cabot Fitzgerald's face could have skinned a cactus. It preceded him into Col. Patt Thomas's office, followed, in degrees, by his maroon bow tie, closely cropped haircut, and tweedy shoulders. Taken by surprise, the colonel swiveled to greet him. He'd been sitting with his back to the door, gripping in his fist, Mayflower observed, a nine, a jack, and a queen. All clubs. Two subordinates—a tech sergeant and a lieutenant—sat opposite him, looking sheepish.

"Poker at this hour of the morning?" asked Mayflower incredulously, although surely his powers of observation, so finely honed on the grindstone of his country's secret service, must have enabled him to instantly analyze the variously aged strata of cigar smoke and the overflowing ashtrays and conclude that the men had been at the cards all night. As he stared at Colonel Thomas, who was aching to draw to his flush, the scowl became a sneer.

Well, the operations officer thought, *what can one expect of a man whose mother named him Pitter Patt because the white lady for whom she worked remarked, upon noticing an obvious pregnancy, that her maid would soon be hearing the pitter-patter of little feet?* What most perplexed Mayflower was that the man, already burdened by the color of his skin, had not deigned to change that unfortunate appellation. Or that the air force, before granting him a commission, had not insisted upon it. God knows he, Mayflower, had endured a few schoolboy taunts and debutante snickers as a result of his own christening, but his name was a badge of pedigree and quite a different story.

"Excuse your men, please," said the case officer, in a voice that could have wormed a kitten. "We have important business, and my time is short."

Bet your dick's none too long, either, thought Colonel Thomas, eyeing the pot he'd been certain he was about to win but that was now being divided equally among the three players. When the airmen had departed and the door closed, he said, "Good you came in early, Mayflower. I've got a bit of news."

In the process of whisking cigar ash off of a chair before seating himself, Mayflower froze. "Has he talked?"

"Oh, *hell* no. Spent Labor Day weekend reading his favorite book. He—"

The case officer interrupted. "Then your news can wait. I have a flight in little more than an hour, and—"

"You going somewhere?"

"When one has a flight, one usually does. Go somewhere. Yes, back to Washington. A low-level person at State is insisting she's uncovered information about a major terrorist plot against the World Trade Center and/or the White House. Some preposterous scenario, supposed to happen next Monday or Tuesday. It's ridiculous, of course. We'd obviously know about it at Langley if an attack of that magnitude was actually being planned. It isn't credible. And anyway, those grubby heathens aren't capable of anything more sophisticated than car bombings. Nevertheless," he sighed, "the director wants me on hand in case some wild-eyed Abdul does try something and the Administration needs . . ."

"A spin put on it." Thomas, who at one time had considered converting to Islam, made note of the bigotry but kept his composure.

". . . a reassuring statement from the intelligence community. A waste of time, but I shouldn't be away more than ten days. *Meanwhile*"—Mayflower unlocked his attaché case and pulled out a folder—"I have a report on the Foley sisters."

"What those lovely ladies up to? You had a tail and a wiretap, right?"

Mayflower grimaced, causing the colonel to wonder if the man's gallstones were on a roll. "Terms such as those are inappropriate in today's climate," he cautioned. "However, we have judiciously monitored the women's activities. The smart-ass is working temporarily at the circus, of all places. Goes there early and comes home very late. The dingbat . . ."

"That would be sweet Bootsey."

". . . is the problem. She's attempting to retain legal representation. She thinks she can interest a marquee defense attorney to take her brother's case. There isn't any case, of course, but—"

"But there *could* be. If some hot-shot, publicity-loving shyster gets hold of it. Damn!"

"So far, Johnnie Cochran isn't returning her calls. Sooner or later, though, she'll get through to somebody who'll—"

"Be on it like a hobo on a ham sandwich. We got to—let me be appropriate in today's climate—intercede."

The operations officer nodded. "No mischief, though. Give her a pep talk. Perhaps a little scare. And we ought to move Foley. Deny he was ever here. Or that he exists. He's MIA, presumed dead. Sisters have gone around the bend. Et cetera. I trust you can handle it."

Colonel Thomas grinned. So wide was his grin that Mayflower was taken aback. "Relax, my man. There's not a thing to worry about. Ol' Patt's a step aheada you on this one."

"What do you mean?" snapped Mayflower, taken aback still further.

Leisurely, the colonel peeled the cellophane wrapper from a domestic cigar. "I believe I told you that, some time ago, I'd sent our boy's priest threads in for dusting. Mineral content of the dirt in the seams. Any organic detritus. Et cetera, as you'd put it. Well, the results finally came back from the lab. Seems Father Gorodish had been kicking up dust on the high plateaus of the Annam Mountains. That'd be in Vietnam or Laos, most likely the latter since that's where he and his fellow intellectuals went missing. So, I'm gonna head on over there and have a look around. Day after tomorrow. Friday. Taking Foley with me."

Incredulity was the expression du jour, and Mayflower brought out another serving. "On whose authority?" he demanded.

Pitter Patt struck a match, ignited the stogy, and tasted the smoke before answering. "On the authority of the chairman of the Joint Chiefs of Staff."

"You went over my head?!" A second cigar might well have been lit with the heat from Mayflower's face.

"No, I reported the findings to my general, and *he* went over your head. It's a bitch, ain't it? All these levels of command." With some difficulty, he had resumed a sober countenance. "At any rate . . . there's a freelancer in Bangkok, used to be one of your own boys, I hear tell." He mentioned a name and watched the other man flinch. "Supposedly, he's got a handle on the Southeast Asian dope trade, knows all the principal players."

"Yes, he *would* know them," said Mayflower. "That screwball can't be trusted. He'd sell you his own grandmother."

So would you, thought the colonel. *The difference is*, you *would deliver*. "We're not letting him in on anything. But maybe he can steer me in the right direction. And maybe Foley will sing some tunes over there in his 'hood that he don't seem to remember in this country. Anyway, getting him out of America should be a relief for everybody concerned. Ain't no TV cameras in the Annam Mountains, no ACLU, no ditzy sisters, and Johnnie Cochran wouldn't dig the haberdashery. We'll fly military all the way, Foley'll be sedated if necessary, and either Tech Sergeant Canterbury or Lieutenant Jenks, the nasty cardsharks you just ran into, will be along as guard. One way or another, we'll try to leave Foley over there. He's only a headache for us here."

"Yes, but the drug charges? What about the DEA?"

"Fuck the drug charges, Mayflower! And the DEA can go suck a purple doughnut. This is a national security issue. Surely nobody in *your* outfit is gonna be bothered by a bit of drug running? Correct me if I'm talking trash."

In silence Mayflower stared at the ceiling, feigning an indifference to the disgusting stains and discolorations thereupon. Then he abruptly consulted his Rolex and all but leapt out of the chair. Locking his attaché case, he said, "On the whole, it's probably for the best. In retrospect, we shouldn't have brought him here in the first place. It was definitely a mistake to involve his sisters. Sometimes, Colonel, it *is* wise to let sleeping dogs lie. If Foley's crewmen are alive over there somewhere, incognito as it were . . . well, we'll cross that bridge when we come to it." He checked his watch again. "I'm late."

"Need a ride?"

The white man reacted as if the black man had made an improper suggestion. "My driver is waiting," he said, with a virtuous jerk of his head. He snatched a piece of paper from the cluttered desk and without ascertaining whether or not it might be important, scrawled upon it with a pencil. "This is my secure number. Direct line. Not even my secretary will answer. Memorize it and shred it. I want to be briefed at every step along the way. Every step. Never out of the loop for a moment." He shot the other a cast-iron look to emphasize his request and was out the door.

Colonel Thomas saluted the disappearing back. "Yes, sir," he mumbled, and jetted a stream of smoke into the hallway.

That afternoon, on his way home, the colonel stopped by a Mission District gay bar renowned for its unusually aggressive and sleazy clientele. A hush fell over the establishment when he entered, and every eye was on him, but thanks to his uniform, perhaps, his height, his bearing, and his color, not one word, hoarse or falsetto, was directed toward him. Nonchalantly, he strolled back to the toilet, made sure it was unoccupied, and let himself in. He removed a juicy marking pen from his pocket and inscribed upon the wall the following intelligence in large letters:

FOR A GOOD TIME OF EPIC PROPORTIONS, CALL:
And underneath he wrote Mayflower Cabot Fitzgerald's restricted phone number.

Approximately twenty-four hours later, on Thursday, Bootsey Foley stepped off a Metro bus and was examining a maple in a neighbor's yard for signs of seasonal change—"Just a wee touch of fall color. Isn't that sly?"—when a bearded, bespectacled man in a dark suit sidled up to her.

"Ms. Foley, I'd like to walk you home."

Bootsey blushed and stammered, "Oh, oh, I-I don't think so."

"But I insist."

"I-I'll . . ." She glanced over her shoulder. "I'll call the police."

Through his bushy muff, the man smiled. "Don't be silly." He took her arm.

"I'll scream."

"You'll be the laughingstock of the neighborhood."

"Ohhh."

"I'll just walk you as far as your door. Colonel Thomas asked me to speak to you. Colonel Thomas is fond of you."

Bootsey brightened but once again blushed. "Colonel Thomas? Yes. I thought he might be."

"Yeah. Well, 'Thomas' is not his real name, of course . . ."

"It *isn't*?"

". . . but he's a good guy and he wants you to know what's going on."

In appreciation Bootsey nodded, permitting herself now to be escorted. At that point, however, the stranger's tone, which heretofore had been genial, even chivalrous, toughened considerably. "Listen up and listen close. I'm only going to say this once.

Are you listening? All right. Good. Your brother's no longer in custody."

"He *isn't*?"

"Don't interrupt! He escaped several days ago, with the help of a Satanic cult. We have every reason to believe he's being hidden in the Playboy Mansion in Los Angeles. No judge will grant us a search warrant because *Playboy* is so powerful and influential. And believe it or not, Ms. Foley, some of the L.A. judges are themselves into Satanism. So, for the foreseeable future, we're going to let him remain where he is. He'll be very safe, you won't have to worry, and he won't be able to harm anybody else. Just pray for the status quo, because if we get our hands on him again, he'll be put to death as a deserter. Tell nobody of this but your sister. If you flap your lip, your own life could be in serious jeopardy. Never forget a word I've said. Never. Very well, then. Count your blessings, ma'am. And have a nice day."

Back at his rental car, a block beyond the bus stop, Lieutenant Jenks removed his fake beard and theatrical glasses. He burst out laughing. "Just let her go to Johnnie Cochran with *that* story," he said aloud. "Even the hacks at the *Weekly World News* would reach for their butterfly nets."

Madame Ko dismantled her shrine. The incongruous boot went back into her luggage, the old scrap of kimono with the chrysanthemum on it followed. The little paper origami figure she held in her palm, examining it there before securing it in her purse. Grandmother Kazu most likely *had* meant it to represent a tanuki, but there was no reason to share that information with nosy inquisitors, was there? *We human beings need secrets*, she thought, *as much as we deserve the truth.*

After settling her bill and checking out of the hotel, she placed her bag in storage for the day. Then she commenced walking in the direction of the Hong Kanyasin, as the National Circus was known locally. The day was sultry, and she walked slowly. The bump in the roof of her mouth was now the size of a cherry tomato (definitely vine-ripened), and it hurt to swallow. Her belly was also swelling, seeming to pouf out a little more each day. O-Ko hadn't warned her that the pregnancy might advance with such haste.

Located in the northern outskirts of Vientiane, the Hong Kanyasin arena was about two kilometers from the center of town. Midway, Lisa paused to buy a tamarind-flavored ice from a vendor and held the syrupy slush against her "implant." She imagined what it would be like to suck Dickie now. Or Stubblefield. For her, considerably less soothing than the ice, but wouldn't *they* be surprised? On second thought, nothing ever surprised Stubblefield. *At least, not yet*, she told herself, and suddenly, out of nowhere and through the soreness, she chuckled, though it was hardly a laughing matter.

When the arena came into view, her pulse caught like an outboard motor. She might have crossed the Mekong without getting wet. Reminiscing about her life in the circus, she wondered if when other people contemplated the trajectory of their lives, they found themselves shaking their heads at how marvelously strange, in retrospect, the path had been. Sometimes "It is what it is" was an insufficient paradigm: it addressed the ice, all right, but not the flavoring.

The ringmaster had been correct. Not four years had passed before the ruling Lao Marxists, feeling more secure about their revolution now that their enemies, real or imagined, had been exterminated, imprisoned, or driven into exile (and bored, perhaps, by their own burgeoning bureaucracy), reinstated the National Circus. At once the ringmaster and principal performers came out of hiding—and no questions were asked. Such a strong connection had been established with Fan Nan Nan, however, that it was to remain the second home of the circus, the equivalent of the "winter quarters" that American shows have long maintained in Florida. It became the place to repair to when the season was over, the place to rehearse and develop acts, the place where showfolk retired when they became too old, infirm, or chubby to wiggle into their tights.

Ko Ko's foster parents stayed in the mountain village permanently, maintaining practice facilities and watching over the circus properties there. Thus, the child grew up with a foot in two worlds: traditional, rural Fan Nan Nan—and La Vallée du Cirque, with its direct ties to another, more glamorous and extravagant reality. Due to the node in her mouth, she was also connected to an even more exotic reality—to a world behind this world—but she'd have no inkling of that until adolescence, and even then the tidings from her mother would not be easily understood.

The maternal message made no explicit mention of tanukis, and any link between those rambunctious animals and the queer nature of her family legacy registered in Ko Ko's mind only subliminally, if at all. (Indeed, the significance of such a link may be an assumption on our part.) Nevertheless, by the time she was five, she was displaying an unusual faculty for taming the badgers and training them to perform simple stunts. Perhaps this was less the result of any native affinity than the fact that very early on she acknowledged the ardor of their appetites and saw how their rapacity—as well as their almost theatrical exuberance—might be exploited in mutually rewarding ways.

Even so, the girl was well into her teens before it occurred to her that her cherished playtime with tanukis might constitute a lucrative profession. By then, she had tripled her original pair of protégés and with Dickie Goldwire's help was setting traps in the hills to acquire still more. Dickie had often encouraged the girl in her endeavors because he found it amusing and was touched by the joy it brought her, but it was the ringmaster who eventually recognized the potential of performing tanukis, and when she was sixteen or so, urged her to get serious about it. She did, although she was nearly twenty before her act was polished and controlled enough to be taken to Vientiane and the Hong Kanyasin.

In the meantime, she was being taught some tricks of her own. Stubblefield had developed a special attachment to her early on as a result of her aptitude for learning English. Of all his captive students, young or adult, Ko Ko was by far the most accomplished. Whether formal or idiomatic, English came as easily to her as if she had a linguistic chip embedded in her frontal lobe. Her eagerness and aptitude pleased the ex-academic to no end, nor was he completely immune to the girl's delightful yet somehow mysterious ways. It was not until she passed through the red gates of puberty, however, and had pondered and absorbed the knowledge passed on to her by her mother, that he realized that she was starting to affect his own worldview.

One day a windblown candle set her hair ablaze, not only scorching her scalp but also causing her for a month to resemble a charbroiled Brillo pad or the reason Raggedy Ann stopped smoking in bed. Most young girls, even in a place like Fan Nan Nan, would have sequestered themselves and not seen the sun again until the scabs fell off and the patches filled in, but Ko Ko went about her business in the village without a hat or scarf, often pointing out her charred head to those who politely pretended not to notice it, laughing about it all the while. "I was the last monkey out of the forest fire," she'd joke. Another time, when an agitated tanuki bit her wrist, she bit the badger back, drawing blood. Then, she nursed its wound before tending her own.

Ko Ko's fearless disregard for convention—the unassuming practicality with which she defied consensual logic—aroused in

Stubblefield somewhat the same admiration that he felt for the wire-walkers. As she grew older, other feelings were being aroused, as well, and he had to struggle against physically expressing them. He possessed enough self-awareness to know that it was a struggle he couldn't hope to win. She must have intuited that, herself.

According to Stubblefield, there was an almost visible aura of destiny around the small hut that Dickie had helped build for her next to the tanuki enclosure. The aura was especially thick on the afternoon when Stubblefield dropped by to scold her for having ventured alone into the gorge that morning to set her traps. He found her calming one of her excitable charges by massaging its grandiose gonads. Usually, his arrival at anyone's door was accompanied by a torrent of discourse, but the sight of her, not yet seventeen, in a cheap Western blouse and skirt, blithely stroking the overgrown scrotum, took his words away. Nodding in the direction of the gulch, he managed only to mumble, "There may be tigers down there."

She laughed. "I'm not afraid of tigers."

For a long moment, they stared down each other, though stealing glances at the bouncing balls. At last, pointing to his tattoo (he wore a white silk sport coat without a shirt), he said quietly, almost dolefully, "You'd better be afraid of this one."

Ko Ko kissed the pacified tanuki on its nose and shooed it out into the pen. Slowly, she came toward Stubblefield, unbuttoning her blouse as she walked. Her small, pale breasts were like the headlamps of an approaching kiddie car, and he could only blink as they bore down on him. When the blouse fell away, the firm little titties seemed to spring to life like puppets escaping their master's strings, and the next thing Stubblefield knew, she was rubbing them along the length and breadth of his bare chest. "This tiger doesn't scare me, either," she whispered.

For them not to have fucked then and there would have required such a reversal of the laws of nature as to cause Newton to spin in his coffin and NASA to discontinue the space program.

Over the next few years, the bearded MIA taught the delectable Japanese-Lao girl everything he knew about sex, which was of sufficient quantity to fill the *Kama Sutra* from cover to cover, with enough left over for a couple of recipes in a Tijuana cookbook. Those lessons, if one could call such interactive propositions "lessons," she soaked up with all the eagerness and fluency with which she had mastered English.

Once awakened from childhood slumber, her clitoris was inquisitive and inclined to prowl. Certainly, Stubblefield couldn't object to her trying some of the young men in the village on for size. He, after all, had his personal backlog of experience, not to mention a villa full of concubines and a brain full of libertine ideals. When, however, she confided that she was entertaining an itch to sleep with her other longtime benefactor, Dickie Goldwire, an uneasiness overtook the maestro of Villa Incognito. It wasn't, cynics to the contrary, that he'd showered with Goldwire often enough to be thoroughly aware of the younger man's artful appendage and felt threatened by it; nor, sentimentalists to the contrary, that her confession had forced him to recognize that he cared for the girl even more than he cared for his principles of freedom. No, the real reason was that Stubblefield knew Dickie's heart.

It should be noted that Lisa—that's how she was called then by those who didn't call her Madame Ko—was now twenty-three, and home from the Hong Kanyasin, where she'd been appearing for three years. (Her popularity was growing in Laos, but it would be another two years before she and her tanuki troupe began to get engagements throughout Asia.) One twilight during that off-season, when monsoon clouds were piled like fat black boxing gloves just below the heights of Fan Nan Nan, she did slide into bed with Dickie and was made love

to with scant intermission until a cock of a different feather announced the dawn. She awoke around noon, late for rehearsal,
to find Dickie smiling at her almost apologetically. "I guess I'd
been saving up," he said.

"You've given me calluses," she moaned, but it did not
sound like a complaint.

There followed a year during which, on those occasions
when she was home from the circus, she spread her thighs
equally (equal opportunity, equal ardor, equal affection) for the
two Americans, although a woman with half of Lisa's sensitivity
could have perceived that—for different reasons, perhaps—neither of the men was entirely comfortable with the arrangement.
Once, she drew the third American aside to ask his advice, but
Dern brushed off her concerns. Dern wanted to talk to her
about animism. Dern wished to know if she believed there was
a threshold of matter and spirit, a point where distinctions between the two disappeared, and if so, which animals, plants, and
objects, if any, lent themselves most readily to a bridging of
physical and metaphysical realms. She professed ignorance, with
at least partial sincerity, and then proceeded to seduce him, too,
to see if it would distract him (it did); to see how it would feel
(it was nothing special); to see if it would alter the prevailing
dynamic in some way (it did not). She merely learned once and
for all that while sex without love could have its thrills and sat-
isfactions, sex without soul was like salad without dressing—a
bowl of roughage fit for cattle and goats.

The prevailing dynamic *was* destined to be altered, however,
and by the following year, Stubblefield altered it. He invited her
to the villa, wined her and dined her, and sat her on his ample
lap. Having seen her thus ensconced, he proceeded to shock her
silly by announcing that he was giving her to Dickie. "Whatever
part of you that I'm privileged to lay claim to—and I'm vain
enough to believe it a relatively substantial portion—I hereby
bequeath, without prejudice, without regret, without strings attached, to Goldwire. No arguments, please. No discussion. It's

my gift to the pair of you, a boon you both deserve." He smiled serenely and pinched a tear from her cheek.

Lisa studied him, she studied him long and hard, but his countenance betrayed no tinge of spite, bitterness, rejection, facetiousness, hokum, manipulation, self-pity, or false nobility; nor, for that matter, was there any discernible jot of good old Stubblefield perversity.

"Stop looking for motives," he chided her. "I am what I it. It it was it is. We'll keep it to ourselves, so as not to burden our innocent Goldwire, and should you insist on thinking of it at all, think of it as . . . as the shadow of a wild duck flying backward."

Now, any man who has the faintest comprehension of the female mind knows that were any ordinary woman informed by a lover that he was "giving" her over to his rival, she would instantly detest him with a hellish fury—while at the very same time want him twice as much as she ever had before and would neither sleep nor eat until she'd somehow devised a means of impressing upon him the error of his ways, the intensity of her desire to win him back being appreciably magnified by his employment of poetic phrases such as "the shadow of a wild duck flying backward."

Ah, but Madame Ko was no ordinary woman. Rather quickly she understood where Stubblefield was coming from in regard to Dickie, and refrained from questioning it further or uttering a word of objection. From that evening on, she was Dickie's girlfriend, returning his love to the extent to which she was capable, although chronically aware, even after accepting his eventual proposal of marriage, that a time would be coming when her hereditary "condition" would baffle and hurt him and rip them asunder.

The 2001 edition of the Lao National Circus wasn't scheduled to open until November, when the monsoon clouds would have eviscerated themselves and, like empty wineskins, been swept away. It was none too early, though, at the end of the first week of September, to be repainting interiors in the Hong Kanyasin, to be sprucing up props and costumes and testing new lighting and rigging. The hippodrome was abang and arustle with various labors, and as she stood on an entrance ramp watching painters, electricians, seamstresses, and roustabouts preparing for the season, Lisa felt a fluttering in her stomach that could not be attributed to the loaf that was rising therein.

It wasn't long before she caught the eye of the ringmaster, now in his seventies and soon to retire. The gentleman rushed to salute her, told her how grieved he'd been to hear that she'd lost her wonderful animals, and how fervently he hoped that she'd acquire another set of them and be back on the world stage in a year or two. "Your act was unique in the way it affected people," he said. "Nothing ever like it, nothing at all."

Lisa thanked him but, patting the slight bulge in her abdomen, declared that as she was soon to have other priorities, she would be joining him in retirement. The old ringmaster cannot be blamed for shuddering as she said this, for he remembered when her mother had announced her own pregnancy: he remembered how O-Ko had spoken with an identical (and previously nonexistent) speech impediment, and he remembered how much O-Ko changed after that, even as her speech returned to normal, and how she in time went away, vanishing, as near as he could tell, from the crust of the earth.

Too polite, or too puzzled, to give voice to his thoughts, the ringmaster squeezed Madame Ko's shoulder, wished her ten thousand good fortunes, saluted her again, and excused himself to go supervise some activity or other. Lisa wandered farther into the arena then, and took a seat in the front row of the stands, directly facing the ring in which she and her curious companions had once entertained the masses.

The ringmaster had opined that Madame Ko's act was more

than entertaining, that it somehow "affected" people, although he'd failed to support that opinion with any evidence, and it isn't easy to know what he meant. Certainly, the feats the tanukis performed were neither unique nor spectacular, consisting primarily of cartwheels and somersaults and pile-on pyramids, of simulated volleyball games and wrestling matches, of dives through hoops (including, as a finale, a hoop of fire), and the balancing of sundry objects upon bobbing snouts. Thus, their ability to "affect," as the ringmaster would have it, was due to something other than their repertoire; and, also, no doubt, due to attributes beyond those twin globes of testosterone bunched between the male tanukis' hind legs: it's true that the grand gonadal display occasioned snickers from many in the audience and murmurs of disbelief or disgust from others; and it's even true that Christian vigilantes in some American cities complained of the poor animals' natural and involuntary adornments, demanding that the creatures be either castrated or banned; but since the reader has likely never seen live male tanukis, it should be emphasized here that their bulging nut baskets, while prominent, are nowhere near the immensity of the legendary scrotum of Tanuki, Himself. Imagine how *that* one might play at a Saturday matinee!

Ultimately, the appeal of Madame Ko's act rested not on skills but on appearances, not on clever tricks but on the paradoxical and unconquerable dignity with which those bulbous beasts, so awkward, lumbering, and cartoonish in demeanor, went through their routines; and, moreover, on the abject pleasure they seemed to take in themselves. To see wildwood oddities break spontaneously (to their mistress's feigned chagrin) into a hippy-hoppy little dance, a jaunty Chaplinesque jig rife with pathos and a kind of implied defiance, and to hear them suddenly accompany their slapstick steps by thumping their parabolic paunches with a rhythm at once anarchistically explosive and as equanimously elegiac as the fugues of Bach (*pla-bonga, pla-bon-bon-bonga-ga-ga*), was to confront—spotlighted and in three dimensions—what Alfred North Whitehead must have meant when he wrote that "the notion of life implies a certain absoluteness of self-enjoyment."

Maybe the affecting aspect was that Madame Ko's tanukis sparked in an onlooker's muscles a kinetic memory of the innocent freedom of early childhood, when one could let one's body go all akimbo on the slightest whim, could bounce, flop, and skip about in pure corporeal joy without embarrassment, judgment, or restraint.

Or maybe there were more "mature" associations, memories, say, of being falling-down drunk at the company picnic—but now crazy little animals were serving as surrogates, allowing one to vicariously relive those deliciously liberating and rebellious moments while maintaining one's veneer of civilized respectability, protecting, in the process, one's marriage, one's standing in the community, one's job.

Or maybe, on a strictly subconscious level, circusgoers recognized in the antics of the tanukis—antics that appeared goofy and bumbling yet, at the same time, brave and successful—an analogy to their own blindly hopeful gyrations in a complex, impermanent universe where every happy dance was danced in the lengthening shadow of death. And maybe they were inspired, if only for a night, to emulate the tanuki capacity for self-enjoyment, a gift that ought to be the birthright of every Homo sapiens.

Or maybe not. Maybe all those interpretations are just so much god-fodder (*The God-Fodder, The God-Fodder II*), the very sort of bullshit responsible, some say, for keeping alive a modicum of divine interest in our discredited race.

In Lisa's case, surely, it was nostalgia rather than analysis that held her in her seat before that empty circus ring. But there she sat, motionless, quietly staring, and who knows how long she might have remained in that position had she not felt a pair of lips pressing with warm familiarity on the nape of her neck?

Once the government-leased Learjet became airborne after taking off from Hickam Field in Hawaii, the shackle was removed from Dern Foley's left wrist. His right hand remained cuffed to a steel ring in the cabin wall. Ever watchful, Technical Sergeant Canterbury sat directly across the aisle from him. Sergeant Canterbury, who spoke several Asian languages and had mastered several martial arts, was at least as brawny as Dern and four inches taller. In that regard, but in no other, Col. Patt Thomas felt secure.

Never in his career had Thomas embarked on a mission whose parameters were as ill-defined as this one. The objective, assuredly, was to learn if Foley's fellow crewmen on the B-52 known as "Smarty Pants" were also alive somewhere in Southeast Asia, and if so, to what extent they—and possibly other MIAs?—might be involved in a drug-trafficking operation. Yet, should he, with a paucity of leads, a minimum of assistance, and an uncooperative suspect, succeed, against odds, in ferreting out those things, what then? Because of its military desertion aspects, the case couldn't just be foisted off on the DEA. America had one criminal MIA, a hero turned traitor, on its hands. Wouldn't two more only inflate the pickle and make matters worse?

Yeah, and suppose he could find no trace of Goldwire and Stubblefield—a distinct possibility—or acquire no further information regarding the source of Foley's narcotics: what *then*? What did he do, then, with the moon-headed, tongue-tied, Bible-cruising motherfucker? Turn him over to authorities in Thailand or Laos, pressure them to salt him away in some rat-gnawed, backwoods bamboo hell cell and never, ever let the foreign media get wind of it? He wouldn't bet his retirement pay on a happy ending to *that* scenario. *I could kill him*, thought Thomas, although having not taken another man's life—at least, not directly—in twenty-five years of military service, the thought suffered from a deficit of authentic resolve. *Or I could have him killed. One of Mayflower's weaselly smack artists would gladly accommodate, or I could order Canterbury to off him. Dirty business, but the alternative would be to haul his troublesome ass back to the U.S. and start plugging leaks, bamboozling sisters, and grinding the damn sausage all over again. Aw, man!*

Motivated as much by frustration as anything else, the colonel unfastened his seatbelt, strolled to the rear of the aircraft, and exchanged seats with Sergeant Canterbury. Dern was perusing the Bible. Thomas stared at him until he was forced to look up. "What you doing, man?" Thomas asked. "Looking for loopholes?"

To the colonel's surprise, his prisoner actually smiled. He tapped the Bible with his fist. "If I was, I'd be in luck. There's not much behavior that can't be justified by one verse or another in here. Ambiguities and contradictions, that's what biblical guidance is made of."

"You don't say?" Thomas was encouraged. This was the first time he'd ever heard Foley speak three consecutive sentences. "Like what, for example?"

"Well, in one place, we're commanded to seek revenge: an eye for an eye, a tooth for a tooth. In another, Jesus instructs us to turn the other cheek, love our enemies. That's an easy one to reconcile, of course. Given an equally pious choice between altruistic loving and wrathful maiming, what's a real man going to do?"

"I see what you mean. But, you know, it isn't often you find a religious scholar in the dope trade. That's kind of a contradiction, too, isn't it, Foley?" When Dern didn't answer, the intelligence officer nodded at the Bible again. "So, you looking for God in there?"

The prisoner audibly scoffed. "In *here*?" Then, after a moment, he said, "Oh, I suppose you can find God's fingerprints in a book, even in an incoherent hodgepodge of myth, history, genealogies, inventories, poetry, sexual fantasy, and politics like the

Bible, but"—Dern pointed out the window—"there's a whole lot more divinity in that reef down there. If I thought I had to *hunt* for God, I'd be looking in a place like that."

This is a good sign, man! thought Thomas. *If I can just keep the cat talking, who knows?* At the same time, he actually was kind of interested. "I guess that means you're one of them environmentalists."

Dern looked puzzled. "One of *what?*"

"Environ—Oh, hell, I reckon they weren't around much back when you were an American. You know, they're the, uh, they're the people who put the ecology—the boondocks and the swamps and the minnows and spotted fucking owls—ahead of progress. Ahead of our economy. Ahead of our national security. The undeveloped, bug-chawed 'natural' situation is the whole pot of gumbo to them types. We call 'em *tree-huggers.*"

Thomas rather thought Foley might ask what purpose was served by an economy whose success and protection depended on people living in ugly, sterile, unhealthy environments—he'd met that argument before and admittedly had had some difficulty refuting it—but the ex-pilot merely shrugged and said, "There's more to trees than you think. I've run across some trees I'd sooner hug than a woman."

As unexpected as the remark may have been, Pitter Patt saw it as an opportunity for a segue. "Speaking of women . . . you got a wife over there?"

"Over *where?*"

Damn him! Oh, well, it was worth a shot. "Laos."

"You calling me a cootie, Colonel?"

Double damn him! "Just axing if you got an old lady."

For the second time that day, Dern's lips scissored into an approximate smile. "Not in the legal sense," he confessed. "What about you? You a married man?"

"Uh. Yeah. I am."

"Never saw your wife around our luxury suite there in Frisco. You don't let her drop in on you at the office?"

Who was questioning whom here? Out of some kind of

need that was stronger than protocol, perhaps, Thomas deigned to answer. "She's down in Louisiana these days. Looking after my sister."

"Your sister's sick?"

"Pancreatic cancer." The way the words scraped against his palate, he might have had his own "implant" there.

"Damn. What a shame. That's a particularly painful one."

Thomas sighed. "Extremely painful. Extremely. Just goes on and on. None of that shit they give her takes the hurting away."

For the first time ever, Dern looked the colonel straight in the eye. The eyes were as brown as ale bottles and, at that moment, as damp as a bar rag. "They claim heroin's the one thing that'll ease it," said Dern.

"I've heard that. But they can't give her no heroin. Against the law."

"In the U.S. it is."

"Other countries, too."

"True. But there're clinics here and there in the world that will treat with it."

Thomas frowned. "What kind of clinics?" Doubt and suspicion obscured whatever hopeful interest there could have been in his voice.

"You know, medical clinics. Safe and clean, staffed by doctors. I mean, I've never been in one of 'em, I've only helped—" Dern caught himself. The colonel noticed. "I'm told that they're pretty compassionate places. Lots of fresh flowers and soft music, and spiritual guidance if the patient wants it. They don't put the person in a stupor, just administer enough dope to ease the transition. Make dying as sweet and painless as possible."

For a long time after that, Thomas said nothing. That suited Dern just fine. He felt he'd talked much too much as it was. He returned to his Bible, meditating on that verse about how the lilies of the field don't bother to flip burgers or climb the corporate ladder. Ten minutes must have passed before Thomas inquired in a low voice, "Can you tell me where the best of those clinics is located?"

Dern sniffed. "I'm not a referral service."

"But you *could* tell me?"

"Maybe. There'd have to be considerations."

"What kind of considerations?"

Dern closed the Bible, leaned his glossy head back, and shut his eyes. After a lengthy interval, he said, "Forget about it."

"You can't be induced to—"

"No!" snapped Dern. "I can't. You're not to be trusted. I know about that oath you took. I took it once myself. You're sworn to uphold and defend whatever wrongheaded, incompetent, self-serving, slicky-slicky, totally corrupt interpretation of the Constitution that a gang of avaricious hillbillies and lying shysters decide to. . . . Forget it. You're sworn to duty, Thomas, and your type has never let the suffering of innocent people stand in the way of doing that duty; even your conscience, if you still have one, wouldn't stand in the way. Sooner or later, the narrow channel that's open in your mind would be flooded with fear and ambition; you'd hear duty calling, you'd hear the Pentagon calling, you'd hear the power and the glory and the right and the might and the yankee and the doodle calling. You'd . . . listen, you may be black and, for a field-grade officer, halfway hip, but you're still a willing cog in the big ugly wheel of patriarchal progress, and those birds on your epaulets are predator birds. You're going to have to dance with the ones who brung you, Colonel, sir, and may the gods, including the ones in the trees, have mercy on your poor sis."

Although Dern's passionate speech was delivered in fairly measured tones, the vocal effort—so uncharacteristic of one of his reticent inclinations—seemed to exhaust him, and he reopened the Bible with a weary gesture, as if taking refuge in an all-too-familiar asylum. Colonel Thomas looked away. Then, he rose and returned to his seat at the front of the cabin.

Madame Phom—the young Madame Phom, grand-daughter of the wire-walking patriarch—and Lisa Ko had grown up together. Best friends, they had always hugged, kissed, and fondled each other, and the fact that her little fling with Bardo Boppie-Bip had cast a permanently different light on such intimacies only slightly inhibited Lisa's reciprocation of the circus star's caresses.

"Phommie! Mmm. Darling. What are you doing here?"

"I've just come to check the set-up we'll be using this season. What are *you* doing here, my love? And why are you talking funny?"

"Oh, well, I have a sore tooth. An abscess, I think. I'll go to a dentist tomorrow. But in Bangkok."

"Yes, yes, Thai dentists are much better educated. I wish I could go to Bangkok with you! Wouldn't we have fun? But I must return to Fan Nan Nan in a day or two."

The instant Madame Phom disclosed her plans, a lamp flashed on in that chamber of Lisa's cerebrum where the Dilemma Twins had been playing Ping-Pong in the murk. For better or for worse, she knew then what her next course of action would be. "Phommie, would you do me the huge favor of delivering a letter for me in Fan Nan Nan? Actually, *two* letters. Would you?"

When Madame Phom gladly consented, Lisa excused herself to seek out pen and paper and a private place to write. "Take your time," said her friend (in reality, she said the Lao equivalent of *take your time*). "I have to go look over the shoulder of the lighting designer. Sometimes I think management wants to blind us aerialists with lights in order to give the bloodthirsty mob an extra titillation."

Borrowing the ringmaster's office, Lisa sat with the index finger of her left hand pressed so pensively, so firmly against her slightly lopsided nose that the feature became temporarily symmetrical. A Hollywood attorney could probably have written the first draft of a prenuptial agreement in the time it took Lisa to compose two short epistles. As brief as they were, however, when she at last sealed them in their respective envelopes (licking the flaps put unpleasant pressure on the lump in her mouth), there was an air of finality around them you could stir with a fork.

> No news is good news in Cognito,
> Addresses are damn hard to find.
> The queen of spades runs the mailroom
> And all the postmen are legally blind.

Although Colonel Thomas had been informed by reliable sources that the Green Spider Hotel was an obscure but comfortable hideaway where the wrong kind of questions were never asked, he frowned uneasily when the desk clerk appeared to recognize Dern Foley. He would frown frequently and with even steeper displeasure over the next thirty-six hours as he waited in vain for the elusive freelance agent and reputed hacker to return his calls.

Thomas and Sergeant Canterbury had adjoining rooms. Dern was held in Canterbury's quarters, handcuffed to the water pipe, the only piece of metal in the place. The door between the rooms was left open, and through it, Dern and the sergeant watched Thomas pace the floor, back and forth, back and forth, like a zoo cat in a cage. He didn't seem alarmed, particularly, but he was restless, a bit frustrated, and obviously had things on his mind.

When, eventually, the phone did ring, interrupting the air conditioner's emphysematous wheeze, all three of the men jumped. It was not the freelancer on the other end, however. It was the American businessman and sometime informant who, without knowing the details, had recommended the freelancer to his old pal Thomas as a knowledgeable, discreet, and effective contact. "Sorry, Patt. No go. When our man learned who you've been playing spook with, he backed out."

"You mean he don't dig the saintly Mayflower? That's good, that's a very good sign. I like the cat already. Just set it up for me to talk to him, and in three minutes I'll put his mind at rest on that account. Just set up a meeting."

"Can't do it. He's left town. Gone down south somewhere with one of his wives."

"*One* of 'em? How many wives the dude got?"

"Just two, I guess."

"Only two. What a pity. These Thai ladies are *fine*, man. I didn't realize they into polygamy over here."

"They're not. One of his spouses is European, and the other's a Yank."

"No way! You jiving me?"

"That's the way I hear it, and they're not Mormons, either. It's a weird time, Patt. This is 2001. Crazy stuff going on everywhere. You've been cooped up in an office too long."

"You're right about that, brother man. How right you are. I got every intention of blowing this stuffy room tonight and checking out the Bangkok scene. But meanwhile, stay on our bigamist, will you? Stay on him, track him down, press him, tell him I'm the sharp rock in Mayflower's gallbladder, and if he relents, buzz me on my satt phone. Thanks, man. Bless you."

An hour or so later, the colonel, the sergeant, and the MIA—in nearly identical khaki trousers and blue polo shirts—approached Patpong three abreast. The handcuffs (which had elicited not so much as a raised eyebrow at the Green Spider) having been dispensed with now, Thomas and Canterbury leaned against Dern, holding onto his elbow or his shirt as surreptitiously as possible, while at the same time allowing him to be their guide. As the crowds thickened, that configuration became increasingly difficult to maintain, and often one or the other of the guards found himself either in front of or behind his fellow officer and the prisoner. In that way, they entered Patpong proper.

Suddenly, rockets of racket, loud and competitive, attacked their ears from every direction: squadrons of musical missiles launched by ceiling-high stacks of Japanese amplifiers and super-charged jukeboxes. Through the meat-heavy tropical air, a hundred lovely smiles and attractive entreaties glided to greet them. The very gutters seemed to run with intoxicating perfumes, a fluid mixture of Buddhist incense, coconut cocktails, bubbling cooking oils, tongue-peeling spices, marijuana's merry musk, and sweet girlie scent-signals dabbed from makeup kits or biologically secreted. The Americans felt a tingle not unlike carbonation in their blood as they were enveloped by mysterious and sleazy splendors almost as ancient as nature. It was as if they were turning the three-dimensional pages of a virtual-reality men's magazine, published in Gomorrah by the Dragon Lady's nymphomaniacal nieces. The pages were thick and steamy, and the "readers" were developing a thirst.

Their course was set for the nearest gin garden when they found the path blocked by a small elderly man in a stained and rumpled suit. Although more than a trifle seedy, there was a seriousness and a kind of dignity about the gentleman that prevented them from brushing him aside. Colonel Thomas had been leading the way, and the old man addressed him directly. "Hey, mister," he said earnestly, "you want to see a girl fuck a tanuki?"

"Say what?!" Thomas could scarcely believe his ears.

The Professor politely repeated the invitation. "You want to see a girl fuck a tanuki?"

Thomas laughed in amazement. He turned toward Canterbury. "Did you hear that?" But Canterbury had not heard because Canterbury was distracted by a pair of gorgeous teenage hookers costumed as Catholic schoolgirls. Thomas turned toward Foley.

But Foley had not heard either—because Foley was no longer there.

Dern Foley was already half a block away, running, running hard, running at full speed through the throng; cutting, side-stepping, stutter-stepping, dodging, pirouetting, stiff-arming pedestrians, or bowling them over; running brilliantly, like the star collegiate fullback he had always dreamed of being. With an oath, Sergeant Canterbury set out in hot pursuit, but Dern was running into the chaos of Patpong rather than away from it, barreling into a convolution familiar to him but not the others, running with inspiration, and Thomas knew that the sergeant, though more than twenty years Dern's junior, had not a prayer of catching him. *He's gone,* reasoned Thomas. *This MIA is now twice missing.*

Thomas turned back to the Professor. The little man had been standing by, stoic, imperturbable, inscrutable. "You want to see . . ."

The colonel smiled. "Lead me to it," he said. "And name your price."

W hen the equilibrist Madame Phom returned to Fan Nan Nan, she did not find Dickie Goldwire at home. Dickie had hiked up to the Hmong village that noon to see if he might acquire enough rubies on credit to jump-start his financial battery, and though it was late in the day, he hadn't yet returned. Because she needed to get over to Villa Incognito and back before darkness made walking the wire impossible, she placed Lisa Ko's letter atop the belongings that Dickie had piled in the center of his hut, as though he were preparing to leave on a long journey. Madame Phom wondered what was going on, but the moment she deftly slid her balancing foot onto the cable, she erased all thoughts of Dickie and Lisa and concentrated every erg of her energy, mental and physical, on the wire. "To perform without a net is ecstasy," Papa Phom had often reminded her, "to perform without focus is fatal." Consequently, she took very little notice of such extraneous things as the cuckoo that sailed past the wire with something like a glowing golden noodle in its beak.

The houseboy named Lan admitted her to the villa but gestured to her to be silent, for Mars Albert Stubblefield was then speaking to a roomful of people. Lan whispered that the lecture was just beginning, so Madame could be happy she hadn't missed anything. Before the aerialist might reply, Lan moved off to squat on the parlor floor in front of his master.

When Lan was settled, Stubblefield, nodding to Madame Phom, rinsed his tonsils with cold champagne and began anew. "As I was saying, many of you have no doubt noted the prolonged absence of Monsieur Foley. Indeed, there are a couple of young women among us who are beginning to exhibit symptoms of neglect." Stubblefield smiled, but as there was no need to point out the young women in question—they being discernibly possessed at the moment of dry, brittle, antsy, irritable dispositions—he continued. "Most of you, however, have made not the slightest reference, subtle or overt, to the fact that my friend and yours has been lacking for several weeks now. To be sure, there is an admirable discretion, native or acquired, always on exhibit around here, and Foley may not have been away long enough yet to arouse alarm, but I'm convinced that should his absence prove to be of infinite duration, you would behave no differently. That is because you Asians acknowledge and accept the impermanence of that material world to which we in the West cling with the last torn finger and broken nail. Oh, yes."

Stubblefield was outfitted in his favorite three-button suit of purple silk. He was barefoot and bare-chested, tattoo resplendent. During the morning toilette, when he was customarily bathed and anointed with oils, one or more concubines had plaited his beard, weaving fresh flowers (probably wild chrysanthemums, considering the season) into the braids. *For all of their reverence*, thought Madame Phom, *the girls seem to treat him like their toy*. She waved the letter to get his attention, but he was warming up to his subject and would not be distracted.

"In the West we have a desperate need for the certain, the explicable, and the absolute. In fact, one of our euphemisms for our lonely monogod is 'the Absolute.' Ironically, perhaps, that happens to be an appropriate title. God *is* absolute. Absolute mystery. Absolute ambiguity. Absolute uncertainty. Ha-ha!

"In this world that God (or Mother Nature) created, it is always hazard and novelty—*hazard* and *novelty*—which assert themselves, thereby rendering notions of fixity absurd. Incongruously enough, however, when we allow ourselves to fully accept uncertainty, to embrace and cultivate it even, then we actually can begin to feel within ourselves the presence of an Absolute. The person who cannot welcome ambiguity cannot welcome God."

There was something hypnotic about Stubblefield's pontificating, and though Madame Phom comprehended little of it, she would have liked to have remained for the rest. Even more, she would've liked to have stayed around for the post-lecture supper, whose preparatory aromas were wafting in from the kitchen. Alas, as the sun would soon be setting, she had no choice but to exit. Once again, she waved the letter, but Stubblefield disregarded her, swerving off, instead, on a tangent about terminally insecure, ego-addled American patriots and their propensity to deny the lessons of history and the inevitability of change.

"In their secretly nervous hearts, they've convinced themselves, poor little delusional narcissists, that their nation is the most powerful that ever was or ever will be, ignoring the still vaster empires that have crumbled in the past, conveniently forgetting that the U.S. has only existed for a mere two hundred twenty-five years, and refusing to consider for a nanosecond that in another two hundred twenty-five years it very well might be gone. Those towering skyscrapers that to everyone in this room constitute such vivid symbols of America, its wealth and its strength, can—by acts of nature or acts of men—literally topple overnight. Contradictorily, while insisting on America's abiding permanence, the many Christians among them profess also to believe that the world is scheduled to end forthwith and the sooner the better—so, you see, they do embody the absurd, even though they can neither recognize nor benefit from it." He sighed. "I confess, I almost miss their cocky brand of schizophrenia. Yes. I do sometimes miss it. It's good tragicomedy. Holds a snakelike fascination."

Those last few words, and the many that followed them (was the speaker preparing his audience for his own imminent departure?), failed to reach Madame Phom's ears, for having finally slid Lisa's epistle across the teak threshold of Stubblefield's private study, she slipped out through the big front door. She crossed the wire—though it should have been routine by now, the crossing was always daunting, in an exhilarating way—and headed home, where, drained by that day's long journey from Vientiane, she soon went to bed. She was dreaming (of birds and glowing noodles, oddly enough) by the time Mars Stubblefield and Dickie Goldwire discovered and read their respective letters.

My dearest one, my mentor, my friend, my lover, and, yes, my "father," I have long told you that a day was coming—and now that day is here.

Thus began Lisa Ko's letter to Stubblefield. It went on to say that all of her life the clues to her future had lain locked in her mother's past, in her grandmother's and great-grandmother's pasts. She wrote:

At last, I stand on the verge of discovering the family secret, of learning what it was that marked me, that left me different from ordinary women. Perhaps it will turn out to be but a small thing, a ridiculous thing, an anticlimax. Yet as conditions grow more dramatic in the top of my mouth, I tremble with fear that I shall learn something too strange to explain or to bear. Okay, it is what it is and I am what I it, but its isness and my itness seem to be stretching the meaning of "is"and "it." Nevertheless, I am simultaneously (and I remember how you appreciate paradox) flooded with an unearthly happiness!

There is a sense, an intuition, that this thing that makes me so unusual is actually shared by all human beings. It's just that in me, in my matriarchal lineage, it is uniquely pronounced. Am I some kind of throwback, a living echo of a more ancient, primal age—or am I a premature herald (an early warning) of a time that is yet to come? Or, as I've suggested, am I imposing exaggerated and wholly theatrical importance upon a physiological condition that I've inherited from, and that has been embroidered by, two or three generations of rootless, foolish, Zen-piqued, superstitious women? I hope someday to provide you with an answer, beloved, although at the moment it is difficult to believe that we shall ever meet again.

Lisa went on to reveal that she was pregnant:

Believe it or not, this was forewarned, as well. I cannot tell you who the father is. It isn't that I will not: I cannot. I'd intended to give birth in Dickie's house as Dickie's wife, and that when the day came for me to go away (to meet my fate, if that doesn't sound too

pretentious), I'd entrust the child to his care, for I know
that he would make it the most wonderful father. But
Dern's arrest threw a monkey tool, as you say, in the
machinery. Now Dickie—and you, too—must likely
flee, must bolt and perhaps be pursued. To live on the
run, or in hiding in a large city, would not be a life for
my little daughter, who I strongly feel must grow up in
close proximity to what's left of the natural world. And
if Dickie is caught and imprisoned, what then?

About my pregnancy, and my need to go away, I've
written to Dickie, also. Naturally, he will not take it well.
He is as dear to you as to me, and you must help him
to—not to understand, for he can never understand, but
to accept. Dickie has in his heart a great capacity for joy,
an easy joy less complicated than your own aggressive
joie de vivre, and you must promise me that you will not
allow him to lose it or fall into despair. That is my parting
wish.

There followed a few lines of fond reminiscence about their
time together, hers and Stubblefield's, lines that walked as gracefully as a Phom the slender strand that separates the spiritual and
the erotic. They concluded thusly:

The fine things you taught me (except, of course, for
the fine you-know-what) can be seen on one level as a
negation of the wisdom passed down to me by my
ancestors—but I am, I think, the better for the lessons.
One cannot arrive at no-mind unless one has a mind to
start from. The brighter the mind gleams, the softer the
silence of the eventual no-mind, just as the overturned
bucket that was once brimming seems so much emptier
than the bucket that never held milk in the first place.
Thanks for filling my little pail.

The venue—it was too small to be called a theater or a club—
was up a rickety, dimly lit staircase above a bar. The bar was particularly seedy, a dive more frequented by pimps and tuk-tuk
drivers than by tourists. Conversely, the theater (we might as
well call it that because it did boast a tiny bamboo stage) possessed
a kind of ersatz elegance, due to the fact that it was draped
here, there, and everywhere with folds of blood-red silk. No
more than a dozen café tables with wire-back chairs filled the
room, lending it the feeling—enhanced by the absence of air
conditioning or fans—of an ice cream parlor on Main Street in
Hell.

At one end of the little stage was a cage, covered by something resembling a banquet-sized linen tablecloth. At the other
end, to the right of the cage, separated from it by a stained cotton pallet, a plain, rather plumpish young Thai woman in a
loose-fitting robe sat on a low plastic stool. The woman was motionless, expressionless, eyes half-closed, but there was movement inside the cage, a constant stirring accompanied by growls
and grunts, as if its occupant was anxious to consummate . . .
that which was promised to be consummated.

Colonel Thomas and Sergeant Canterbury had seated themselves at a table in the rear. The sergeant appeared agitated;
brooding, no doubt, over his failure to foil Dern Foley's getaway,
but the colonel looked to be taking the escape in stride. If he was
upset about anything, it was the amount they'd been charged for
their beers.

Most of the tables were occupied by middle-aged Japanese
men in business suits. They were gulping bad Thai whiskey, jabbering, giggling, sweating, and fidgeting with their cameras. The
exception was the table adjacent to the Americans. At it, there sat
a pretty Asian woman of about thirty in a jade green, high-

collared dress. She sat alone, self-contained, cool, strangely bright-eyed, sipping a cola. Colonel Thomas found himself staring at her. He nudged Canterbury. "That woman," he whispered. "That woman next to us."

"Sir?"

"That's the woman from the circus. In San Francisco. She wasn't at the show I went to, but she was in all the ads. I saw her on TV a bunch. She had the tanuki act, the one the drunk clown screwed up. I'd bet my retirement it's her." Thomas hadn't suc-ceeded as an intelligence officer by being unobservant. "See, she's wearing the black boots. Maybe she's recruiting talent or something. Researching her new act. I'll be damned."

Confident, Thomas caught the woman's attention. He leaned toward her (politely, he hoped), intending to speak. Be-fore he could open his mouth, however, two things happened: the lights dimmed, signaling the beginning of the show, and his satellite phone beeped.

Thomas almost switched off the phone. The covering was be-ing removed from the tanuki cage, the girl onstage was slipping off her robe, and the woman he'd been about to address was smiling at him. Talk about bad timing! Who said irony was dead? In the end, his sense of duty (so wobbly of late) prevailed. "Yeah?" If it turned out to be Mayflower, he'd really be pissed.

"Colonel Thomas, sir, have you heard the news?" The voice belonged to Lieutenant Jenks, and it sounded shaky. Disturbed.

"What news would that be?"

Until that moment, Canterbury would have bet *his* retire-ment that a black man couldn't turn pale. Thomas whirled to him. "Come on, Sarge! We're out of here!"

The sergeant rose quickly. "Foley?" he asked hopefully.

"Fuck that peanut. The shit has hit the fan in New York and Washington. Terrorists. Big time!" He led the way out.

As they rushed downstairs, a strange *pla-bonga pla-bonga* sound followed them. Funny. They hadn't noticed any drums on the stage.

At the Queen Anne branch of the Seattle Post Office, the clerks that Tuesday morning were inattentive. No customers complained, for they were equally distracted by the terrible news that poured continuously from a radio near the rear of the mailroom. Bootsey Foley was not the only person present with tears in her eyes, though she may have had a few more than most.

On her lunch break, however, Bootsey didn't join those workers who repaired to bars, cafés, or appliance stores to watch reruns of the death planes ramming the buildings. Instead, she went looking for Pru, who had neither answered her cell phone nor returned a call all morning.

Luckily, Key Arena was but a few short blocks from the post office. When Bootsey (uncharacteristically oblivious to any "adorable" undertones of fall in the air) arrived there, she found that, according to the arena reader board, the circus performance that evening had been canceled. As the arena appeared deserted, Bootsey joined the line at the box office, where people were turning in their tickets for refunds. The ticket seller informed her that because of the tragedy, all circus personnel had been sent to their railcars or hotels but would doubtlessly return on Wednesday, if only to strike the show.

Since Bootsey hadn't taken so much as one sick day in nearly fifteen years, her boss was sympathetically agreeable when she requested the afternoon off. She splurged on a taxi, and was both relieved and concerned when she saw Pru's old black and gray Hyundai (it made one think of a campground stewpot) in their driveway. At the cottage door, Bootsey paused, surprised not to hear the sound of television. "My goodness," she muttered.

When she opened the door, she "my-goodnessed" some more. It was "my goodness" squared, "my goodness" cubed, "my goodness" to the thirteenth power. There, on the sofa, hair disheveled, lipstick smeared, sat Pru Foley with her arm around a clown.

Dickie felt that the wind had been knocked out of him. His breath was knotted. He went so far as to drop to his knees. The letter fluttered out of his grip.

To be sure, it was a gentle letter, loving and warm, but at bottom it was a rejection, and rejection of that magnitude is a pill so bitter all the ladles in Candyland could not coat it nor all the molasses in Africa aid in its ingestion. Dickie was stunned and stung. He was sickened by loss. And, finally, he was angry.

After retrieving the letter, he paced the floor. Lisa Ko wasn't going to get off that easily. She had some serious explaining to do. If the baby was his, how dare she take it away! And if it was not his, how dare she have conceived it! After so many years, did she think she could just drop off a note at his hut and . . . ? Where was she? Oh, but of course! There was only one place she could be, would be.

Dickie was in such a state when he stormed out of the hut that he neglected to secure the treasure he'd acquired that afternoon. After receiving a half-dozen especially rude, small, undistinguished rubies on consignment, Dickie had been about to bid the Hmong widow farewell when she'd reached into her skirts and, looking around anxiously to ascertain that no one was approaching, pulled out a pigeon-blood stone of extraordinary size and clarity. He'd never seen anything to equal it. He couldn't believe that she would entrust such a rare, valuable specimen to him—it should have been turned over at once to the Hmong elders—and under ordinary conditions he would not have accepted it. Nor, under ordinary conditions would he have done what she expected him to do in return. But these were hardly ordinary conditions. He assuaged his guilt and disgust by reminding himself of Miss Ginger Sweetie and the violations of intimacy that wonderful girl regularly and cheerfully endured in exchange for control over her destiny.

In the end, Dickie's spirits had been immeasurably buoyed by that grand ruby. His share of its sale could have taken him—and eventually Lisa Ko—a long, long way. Now, however, he walked off and left it on his table as if it were a forsaken morsel of chili pepper (or a little Janis Joplinized piece of his heart).

What he required was an aerialist. Alas, at Madame Phom's house, everything was dark and still. He hurried to the home of her cousins. They were eating dinner and invited him to join them. "Very good *tam màak hung*." When he explained that he wanted to cross over to Villa Incognito, they laughed and pointed out that it was night. "Nobody can walk wire in dark. Not even ghost of Papa Phom." They laughed some more.

Obviously, Dickie should have just let his emotions settle down. He'd survived rejection before (remember Charlene in Chapel Hill?), and he wasn't one of those fragile or self-obsessed types who allow themselves to become embalmed in the crawling formaldehyde of prolonged depression. But the green worm had him by the brainstem, and he was unwilling to wait quietly for it to relax its bite (as, with patience and perspective, it always will). He was driven to act, even if the action was muddleheaded, futile, and wrong. He may have successfully dropped out of dream school, but his name, like the names of so many lovers, was obviously still on the rolls at Cupid's Academy of Needless Melodrama.

Out by the gorge there were no lights, and the moon, pale and waxen as a junky's jowls, was just rising. Dickie, however, had no need of lamp or lantern. His eyes were bright and bulging, like a lemur's, like a hungry prosimian awakened from its diurnal slumber. Standing on the platform, he saw with those big bush-baby orbs every inch of circus cable that separated him from Villa Incognito, where there were lights aplenty and where things he fought not to imagine were likely going on.

He stood there for at least ten minutes, reasoning with himself, reminding himself of the last and only time he'd crossed the gorge on his own. Although human beings are by and large a fearful lot, every bit as fearful behind their civilized, technologized masks as they were in jungles and caves, there are emotions capable of turning the charcoal sweat of fear into pink lemonade. Not that Dickie didn't have an electric drill in his stomach: he was scared, all right, but his fear, like his judgment, was simply outvoted and overridden. Then, too, there was that crazy attraction he had, not to heights but to falling.

A round the wire he closed first his right hand, then his left. Against his palms the steel felt as cold and solid as his mind was hot and turbulent. Although it led out over a near-bottomless gulf, there was something grounding about it. Gripping it, he felt purposeful, calmed, in control. There was no single moment when he decided to go for it. Rather, one second his feet were on the ground beside the platform, where little Ko Ko had so often stood, and the next they were dangling in air.

Hand over hand, he went. It was cool out there in space, and silent and peaceful. Dickie couldn't remember when he'd felt so alone: not lonely but, rather, alone in an oceanic sense, as if there was only one great all-encompassing throb of life in the universe and he represented it. True, his arms were starting to register the strain, but he was making good progress. It definitely was easier crossing the wire in the dark. Hand over hand. Hand over hand.

About that time, the moon broke free of the teak boughs. Its rays fell over him like a net. In its web he felt like some kind of huge silver insect. *My God*, he thought—and he hadn't thought anything along those lines in years—*if the folks back in Carolina could see me now!*

The wire was sagging now, so he reasoned he must be nearing the halfway point. It seemed to sag more than he remembered it sagging, and to shake more, too, but he supposed he'd put on a pound or two since then. Apparently, the added weight wasn't muscle, because his shoulders were starting to ache in earnest.

The cable sagged further still. A mighty quiver ran along it, making it difficult for him to maintain his grip. Panic rose in Dickie like gasoline in a siphon. He heard noises, human noises, like someone swearing and laughing. They sounded close by. Swiveling his neck toward the villa side of the gorge, he saw then a shadowy shape a few yards away—and realized with a frozen prickle that someone else was on the wire.

Ach! Lieutenant Goldwire, I presume."

"Stubblefield? What th—?!"

"We've got to stop meeting like this."

"Stubblefield! What're you doing?!"

"Taking the air, my boy, taking the air. Mmm. An evening redolent with gossamer delights." He was taking air, all right, breathing very hard. "I'm in my element. Oh, yes. Where the bee sucks, there suck I/On a bat's back I do fly." His words from Shakespeare were punctuated with huffs and gasps.

"What the hell are you doing out here?" There was desperation in Dickie's voice, and a growing pain in his arms.

"Coming to call on you (*gasp*). Foley left the chopper in Thailand. I knew I should've gone and fetched it. Jesus! Think I'm too old for this (*grunt*). Gymnastics never my sport. Wrong body type."

"But . . . where's Lisa?"

Stubblefield groaned. "Lisa? Not hanging seven hundred fifty feet above the goddamn terra firma, I'll tell you that." He groaned again. "Don't know about Lisa. Madame Phom (*gasp*) left me her letter. She wrote you, too, I gather. Thought you might be upset. Was coming to see if I could cheer you up. Jesus! My shoulders are killing me."

Dickie didn't know what to think. "Lisa's not been here at all? Okay, I get it now, yeah. And you were coming to comfort me?"

"I'm your officially designated bluebird." Puffing, but with a childish lilt, Stubblefield broke into an old Sunday school song. "If you're happy and you know it, clap your hands." He glanced at the sagging wire to which they clung. "On second thought . . ."

"You're crazy, Stub."

"No, *you're* crazy. I'm here to straighten you out."

"Look, we got to get off of here. You start moving backward." Dickie's supraspinatus and infraspinatus muscles were frying in napalm, and his brachioradialis tendons seemed ready to pop.

"Don't know if I can. . . ."

"Go back the way you came. It's shorter. I'll follow you. Get moving!" Dickie proceeded, but Stubblefield hadn't budged. Now they were almost cheek to cheek.

"You're (*groan*) in my space, Goldwire. I swear, you have no more respect for privacy than those women I live with."

In the near distance, an errata of bats zigzagged by, their squeaks and beeps providing a science-fiction soundtrack to the spectacle of the two men hanging there in midair, side by side. Had there actually been a fairy on a bat's back, it might have thought the men, silhouetted against weak moonlight, to be a feature of the skyline of a faraway city.

"Get moving, damn it!"

"Okay, okay. You're pressuring me to retreat, Goldwire. Are

you not aware (*gasp*) that I owe my reputation to (*gasp*) pressing ever forward? Ow!"

Slowly, with painful effort, they were making their way to the rim. Despite the gravity of the situation, Dickie was unable to prevent himself from calling out, "What about the baby?"

"Baby (*gasp*)?"

"Who's the father?"

Stubblefield abruptly stopped, and Dickie almost collided with him. "None of our business." He huffed and heaved. "None of our business, Goldwire. Women have their mysteries. Honor that." His voice was weakening. "Our Lisa has some . . . some enchanted sickness—or haven't you figured that out? Lisa's dealing with significant forces (*puff*). Forces worthy of awe and respect. You and I, we only have to deal with the government." He chortled at that, and when he laughed, his right hand slipped off of the cable. His luxurious, purple-suited body was left dangling by one flabby arm.

"Hang on, Stub! Jesus! Grab the wire!" Dickie understood the difficulty, for his own fingers were growing increasingly numb. "Grab it! Grab it! Please! Stub! Hurry!" He was sobbing. "Please!"

"I'm . . . disillusioned . . . with this method . . . of travel." Stubblefield was swinging somewhat wildly. "It's . . . undignified. Think I'll . . . take a . . . different route." He shouted something that sounded vaguely like, "Keep 'em guessing!"

And then he was gone.

Gone. Just like that. Dickie never really saw him fall. Stubblefield simply was there one moment and not the next. The soles of Dickie's feet felt the emptiness beneath them as plainly as if they were standing on a pile of sharp rocks. And from the depths of that vertical desert, no cry, no splat, thud, or parting champagne burp rose to signal a conclusion. There was only a bat squeak, a cuckoo's *cu-koo*, and the flirtatious hum of oblivion.

Followers of Carl Jung maintain that there's no such thing as co-incidence. There're some people of our acquaintance, moreover, who'd have us believe that there are no mistakes, and, by inference, we might conclude, no happy accidents. Well, who's to say whether it was by random chance or unconscious design, but there Col. Patt Thomas was, on September 15, at the Chingo-do temple in Tokyo. Chingo-do happens to be a temple consecrated to tanukis, and Thomas definitely had not gone there on purpose.

Immediately after receiving news of the terrorist attacks, the colonel had reported via phone to the commanding general of air force intelligence. Thomas and Sergeant Canterbury were ordered to proceed at once to the U.S. embassy in Tokyo and stand by for possible Asian assignments. Toward the end of their brief conversation, Thomas had mentioned that the deserter Dern Foley had been "neutralized" and wasn't likely to cause further trouble. (Ol' Pitter Patt had his fingers crossed.) The general growled, "Good," and that was the end of that. Mayflower Cabot Fitzgerald could like it or lump it, though the dweeb doubtlessly had more pressing matters on his mind now than inconvenient MIAs. It's an ill wind, indeed, that blows no good.

In Tokyo, the colonel had looked up an old friend. Bill Leworc was a former intelligence officer who worked for the Public Affairs Section at the embassy. On Saturday afternoon, with no orders yet and nothing on his plate, Thomas accepted Leworc's offer to show him around town. Thomas, who hadn't been in Tokyo in nearly twenty years, listed several points of interest he'd like to visit. Among them was a certain temple—but it was *not* the Chingo-do temple. Leworc's knowledge of temples was incomplete, and he had taken his pal to Chingo-do by mistake. (Mistake?)

It might be more accurate to say that Leworc took him to Senso-ji, the large, lively Buddhist complex in Asakusa, that quarter of the city that, along with neighboring Yoshiwara, was once to Tokyo what Patpong is nowadays to Bangkok. Chingo-do temple is situated very near Senso-ji, on the temple precinct's (Senso-ji's) shopping street, where everything from tourist trinkets to genuine Edo antiques are sold, and is loosely associated with the much grander Senso-ji. (The five-story pagoda of Senso-ji is surrounded by gardens, whereas the entrance to Chingo-do is next to a shoe store.)

Confused? So was Bill Leworc. "Naw," he said, "this isn't the place." He'd paused to read the plaque by the vermilion torii gate, and now he informed Thomas that in 1872 the head priest of Chingo-do temple—the so-called Hall of the Guardians—had dedicated it to a deified animal, a "raccoon dog," that had formerly lived in great numbers on the grounds of Senso-ji and that was popularly believed to fend off robbers and prevent fires. "Sounds like a combination of Smoky the Bear and Sergeant McDuff," sneered Leworc, and he was about to move on. "Maybe your place is around here somewhere."

"Wait a minute," said Thomas. "Let's pay our respects. If it works, I can cancel my home insurance. Damn fire and theft premiums are bankrupting me." Despite the tragic events of that week, the colonel was in an oddly ebullient mood. Maybe it was the prospect of action, maybe it was related somehow to the note in his uniform pocket: when he'd returned to the Green Spider Hotel late on the night of September 11, he discovered under his door a scrap of paper upon which was scrawled the name and address of a hospice in India where his terminally ill sister might have her suffering eased with heroin. The note was signed, "Tree Hugger."

The Americans walked through the torii, paid a nominal fee at the ticket office on their left, passed between two quite large stone lanterns, and approached the shrine. It was in no way remarkable, the shrine, except that just to the right of it there stood two ceramic statues, each of them a funny-looking animal figure up on its hind legs. Four or five feet tall, the figures were painted black, with round white bellies and wide white circles around their decidedly crazed eyes. As the representations were rather mannered and stylized, it didn't dawn on Colonel Thomas what they were supposed to be until Leworc said, "Oh, I get it. These 'raccoon dogs' are the legendary Japanese badgers, the, uh, *tanukis* I believe they're called."

The words were hardly out of his friend's mouth than Thomas saw her. High-collared green dress, black patent-leather boots, lovely if marginally lopsided face, gleam in her eye that lent her a playfully menacing air. She was dropping five-yen coins into an offering box. Without a word to Leworc, he went straight to her.

She returned his greeting with icy politeness. Then, she brightened. "Ah so. From Bangkok. Yes, I 'member you. You alla time go for tanuki, *ne?*"

"Say what?" He followed her gaze to the ceramic statues. He laughed. "No, no. Not me. Just a coincidence."

"I no think so. I think you—how you say?—got big thing for the tanuki. Tanuki fan. You for secret alla time belong Tanuki cult."

"No, really. I don't know diddley-damn-squat about tanukis. I was looking for another temple, a different temple altogether. My buddy thought it might be in this area." She'd been seated at a table when he'd encountered her in Thailand, and now he noticed for the first time that she was about six months pregnant, straining the seams of her cheongsam. Nodding at her stomach, he said, "I got a feeling you might know where it's located."

"Oh? What you speak?"

Thomas said there was supposed to be a temple in Tokyo, he couldn't remember its name, where pregnant women went to petition the gods for healthy babies and childless couples went to pray that they might conceive. Kind of an obstetrics/fertility temple.

"I not know such place. I live Tokyo short time." She looked at him quizzically. "Why you want go such temple?"

For reasons he couldn't explain, the colonel had recently found himself giving frank answers to personal questions, not ordinarily a trait of his trade. "Uh, well, you see, my wife and me haven't been able to have kids. I'm forty-five and she's thirty-eight, so the clock's ticking itself to death on us. My wife saw on TV that there's this temple in Tokyo where infertility is cured, so when she heard I was coming here, she bugged me to drop by and give it a whirl. She tried to sound like she was joking, but she's a Louisiana woman, got a lot of them ol' voodoo superstitions." He glanced back at the statues, noting the one's huge scrotum. "I don't suppose these critters here would help us?"

Smiling, Lisa shook her head. "No, no help you here. This nice temple but alla time crazy silly place."

"Yeah? Why do you say that? Why crazy silly?"

"Japanese people think Tanuki is keep them safe from robber, but Tanuki is biggest robber of all. Tanuki alla time stealing food, stealing sake, stealing women."

Sounds like some of my buddies, Thomas thought. He said, "We have a saying in English: 'Takes a thief to catch a thief.' In fact, what passes for law enforcement in the U.S. these days seems to be operating pretty solidly on that principle. So maybe these tanuki guardians are just right for the job."

Lisa looked at her wristwatch. "I go now more better Tanuki place. More better. You like Tanuki, you secret Tanuki fan, you come with me I show you. Best Tanuki shrine. *Ichiban*. Number one. You want see?"

With one of his long fingers, Thomas beckoned to Leworc, who'd been waiting at a discreet distance. "Bill. Come here. I want you to meet Madame Ko. She's offered to take us to tanuki world headquarters." He turned back to Lisa. "This isn't anything like that showbox in Bangkok, is it?"

Leworc's bow would have been almost imperceptible to anyone but a Japanese. Madame Ko, blushing incandescently at the colonel's reference, acknowledged the greeting. "More tanukis?" asked Leworc. "What the hell for?"

"I'm a fan," the colonel said, winking. "Secret member of the cult." He dropped a coin in the offering box, and the three of them, chatting away, walked to the nearby train station. The men wondered if Lisa didn't have some kind of serious speech impediment (she spoke as if there was a gumball in her mouth), but neither of them inquired about it.

The shrine to which Lisa had referred was called Yanagi Mori. Oddly enough, it turned out to be located in Akihabara, one of Tokyo's most nondescript districts, known primarily for its discount electronics stores. Surrounded by a red picket fence, Yanagi Mori faces a narrow plebeian street lined with small shops and stalls. Its rear is on the cement banks of the Kanda River, an urbanized trough whose imprisoned green waters course pitifully across Tokyo in much the same way that the Los Angeles River trickles through L.A.: a liquid indictment of the failed imagination of man.

Although the shrine grounds were no larger than, say, the parking lot at a suburban McDonald's, it was filled with Tanuki images in stone, wood, clay, rusty iron, and other media not readily identifiable. Some of the carvings were quite fanciful, and the Americans had to admit the place had a pleasing atmosphere. Certainly it was reverential, but with comic undertones, as if refusing to allow that reverence to puff up into piety.

After they'd wandered among the statues for a while, Thomas pointed to a building on the grounds. "Looks like more tanukis over there."

"No," said Lisa. "That Kitsune shrine. Kitsune not same-o same-o Tanuki. Kitsune is what you call . . . *fox*. In Japan, fox and badger have special powers and people worship, but are not true gods. Kitsune the fox is messenger of gods. He run between worlds. Between other world and this world. Sometime cause trouble, make joke, but he work very hard. Tanuki never work. He for fun. Eat, drink, dance, make sex. Alla time big fun."

"I see," said the colonel. "So why aren't we hanging over there with Kitsune? Sounds like Br'er Fox is the important one."

From the curve of his visor to the blunt tips of his military shoes, Lisa looked him over. Her eyes, he thought, were luminous, like the interior of a bell pepper from which a slice has been cut out. Her smile, having no real color of its own, seemed to usurp color from everything around her. It mixed the hues and threw them back at him. "Oh?" she asked. "You no think fun important? Fun not important same-o same-o work? Maybe fun more better? You no think so?"

"It wouldn't take much to convince me, Madame Ko. And you're doing a pretty good job." His laugh, deep but unsteady, had a lot of bayou silt in it.

Leworc spoke up. "The colonel here is not entirely averse to fun."

"Not entirely," agreed Thomas. "Not entirely. I plan to have me a heap more of it when I get out from under the weight of these eagles." He tapped his epaulets and explained to Lisa, "I'll be retiring in five years."

"What you do then?"

"Oh, we bought us a nice cedar lodge out in Oregon. In the hills near Grants Pass. Hook me some fine trout, buy me a pair of them Timberland hiking boots, meet a few *amis*, maybe, who'll just want to play poker with me and not always be woofing about current events. Most of the time I'll just sit on the porch and sip whiskey and talk to the woodpeckers. Hell, maybe I'll rise up now and then and hug a tree or two." Unnoticed by the others, he fingered the note in his pocket. "Of course," he sighed, "since we haven't located that knock-up temple, there won't be any pitter-patter of little feet around the place."

Leworc grinned at the reference. Lisa thought, *Don't be too sure of that!* She was remembering, obviously, her escaped tanukis, how they were at large at Grants Pass—but then, suddenly, something else came to mind. A notion buzzed in her skull like a diamondback. She turned to one of the stone badgers and pretended to study it. The way she was working her jaws, one would have guessed she was chewing gristle, but it was due to the thought process—and the increasing pain in her palate. Several minutes passed before she rejoined the men. With unexpected boldness, she grabbed the colonel's right hand and placed it on her belly. "In short time," she said, "I have baby-san. I go away. No can keep baby. Maybe I give baby you and you wife."

Thomas was speechless. Leworc asked, "Are you serious?"

"Yes. Is so." She clasped Thomas's hand more tightly. "You think alla night, you talk you wife. Tomorrow or next day, you come here to shrine." She pointed, then, to a building on the premises, a house not much bigger than Dickie's hut. "Caretaker house. If I not here, you leave answer with caretaker. Okay? If answer is yes, then you come back this place in one year." She consulted her watch. "One year. September 15. When baby no more suck tit. If I no here, baby girl be in caretaker house. For you. Your child. I sorry, no legal papers."

For someone with his military and CIA connections, getting an undocumented infant out of Japan would scarcely be a problem, but Thomas was still shaken. He could tell, however, that although Madame Ko's speech was worsening, she was totally sincere. All he could mumble in reply was, "Thank you. This is unbelievable. Thank you. I'll let you know. We'll give it some serious thought and let you know. Thank you."

At that precise moment, Lisa's eyes widened, and her face contorted. She covered her mouth with her hand and doubled over. Thomas was convinced she was about to vomit. Embarrassed but concerned, the men stood there looking helplessly at each other. Lisa made a horrible choking sound and turned away from them. Then, she commenced to pull something out of her mouth. Something brightly colored. And soft. And surprisingly large.

For a full minute, she stared at what appeared to be a lovely fresh chrysanthemum. It glistened with saliva as with the dew. She held it up for the men to see. She smiled apologetically, yet with just a hint of pride. Then, she turned, walked swiftly to the caretaker's shack, and disappeared inside.

"Jesus!" Bill Leworc swore. "What the hell was that all about?"

"Oh," said Colonel Thomas dismissively, leading his friend out of the Tanuki shrine, "Madame Ko's with the circus. It was some kind of trick."

EPILOGUE I

Stubblefield's body was never found. The logical assumption was that his remains were eaten by a tiger. It was a bit odd, however, that a combing of that portion of the gorge turned up not a bone, not a shred of purple suit, not a piece of the backpack he'd been wearing (apparently, he'd planned to spend the night at Dickie's).

The search party, which included Dickie and a half-dozen weeping young women, observed two deep indentations in the mud at an eddy where the stream had been overflowing, and since each was about double the circumference of a human leg, it inspired the theory that Stubblefield had landed feet-first in the ooze and miraculously survived the fall. Such a "miracle" is not without precedent. For example, once in New Zealand, a skydiver whose chute failed to open landed in a nasty duck pond and walked away with barely a bruise.

There were a couple of elders who insisted that Stubblefield was protected from tigers by his tattoo. They reasoned that he was alive and well, perhaps living in a cave with a family of tanukis.

A slightly more credible rumor, brought to Fan Nan Nan by some well-traveled circus performers, insisted that he'd made his way to Hong Kong, where he'd long had funds on deposit, and, indeed, had been spotted there on more than one occasion. He was reputed to be holed up in a splendidly appointed junk in the harbor—writing his memoirs. Now *there's* a book that might knock a hole in a library wall or two. It would probably be called *Keep 'em Guessing* and be roundly attacked by all those who cannot abide the idea that in the life of an individual, an aesthetic sensibility is both more authentic and more commendable than a political or religious one. Until such an autobiography should appear, however, we can only presume that Mars Albert Stubblefield is dead. Long live Mars Albert Stubblefield.

Following a final, sputtery, perilous flight in decrepit Smarty Pants II, Dern V. Foley reoccupied Villa Incognito.

He dismissed the staff, paying them off with rugs and pieces of furniture. The concubines, including his favorite, were rewarded with valuable objets d'art and sent away. That same day, Dern took a hacksaw and cut the guy wires on the villa side of the gorge. Then, he sawed through the circus cable. When he was done, it dangled uselessly from the opposite rim, resembling, as it reflected the afternoon sun, a giant glowing noodle hanging over the edge of a bowl.

Having carefully examined with an open mind every single one of its verses innumerable times but finding in none of them any rational justification for the popular belief that they constituted "the word of God," Foley now tossed his Bible aside and turned full attention to the surrounding flora and fauna. And should the invocation of "nature spirits" prove in the end to be yet another dance around the suck of a spiritual black hole, just one more bloodless squeezing of the cosmic turnip—well, there was always the wine cellar and the chandoo.

Not to mention that special, splendid joy he took each waking moment at having once again slipped through the steel net of authority.

Speaking of authority, Col. Patt Thomas was assigned to temporary duty in Pakistan. Before leaving for Karachi, he met with Lisa Ko again at the Tanuki shrine, where he informed her that he and his wife, after an hour-long telephone conversation, had enthusiastically decided to accept the offer of her baby girl. In the past, they'd been lukewarm about the prospect of adoption, but this was somehow different.

Naturally, there were questions. The identity of the father, for example. When Madame Ko said she could not provide that information, Thomas shrugged and wrote it off to the promiscuity that seems always to abound in show business.

Lisa was almost equally vague concerning where and how the couple might reach her during the intervening year, but Thomas was left with an impression that she would be spending much of her time at the Yanagi Mori shrine and might possibly be contacted through the caretaker there.

Regarding her whereabouts once the Thomases had picked up the baby, she alluded to the Lake Biwa wilderness area, wherever that was. What she would be doing there she would not or could not say, although she made it rather clear that she wouldn't be coming back. Not ever. However, she would provide a sealed envelope that her daughter should open upon reaching puberty. Since that was Madame Ko's sole stipulation, the colonel gave his word, and final arrangements were made. (Her speech was fine, incidentally, and there were no more magic tricks.)

Prior to his departure from Tokyo, Thomas made one additional set of arrangements. His wife, it seems, would very soon be escorting his sister to a certain clinic near New Delhi, where she might die with the grace and ease that every being deserves, and for which purpose God—or Mother Nature if you prefer—surely put the opium poppy on earth.

Pru Foley ran off to New York with Bardo Boppie-Bip, becoming shortly thereafter the producer of her cable TV show: buffoonery for the gay, the would-be gay, and the unsuspecting. In Pru's e-mail messages to Bootsey, she sounded happy enough, although she once let it slip that she was unable to respond romantically to her partner unless the clown was in full polka-dot suit and whiteface, a kink that seemed destined to create trouble somewhere down the line.

As for Bootsey, she was not quite as lonely as everyone had feared, due to the fact that, to great astonishment at the post office, she dyed a green streak in her hair, painted dark circles around her eyes, pinned on a corsage of black paper roses, and began frequenting late-night venues such as the Werewolf Club. Her intention was to infiltrate a satanic cult, in the hope that she might make contact with fellow Satanists down in Los Angeles and eventually rescue Dern from the Playboy Mansion. Her standing in local Goth circles received a lethal blow, however, on the evening when she was overheard to refer to Halloween as "the cutest holiday" and the first wild storm of autumn as "precious."

Dickie Goldwire peddled the inferior rubies in Bangkok. Then, using his fake French passport, he traveled by train to Singapore, where he sold the pigeon-blood gem for a small fortune. Back in Thailand, he arranged for Xing to deliver to the Hmong widow her share of the proceeds, and shortly thereafter, he looked up Miss Ginger Sweetie.

"Dickie!" she squealed. "You no go now dream school? Where you guitar?" Within a month, they were married. The vows were Buddhist, but it was a Western-style wedding at which Elvisuit sang, and sang beautifully, although his beeper went off twice during the ceremony, and immediately thereafter he rushed off to another gig.

The newlyweds moved to Nakhon Pathom, near the university, but not three months passed before the bride was granted an American student visa, and away they flew to Colorado—Mr. and Mrs. Pepe Gazeau—so that she could study the writings of Allen Ginsberg at Naropa Institute.

Shocked by the deterioration of liberty and the all-pervasive proliferation of advertising in the U.S. during his absence, Dickie experienced some difficulty in adjusting. As much as he missed Fan Nan Nan, however, he bore no rancor, no regret, and thanks to the ruby money, he and Miss Ginger Sweetie lived quite comfortably in Boulder. Aware of the various consequences of contacting family or running into acquaintances, he kept a very low profile—although he was inclined on occasion, in tribute to Stubblefield, to scrawl *LIE!* with a marking pen across "Vine Ripe Tomatoes" signs all over town. As of this writing, he hasn't been caught.

How often and with what depth of feeling he thought of Lisa Ko, it's unprofitable to speculate, although we may be certain that at many a quiet moment alone he pondered what

Stubblefield had meant exactly when he said that "our Lisa has some kind of enchanted sickness."

Regarding guitars, Dickie did buy a new Martin D-28, a genuine one this time. And he finally finished the words to his song.

Just because you're naked
Doesn't mean you're sexy,
Just because you're cynical
Doesn't mean you're cool.
You may tell the greatest lies
And wear a brilliant disguise
But you can't escape the eyes
Of the one who sees right through you.

In the end what will prevail
Is your passion not your tale,
For love is the Holy Grail,
Even in Cognito.

So better listen to me, sister,
And pay close attention, mister:
It's very good to play the game,
Amuse the gods, avoid the pain,
But don't trust fortune, don't trust fame,
Your real self doesn't know your name
And in that we're all the same:
We're all incognito.

EPILOGUE II

K nock! Knock!

"Who's there?"

"Me. Himself."

"What? Tanuki? Is that you? Come on in—if you can get in. My den looks like a typhoon passed through it. Even the God of Bachelor Apartments would be appalled at this mess." Kitsune watched Tanuki waddle in. "It *is* you. Where have you been, old rascal, and how have you been getting along?"

"Aw, you know. Same as you."

"Yes, I do know." Kitsune sighed. "Those damn men. But we might not have to worry about them much longer. They seem more intent than ever on committing mass suicide."

"Yeah, global hara-kiri. But they don't call it that."

"Of course not. They call it *progress*. They call it *growth*. They call it *national security* and *energy policy* and all sorts of fool-ish things, but both the motives and the end results are the same.

The good news, perhaps, is that they're starting to relearn the art of species-wide communication. I mean, they do it with those machines they call computers, they do it on the 'World Wide Web,' but . . ."

"That goes all the way back to the Animal Ancestors. They forgot how to do it, I guess, when they forgot that they were animals."

The fox nodded. "All that showy technology in the paws of a band of primates who in terms of their emotions are barely advanced beyond the level of baboons. They're chimpanzees with bulldozers, monkeys with bombs. It's a dangerous situation, but that's okay: danger is the perfume of change, and change is the future's vocation. There's hope for us in this realm yet. Meanwhile, your clan is faring better than most. Much better. Why, your fame is even spreading to America."

"Ha!" snorted Tanuki. "That and two thousand yen will get you a cup of sake."

"Oh, I'm so sorry. What a rotten host I am! But I swear I haven't a drop of drink on the premises. All I can offer you, I'm afraid, is a rump of leftover owl."

In the mouth of the perpetually hungry badger/dog/raccoon, saliva pooled like runoff from a shower. Nevertheless, he said, "Don't bother. I've got to be trotting along. I'm on my way to an appointment."

"Ah so! Yes, yes. You have to meet someone. I remember. It continues, doesn't it? Your greatest folly or your greatest triumph. As the humans say, only time will tell."

Again Tanuki snorted. "Time has a big mouth and a small brain."

"Well put," said Kitsune. "Well put." They chuckled together at the various misconceptions surrounding the phenomenon of time. Then the fox said, "Okay, you're Tanuki. You're going to do what you're going to do. I must say, I remember Miho and little Kazu with a certain fondness." He nudged his visitor with his snout. "Here, I'll walk outside with you. When you come again, I'll have a bottle for you. And we can do something more productive than complain about human beings. We should follow the example of the gods, no doubt, and just ignore them until they wise up."

Tanuki was about to retort that it was easy enough to ignore mankind when one was in the Cloud Fortress or the Other World, but he was suddenly struck by what a gorgeous day it was in *this* world, and his tongue seized up with joy.

All across the clearing, the dying grass and the sun were practically the same shade of yellow. Last-minute shoppers crowded the pollen parlors, and every other flower-head drooped from bee-weight. A breeze with only a calorie or two of warmth left in it slid down the mountainside as if on its way to one final dip in Lake Biwa. Already rubbed red by nights of foreplay, boughs, each leaf alert, awaited the transformative ejaculation of frost. The air was musky with the fate of fallen fruit and collapsing mushrooms, brisk with the historic hustle of harvest, and a flock of crows flapped through it, teasing everybody and everything with their impenetrable koans. In flight, a twitchy curve of ebony luster, they formed the false mustache of the world.

"There's something about summer turning into autumn," said Tanuki, "that always makes me want to . . . to roll around." With that, he gave his belly a smack that jiggled his mighty scrotum and lay right down in the dry grass and rolled.

"I know what you mean," said Kitsune, "though we foxes are not quite so demonstrative. This is the only sort of time men have ever needed to take seriously, you know. The changing of the seasons." Then, laughing, he dropped down on the ground and joined his friend in a roll.

Could it be, do you suppose, that despite her unfortunate vocabulary, Bootsey was on to something all along?

ACKNOWLEDGMENTS

A tip of the hatless hat to my fellow Southeast Asia enthusiast, James Gierman; to my fellow Tanuki fancier, William Crowell; to Zen Maestro Rudolpho (he are what he ain't); to my "lazy diamond-studded flunky," Barbara Barker; to my dear agent, Phoebe Larmore (as well as her evil twin, Skippy); to my editor, Danielle Perez, with a carload of chocolate; to my line editor, Danelle McCafferty (who knows which way the geese fly); and finally, to the Godfather himself, my intrepid and ever scintillating longtime publisher, Irwyn Applebaum. *Bien joué!*

T. R.

ABOUT THE AUTHOR

TOM ROBBINS, maverick author of eight juicy, daring, and sagacious novels, is one of those rare writers who approach rock-star status, attracting SRO crowds at his personal appearances in Europe and Australia as well as in the United States. He lives primarily in the Seattle area.